'Nyathi's book is rich in detail ar
from her characters for South Afr
beginnings to success against all odds.'
– *Business Day*

'Nyathi has woven a work of fiction which is vividly authentic …
in a lyrical and beautiful way.'
– *Destiny* magazine

'This book gives you a much-needed glimpse into the hard-
ships, losses, pain and unrelenting fight for survival that illegal
immigrants face on a daily basis in the unwelcoming streets of
Hillbrow. *The GoldDiggers* is tough to take, but it makes for a
remarkable read and Nyathi is a writer to watch.'
– *Cape Times*

'If there was ever an author who could do a book like *The
GoldDiggers* justice, it would be none other than Sue Nyathi.'
– *Drum* magazine

'Don't let the title fool you, *The GoldDiggers* is not about women
dating men for money. Nor is it about toiling miners. The book is
a page-turning tale of struggle and triumph.'
– *Sunday World*

# THE
# GOLD-
# DIGGERS

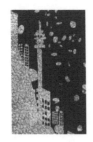

# THE GOLD-DIGGERS

*A Novel*

## SUE NYATHI

MACMILLAN

First published in 2018 by Pan Macmillan South Africa

This edition published in 2019
by Pan Macmillan South Africa
Private Bag X19
Northlands
2116
Johannesburg
South Africa

www.panmacmillan.co.za

ISBN 978-1-77010-681-9
e-ISBN 978-1-77010-682-6

© Sukoluhle Nyathi 2018, 2019

*This is a work of fiction. Any resemblance to actual events, places or persons, living
or dead, is purely coincidental. The Bible verses quoted on each Part page are taken
from the New International Version.*

Editing by Jane Bowman
Proofreading by Pam Thornley and Katlego Tapala
Design and typesetting by Triple M Design, Johannesburg
Cover design by publicide
Author photograph by Shaun Gregory Photography

Printed and bound by Bidvest Data, Cape Town

To Sabelo
My darling son,
You have taught me the true meaning of love

# INTRODUCTION

It has been a year since *The GoldDiggers* was published. The novel was received to much critical acclaim; a huge affirmation for my writing. I reckon writing your second novel is the hardest. My debut novel, *The Polygamist*, was well received but I was afraid I was not going to live up to expectations the second time around. When literary critics said things such as, 'This is a literary masterpiece' and 'Sue's writing has matured like fine wine', I got warm and fuzzy feelings inside.

For the most part, writing is a lonely craft. Apart from the company of the characters that live in your head, in a world you have created, you tend to be cut off from the real world for long periods of time. So once the book is out there and readers are engaging with you, it really is the greatest compliment for me as a writer.

I have enjoyed talking about my book on the book club circuit and interacting with readers who are ardent fans of my work. Some readers might not have the opportunity to meet me in person or have their questions answered, so here are responses to some of the issues I have been frequently asked about when discussing *The GoldDiggers*.

# THE TITLE IS MISLEADING

Yes, the title is a bit of a misnomer because when the word 'gold-diggers' is mentioned, the first thing that often comes to mind for some people is beautiful, young women trying to make money by milking rich men. But I think after reading the book, most readers agree this is far from the truth.

The book is predominantly set in Johannesburg, a city that grew as a result of the discovery of gold in the 19th century. 'Egoli' is synonymous with gold and finding your fortune, so it made sense to use 'gold-diggers' in the title.

Centuries later, it might not be gold bars that people are looking for but it is still economic wealth. As such, it seemed appropriate to call the book *The GoldDiggers* because most people who come to this city are in search of their fortune – whatever that fortune might be. However, like most people in search of things, some succeed while others fail. In line with this, I pictured Johannesburg as a woman. If we think of Cape Town as the 'mother' then why can't Johannesburg be the 'daughter'? Hence the image of a woman on the cover.

My journey in writing this book started in 2013 but the idea was implanted in my head as a result of the conversations that arose around the xenophobic attacks that broke out in Alexandra in 2008. I would turn on the radio and hear vociferous callers saying, 'But why are foreigners here? Why don't they return to their own countries?' I felt I had a responsibility, as a foreigner myself, to answer those questions. Plus, there was no way I could express what I felt in a few minutes on a radio show or in a 280-character tweet. What better way than write a book at your leisure without interruptions?

Sadly, at the time of writing this, a spate of xenophobic attacks had erupted once again and the topic continued to dominate headlines and spark conversations. It would appear that xenophobic sentiment remains high. This is echoed on a global scale with many countries closing their borders in an effort to try to curb inward migration. So not only is the issue relevant, it has also become a topic on the lips of many citizens and policy makers.

I finished writing *The GoldDiggers* in 2016 and during the process I fell pregnant and had my son, Sabelo. The drafting and planning of the book took place long before Sabelo was conceived and a large part of it was written whilst he was gestating in my belly. I remember being seven months pregnant and taking a walking tour of Hillbrow, which forms part of the setting for the book. I have walked the streets of Joburg's inner city over the years and know it intimately, and this is reflected in my writing.

I once worked for an economic development consulting firm that was contracted by the Department of Economic Development, an arm of the City of Johannesburg, to work on a project that looked at decking the railway lines running through the inner city and building above them. In conducting a baseline assessment of what was in the city, I literally had to map the retail, residential and commercial uses of the railway in the CBD. And, yes, it was a tedious exercise that involved me walking the streets and writing everything down, but those notes later fed into my writing of *The GoldDiggers*.

These geographical details were important to me, so that all readers, especially those not from Johannesburg, could get a picture of this so-called Mecca of a city in southern Africa that has lured so many people to it. I enjoyed the research immensely as it gave me historical insight into a city that I was not born in but have resided in for the past ten years. I've always enjoyed history, even in high school, so I loved learning about the stories behind the landmarks. While a lot of the history was cut from the final novel for the sake of narrative flow, my mind is all the richer for it!

After Sabelo's birth in 2014, motherhood overtook my writing efforts, so the book was set aside for a while, and I eventually resumed writing in April 2015, which resulted in the second draft of the book. Coincidentally, this was at the same time I returned to full-time employment in my day job.


## WHY DO I WRITE?

I often introduce myself as a writer by passion and an investment analyst by profession. I write because I simply love it and because it makes me feel alive. But I have a day job because the reality is that most writers cannot make a living solely from their writing – not unless you are in the company of authors such as JK Rowling or Chimamanda Ngozi Adichie.

I was trained as an investment analyst and have a Master's degree in finance and investment. During the day my head is buried in economic shop talk, building financial models and preoccupied with the volatility of the Johannesburg Stock Exchange. And then my writing keeps me busy at night.

You're probably wondering how a creative like me got stuck in the world of finance and it turns out that it was actually a random decision. I always knew from a young age that I wanted to write so by the time I was eight years old, I was cutting pictures out of magazines and writing stories around them. Even when I played, I was acting out stories. By the time I got to high school,

I was writing my own books in A5 exercise books with my own cover design and blurb. Just like profesionally published books are delivered except mine, of course, were handwritten and there was only ever one copy, which was circulated amongst my fellow students. These books soon migrated from one High School to the next and everyone got to know about 'Sue's Books'. Soon it became like hiring a DVD for 'one night only' because the demand was so high. Those students treasured my books and although they became torn and tatty, none of them were ever lost or misplaced.

I probably spent more time reading and writing in high school than I did on homework, and on many occasions my mother threatened to suspend my library subscription because I preferred to be buried in a novel rather than my maths or physics textbooks! When I left high school everyone thought I would go on to study something literary. I had my heart set on journalism but the only university in Bulawayo at the time only offered science and business courses. As my parents were set on me getting a degree, I looked at what was on offer and thought finance sounded interesting. And that is how I ended up in a field that I initially did not enjoy but grew into, and I now have a greater appreciation of financial markets and the mechanics of financing things.


## WHEN DO I WRITE?

I have always made time to write despite my very demanding day job. Whether it's contributing to a column or writing a book in my spare time, I have not let the financial markets stifle my creativity.

I am one of those writers who needs complete silence in order to write. You won't find me typing away in the corner of a

Starbucks with an untouched cup of coffee next to me. I hate noise when I am writing because I find it very distracting. During my pre-Sabelo days it was easy to shut out the world and write. There were weekends when I wouldn't leave the house and would write from the time I woke up until I went to sleep. I remember being so caught up in the writing I would even forget to eat! That's how consumed (or possessed!) I was when I was writing *The Polygamist* and as a result I was able to finish writing the book in six months.

Writing when I became a mother was much tougher as I had to set aside that 'quiet time'. I would write between 3 am and 6 am every morning and then get ready for work. I kept up this routine until the manuscript was completed.

Writing is not glamorous; it requires determination and dedication to a process, to which I was committed because once I start something I have to finish it. *The GoldDiggers* was completed in 2016 and it took me a year before I found a publisher interested in publishing it. I had resolved to self-publish if I did not find a publisher by the end of that year but then Andrea Nattrass, the publisher at Pan Macmillan, responded positively and offered me a publishing contract and, as they say, the rest is history.


## ARE THE STORIES IN THE BOOK TRUE?

The stories of the characters in *The GoldDiggers* are unfortunately real. Very real. The characters themselves are fictitious but the stories are all based on truth.

Fiction gives a writer more leeway and makes room for your imagination to come into play. Writing a novel allowed me to weave fiction into fact as I find non-fiction more limiting in this regard.

Also, I feel that there are already a lot of non-fiction titles that tell of the plight of Zimbabwean immigrants in South Africa. One of the most notable, for me, is written by Christa Kuljian and is entitled, *Sanctuary: How an Inner-City Church Spilled onto a Sidewalk*. This book provides an intimate account of the plight of immigrants based on face-to-face interviews. *Washing Dishes and Other Stories* written by Oswald Kucherera, a fellow Zimbabwean, provides an account of the migrant experience from a more personal perspective.

The character of Chamunorwa is fictitious, but was inspired by the death of Ernesto Alfabeto Nhamuave, a Mozambican who was beaten, stabbed, set alight and burnt to death in the informal settlement of Ramaphosa in 2008. Ernesto became known as the 'burning man' and disturbing images of him were splayed across many media outlets. Those images will haunt me forever.

Ernesto was a builder who was trying to earn an honest living before he met his untimely and brutal demise. Through Chamunorwa's character I pay homage to Ernesto and his short-lived life. For me, he will always portray the brutal image of what xenophobia really is.

Portia is another fictional character but she represents the realities of the lives of many wives of migrant labourers. My grandfather was a migrant labourer who worked in the gold mines on the reef. His home was in Empandeni Mission in Plumtree in Zimbabwe and he was often gone for up to three years at a time, leaving my grandmother to look after the homestead and keep the home fires burning.

It was not uncommon for migrant labourers to have wives or girlfriends with them in Johannesburg, and some of those unions bore children. This is represented in Dumisani's story when he eventually abandons his wife back home in Zimbabwe and marries Nomonde. What saddens me is that this narrative hasn't changed. We are living in the 21st century and men are still going away to work in foreign countries, leaving their wives and children behind. The nucleus of the family continues to be destroyed, and so Portia represents those women who decide to follow their husbands and try to make something of their lives, often with tragic results.

Dumisani's story is one that is so common amongst many professionals from Zimbabwe who, because of the circumstances under which they came to South Africa, end up as waiters. Some never manage to find alternative work, while others find employment as gardeners and domestic workers with degrees and years of professional experience behind them.

Some people think Dumisani's character is based on my own and while there are similarities in terms of his professional career, that's where the similarities end. I was privileged in the sense that I came to South Africa on a work permit in 2008, which is when the book begins. Furthermore, I had siblings and friends who resided here and so I had a great support system when I arrived here. The journey of someone on a work permit differs so much from that of an illegal migrant and so that is the story I chose to tell on their behalf. This book was my way of giving a voice to the voiceless who are so often exploited by the system.

Gugulethu's story represents the stories of thousands of children who end up being sold into human trafficking. Typically, there are millions of Zimbabweans working illegally in South Africa and their families reside in Zimbabwe. During the school holidays many parents send for their children because they cannot take leave and go across the border to be with them. The children may or may not have the correct documents to cross the border, but they will be illegally ferreted across the border, often unaccompanied.

A huge case hogged media headlines on 11 November 2017 when eight children were apprehended in a truck in Rustenburg while travelling unaccompanied and without any identity documents. The children were headed to Cape Town to spend the Christmas holidays with their parents, but for three months the Department of Social Development held the children in custody whilst awaiting repatriation. Even though the parents of the children came forward to claim them, the department refused to grant them access.

It is incidents like this one that give greater motivation to the Department of Home Affairs' decision to introduce the unabridged birth certificate system for minors in 2015. There are thousands of children who were not as lucky as the ones who were found and who have disappeared with their whereabouts unknown. Children, who like the character of Gugulethu, are sold into child prostitution. After reading *The GoldDiggers,* you may become aware of a lot more of these stories concerning child trafficking and hopefully because of Gugulethu, the plight of these children will be closer to your heart.

Lindani is a character carried over from my debut novel, *The Polygamist.* Readers seem to have fallen in love with her character so I brought her back to narrate the drug-trafficking storyline. Once again, the media is awash with stories of young women tricked into becoming drug mules. Some die in jails in foreign lands while others return to South Africa with heart-wrenching testimonies of the ordeals they suffered in prison. I often get asked what happened to Lindani on that flight and as a reader you can rightly assume, and I allude to this in the book, that she suffered the fate of many drug traffickers and ended up in a Malaysian prison. Many readers have appealed to me to be merciful and bring her back in a third book!

## THE STORIES SEEM INCOMPLETE

This is criticism I have seen in various reviews or critiques. For example, I have been asked a number of times what happened to Thuli, who was accosted into the wilderness by *ogumaguma*. I have left it up to the reader to decide her fate. The incompleteness is deliberate. The truth is that many families never get any closure and that's what that chapter represents. Many adults, young and old, would leave home in search of their fortune in Egoli, never to be seen again.

Although it is not so common nowadays, many illegal border jumpers traversed the treacherous Limpopo River to get into South Africa. Many drowned while others might have been killed by *oma-gumaguma*. Some who made it then disappeared and were never heard from again. I have cousins who are not accounted for after travelling to South Africa.

Imagine for a minute an illegal migrant arriving in Johannes-burg, gets a new identity and is then killed in a car accident. The person is then left lying in a mortuary with a fake alias and no one knows who they are or how to get hold of their kith and kin. They are then probably buried in Chiawelo or some other cemetery since their bodies were not claimed.

There is a colloquial saying in Matabeleland: 'wadliwa yiGoli', which is literally translated to mean 'they were swallowed by Johannesburg'. This saying is used to account for those people who disappeared and remain unaccounted for.

# WHY CAN'T THE STORIES HAVE HAPPY ENDINGS?

Some readers, after reading *The GoldDiggers*, accuse me of painting a bleak picture of migrants in South Africa. I think I am painting an honest picture. Yes, there are the happily-ever-after stories of successful Zimbabweans who are residents of Dainfern and Sandhurst, but there's only a handful. My stories represent the plight of the majority of Zimbabweans and for me, those were the interesting stories I wanted to tell.

I tried to bring in a successful happily-ever-after with Dumisani and Portia, but sometimes even that happily-ever-after can be bittersweet. I don't believe anyone has a monopoly on any narrative and if you feel there is a happy story to be told or written, do it.

I always say, I don't owe anyone any happy endings and neither does life. This is a brutal story and it's heartbreaking. It will make you cry when you are reading it, but rest assured I cried when I was writing it. There were times when I could hardly see the screen through the blur of my own tears.

Lastly, dear reader, I want to thank you for buying this book. I hope it evokes empathy in you so that when you encounter a foreigner tomorrow or the day after, you are more compassionate towards them. There are so many stories behind those faces; painful ones too. I wanted to share this Zimbabwean story because it is the country of my birth and it's a story that I know intimately. Hopefully, other migrants will share their stories too.

*Sue Nyathi*
*Johannesburg, April 2019*

# PART ONE

**The Exodus**

'Then the Lord said to Moses, "Now you will see
what I will do to Pharaoh. Because of my mighty
hand he will let them go; because of my mighty
hand he will drive them out of his country".'

*Exodus 6: Verse 1*

# ONE

A gleaming white Toyota Quantum with black-tinted windows pulled into a vacant parking space opposite Max's Garage. Everyone in Bulawayo knew Max's Garage. It wasn't just a fuel and service station. It was more like a busy transit terminal. Max's Garage was the gateway out of Bulawayo to places like Esigodini, Gwanda, Beitbridge and Johannesburg. In the same vein, it was also the entry point for those coming in from the southern parts of the country. It welcomed you into the bosom of the City of Kings. A city whose pulse was faltering as its entire body succumbed to an economic malaise. The Inns fast-food franchise located there also ensured the place was always bustling with activity. The people who thronged there were an easy target for the con artists, petty criminals and vendors milling around.

From his car, the driver had a vantage of the unfolding action around him. His interest was piqued by a woman sitting on the pavement, a child plugged to her breast, punting overripe bananas to every passer-by. How many bananas did she have to sell in a day to break even? Could anyone actually survive on those takings? He shook his head in disdain. Not only was life brutally unfair, it was savagely hard. The thought that in a few minutes he would be driving out of this quagmire gave him a fleeting moment of joy. Fleeting because he would soon return to it and invariably nothing would have improved. In fact, the city's condition would probably only worsen. This is why the numbers of mobile cargo he carried had increased in the last couple of months. They all had one thing in common: the desire to find refuge in the arms of their South African neighbour. He had listened in on many conversations, many that were grandiose and flowered with adjectives of prosperity. So similar to the one taking place in the back seat.

A young man and woman conversed noisily in Shona. They had arrived together and had insisted on sitting together. Melusi assumed they were a couple. They continued to chat animatedly. He smirked in disgust. That language should never have even been allowed in Matabeleland. He had aspirations of becoming president one day. He would divide the country along tribal lines. Matabeleland. Manicaland. Mashonaland. Those who did not fit into these three categories would have to squeeze into Otherland. When he was president there would be no electricity outages, no fuel shortages and an uninterrupted supply of running water. Bulawayo would be a thriving city with employment opportunities for all the Ndebele; many of whom were disenfranchised and scraping by in South Africa. A livelihood, which they should have easily made from the fruits of this once beautiful land. It now looked like a tired prostitute screwed of all sanity and life. He sneered again and was almost tempted to throw the Shona couple out of the car. It was *their* fault. Their fault the country was in the quandary it was in. Now they were also making an exodus to South Africa; an exodus he had been forced to make ten years earlier. Why did they not stay and fix the mess *they* had created? They still had opportunities here; many that had been denied to him.

He'd not been able to get a job simply because he was born of the wrong tribe. Being Ndebele in Zimbabwe was a curse. He had lost his father and three uncles during the Gukurahundi massacres of 1986. His mother now limped around her homestead after she had been beaten by members of the 5th Brigade during a show of defiance when she refused to cook for them. But his family was not the only one that had suffered. Several homesteads from his village just outside Plumtree had been burnt and razed to the ground. Men were denigrated and some killed in cold blood. Women and children were raped repeatedly. Historians called it a period of 'ethnic' cleansing. To him it had been a baptism of fire. The memory of which made his blood curdle. He stared at the couple through the rear-view mirror with sheer contempt. He had been raised to hate *them*.

'In my car we *only* speak Ndebele,' he stated bluntly.

The couple stared at each other in confusion, unsure if they were the intended recipients of the message.

'You heard me,' he sniggered. 'In my car we *only* speak Ndebele.'

'Melusi, please,' chided the woman who sat beside him.

'It's my car!' he replied. 'I can lay down the law in *my* car.'

Shona people could dominate elsewhere but not in his car. This was *his* car, his livelihood. He made a living from carrying goods and people back and forth from South Africa. He was a transporter. *Umalayitsha.* He reached forward and turned on the radio. The voices of Shwi Nomthekala filled the car as they crooned, *'Wangisiz'ubaba'*. The song always calmed him ahead of a long journey. They had a long passage ahead of them. More than 300 kilometres before they reached the Beitbridge border. You would think after driving all these years the journey would be easier but it was not. The roads did not provide the smoothest passage. His car tyres had to be changed at least twice a year because of deterioration. He snorted again. To add to his irritation the Shona couple were screaming above the loud music.

Had Melusi taken the time to question them he might have discovered they were actually not a couple but siblings who not only shared a mom but also shared a womb. His prejudice would not allow him civility towards them. He was tempted to throw them out of the car but his desire for their money surpassed his intolerance. All the passengers in his car were going to be ferried across the border illegally. Just like his name, Melusi, he was shepherding them into the City of Gold. To them it was the promised land; supposedly flowing with milk, honey and other countless opportunities. He held the fate of each one of them in his hands. All nine of them. This was an eclectic bunch he was travelling with.

Beside the noisy Shona couple there was a young woman who he guessed could not be more than twenty-five. She was travelling with her son, a young boy of about five. She was a pretty young woman except for that hideous hair sewed onto her head looking like a hornet's nest. She had big brown eyes that spoke of untold naivety. He knew her type. They had lived in the rural areas all their lives and only came into the city on special occasions. Now she was going to be thrust into the bosom of Johannesburg. A city ten times bigger than Bulawayo and ten times racier. He was convinced Johannesburg was the Sodom and Gomorrah that they wrote about in the Bible. Many had got caught in the clutches of sin and inebriation. Very few survived it.

Beside the woman was a little girl, probably five or six, with

gangly legs dangling from her pretty yellow frock. She was travelling alone. The fear in her innocent eyes was palpable. She had
not said a word since she had entered the car. An old woman had
dropped her off earlier. How she had cried when the matronly
woman had turned to leave. If anything he had been annoyed by
her noisy lamentation. Children were the worst kind of cargo to
carry.

There was also a young man in his late twenties. An upbeat-
looking fellow who walked like he owned the world. They had
conversed briefly earlier. The young man spoke with such exuberance and untold optimism. He was degreed and was going to ply
his trade in Johannesburg. Melusi had disliked him on sight. He
hoped, without genuine sincerity, that the young man would con-
quer Johannesburg before it conquered him. That city had many
fallen heroes and heroines.

The seventh passenger was sitting right beside him. She was
a beautiful young thing called Lindani who he'd met in Bulawayo
the weekend before. Unlike the others she was not a paying passenger, well not in the conventional way anyway. When she looked at
him his heart did somersaults and his loins stirred to life. He could
not wait to bed her again. She was manna from heaven. She had
fallen from the sky into his hands.

'Sweetie,' she spoke, in a soft voice that gently caressed him,
'what are we still waiting for?'

'Givie is not here,' he replied.

Givemore was not a passenger but rather his co-driver. More
than that, he was also his best friend. They were both Empandeni
boys, their homesteads just metres apart. They had sat together at
the back of the class at Mbakwe Mission. Over the school holidays
they herded cattle in the savannah grasslands outside Plumtree

town. During the hot summer days they would lie down by the riverbanks dreaming about a charmed life beyond the borders of Plumtree. A life Melusi's grandfather had narrated to them in many bedtime stories as they sat around a fire. Stories about the glamour and glitz of Egoli. Melusi's grandfather had been a migrant worker employed in the gold mines on the Reef. He told them how he had been to hell as he worked deep below the surface of the earth. He also spoke of the heaven that existed outside the mines. The illicit jazz clubs and the sensuous Xhosa women who frequented them. It was that heaven Melusi and Givemore often dreamt about. A heaven they had pursued and had not yet found. Melusi reached for his cellphone and dialled. There was still no answer. However, before his irritation could gain hold Givemore swung around into view with his hand draped around a young, lanky teenager.

'She's coming with us,' announced Givemore. 'You think you're the only one who can pull a hot chick?'

Melusi shrugged. Who was he to complain? The more the merrier. The door of the Quantum slid shut and the engine roared to life. They were on the road again. He reminded himself that he was doing this journey to keep the home fires burning. People depended on him for their sustenance. He longed for the day when he could retire. The day he would park his car and never again have to set eyes on a uniformed border official. But unfortunately it was not going to be today.

# TWO

The twins could remember vividly the day their mother walked out of their lives. It had been a bright sunshine-filled day in October. They were playing outside in their garden devoid of any grass or flowers. They played 'house', cooking mud cakes oblivious to the brutal sun beating down on their tiny backs. Their mother had appeared then, like a rainbow after the storm. In her hands she carried a battered brown suitcase. She wore a beautiful floral dress clipped at the waist showing off her tiny waist and rounded hips. Her big Afro formed a shade from the glistening sun. They had expected her to berate them for being grubby and dirty. Instead she had crouched down to kiss their dirt-stained faces. Her big brown eyes were filled with tears. Their mother's eyes were often wet.

'I have to go home.' She spoke in her soft lyrical voice. 'I will be back soon,' she promised.

This was a line that had been repeated to them often enough in the past. It was like a line from Humpty Dumpty, their favourite nursery rhyme. Their mother often left but she always returned. Her return was always accompanied with abundant joy, laughter and generous kisses. Even their father would be in a celebratory mood. At that moment he emerged from inside the house. He wore no shirt; the tight black hairs on his chest glistened with sweat like droplets of dew on a cold summer morning. The brown trousers he wore were held in place by a thick leather belt with a shiny silver buckle. A belt that had danced on their backsides and yielded angry welts on their soft flesh so many times. His face was stormy, devoid of any happiness.

'Sibongile! I told you to leave!' he bellowed. 'Go now! I don't ever want to see your face here again.'

Their mother had bowed her head in capitulation. Normally she would have challenged their father but her whole demeanour communicated resignation and defeat. They had often witnessed their father hit their mother. Their little minds could not comprehend the violent display. Often, they would cry with her as she tried to shield herself from the brunt of her husband's brutal fists. At his fierce command Sibongile picked up her suitcase and walked off. She never returned.

Chamunorwa and Chenai grew up motherless. At first they would cry relentlessly, hoping she would return. But they soon learnt that their tears evoked the deep wrath of their father as opposed to sympathy. A year later, their father acquired a new mother for them who came with her own child, Saru, a wily girl who was prone to throwing tantrums. Chenai was convinced their new mother was the evil stepmother from Cinderella and that Saru was their evil stepsister. In the book there were two stepsisters but Chenai was glad she only had to deal with Saru. In her world, the Prince was Chamu. She knew he would grow tall, strong and handsome and rescue them from this drudgery. In her head, her mother was her Fairy Godmother. She prayed to her every night. Prayed that she would appear and wave her wand and they would vanish into a beautiful world, like the one described in the story. For now she was stuck at home scrubbing the floors of their two-bedroomed house until they gleamed. It was a daily chore that awaited her when she came home from school. Afterwards she would have to cook supper. The tiny stool made it possible for her to see the top of the two-plate stove.

Chamu was always there beside her, helping out. She made him slice the onions as they always made her cry. Sometimes she wondered if it was because her tears were always close to the surface since Chamu could do it without shedding a tear. Only after they had finished the cooking would they be able to sit together on the stone floor and do their homework. They would always hear the laughter of their stepmother and child as they watched television. A pleasure they were nearly always denied.

Their father, a train driver, often came home late so he was oblivious to what happened in his absence. Not that he would have cared much as he was enamoured with his new wife and new daughter. The twins faded into the background of the dull concrete walls of their home. Spoke only when spoken to. They knew they were totally sidelined when, come Christmas time, their father went shopping for clothes with his new family and didn't bother buying anything for them. Saru would come flitting into their bedroom, modelling her new party dresses. However, the party was short-lived when the violence erupted. Their father became abusive once more, beating up Saru and her mother until they could no longer stand it. They left unceremoniously one evening never to return again.

It was about this time that Chenai thought she was going to die when she discovered a spattering of blood on her panties. In

11

her confusion she confronted her school teacher, the only trusted female figure in her life. Her teacher explained to her that this was the beginning of womanhood; an important time in her life. When Chenai got home she told her father.

'You and Chamu can no longer share a bed,' he declared with authority.

The true enormity of his words dawned on her when in the dead of the night he made his way into her bed. The springs squeaked in protest as he manoeuvred his gruesomely disproportionate body over it. She almost choked on the overpowering smell of beer that emanated from his breath.

'You are now a woman,' he said. 'I'm going to teach you what being a real woman is all about,' he whispered in her ear.

He shoved his hands up beneath her dress and began to grope her. Instinctively she knew something was wrong, very wrong. He leaned forward and smothered her face with his thick lips. She shoved him away with all the strength she could muster.

'Feisty like your mother, huh? That Ndebele temper I see!'

He pinioned her to the bed and shifted his weight over. Without ceremony, he shoved himself inside her. Her anguished screams jerked Chamu from his deep sleep. Instinctively he raced to Chenai's door. He tried to open it but it was locked. He slammed his fists into the door.

'Chichi!' he called out. 'Chichi!'

There was no answer.

'Chichi,' he screamed.

'Go back to sleep, Chamu,' came the dull voice of his father. 'Everything is okay.'

For a minute Chamu felt like his heart had stalled. Loud cymbals crashed noisily in his head. He wanted to scream out in protest but no sound emerged from deep inside. Instead he slammed his fists against the door. He had no idea when or how he finally collapsed with exhaustion onto the floor. Feeling defeated he dragged himself to his blankets on the floor of the living room. He lay awake staring into the darkness. In the background he could hear his sister's screams once more. Huge teardrops fell from his big eyes. Gut-wrenching sobs that formed deep inside his bowels. He felt a myriad emotions ranging from anger, betrayal, confusion to sheer agony. He yearned for his mother then. Yearned for her more than he ever had in his entire life. Where was she? Why was she not here to protect them from this man? Darkness gave way to the morning light and still the demons raged inside Chamu. He heard his father leave in the morning. Then he ventured into Chenai's room taking guarded steps. She was cloistered in the corner of the room, her knees drawn to her chest. He ran to her and hugged her. She screamed. A scream so deep that Chamu felt something break inside him.

# THREE

The journey south began on Leopold Takawira Avenue, named for a liberation struggle hero who met his demise in the seventies. Some still referred to it as Selbourne, its former name that celebrated a lord from another era. Even when mothers threatened their kids with a hiding they would hiss between gritted teeth, 'Uzaqonda nta njengo Solobhoni.' I'll straighten you out like Selbourne.

The road was wide and welcoming, lined with jacaranda trees that formed a canopy of shade from the merciless heat in summer. When the jacarandas flowered, they painted the city's skyline with hues of lilac, purple and lavender. Leopold was the main artery from the city, which led to the eastern suburbs. It cut through the heart of Centenary Park and nestled on the grounds of the park was the Natural History Museum of Zimbabwe. However, this is not what the park was renowned for; rather it used to be a popular venue for newlyweds to pose for photographs. Cameramen lived off bridal parties that would descend on the park on Saturdays in noisy convoys spilling out of cars in all their splendour and finery. The park, with its blooming flowers and beautifully landscaped gardens, was the ideal background for the nuptials being celebrated weekend after weekend. Couples would wrap themselves around the trunks of trees whilst the ebullient moment was captured on a Kodak camera.

Melusi recalled with fondness how he used to court girlfriends of the past in that park. They would take long leisurely walks, hands entwined. Then they would pause to buy ice cream from either the Dairibord or Lyons Maid vendor. When exhaustion took over they would sit on the lawn under the shade of a cypress tree. He almost blushed at the memory of how, like many lovers in the park, they would kiss and caress unabashedly; bodies rolling over the lush green lawn.

Except the green was gone now, replaced by long overgrown grass. Even the locomotive train that chugged through the park had gone off the rails. The park was now littered with dirt and debris. A few perennials still bloomed but for the most part they were a rare sight. The park had lost its former appeal and was now a refuge for beggars and vagrants. A walk through the park could get you raped or mugged. Even the Anniversary Fountain, which had sprayed out jets of water, had dried up like the rest of the city. Melusi was filled with more angst and turned his eyes back on to the road.

Leopold Takawira cut through the heart of Suburbs, a quin-tessential neighbourhood with palatial homes whose architecture was reminiscent of the city's colonial past. It was the first suburb of Bulawayo and was ironically named that too as if the City Fathers had lacked creativity. Melusi came to a jarring halt at the intersec-tion of Ascot Way almost trampling the population of schoolboys in blue shirts who were waiting to cross the road. At this point, Leopold Takawira Avenue changed identity and became Gwanda

Road. They traversed through Khumalo, another suburb for the rich and uppity.

When things were good, the residents here shopped at the Ascot Piazza and met for drinks at the Holiday Inn. Now that supermarket shelves were devoid of the bare necessities Melusi shopped across the border on their behalf. His clients drew up long grocery lists which included treats like Cadbury chocolate bars to two-ply Baby Soft toilet paper to wipe their delicate arses. So every month when he made the deliveries to their opulent homes he got a glimpse into their luxurious suburban lifestyles.

He admired the sweet-smelling madams who were no longer white but black with long flowing silky hair that reached their waists. Even in the darkest days when the city was plunged into gloom their diesel generators roared. Their money cosseted them from the vagaries of the life that the rest of them were forced to endure. It did fill him with envy because deep down he also wanted a piece of *that* life. Wanted it so badly. The longing made his heart ache even more as they drove further down past Selbourne Park, named after the lord, also housing people with 'airs'. It was a new and mushrooming suburb for Bulawayo's upper middle class. A new breed that had risen by gambling on the rising and falling fortunes of the Zimbabwean economy.

On its left stood NUST, the National University of Science and Technology, which churned out thousands and thousands of graduates into an economy that could not absorb them. Still its doors opened year after year, admitting hopeful students on one end and spitting out disillusioned graduates on the other.

Further and further he steered the car till there was no sight of suburbia; only sprawling plots of lands with lone homesteads falling apart at the hinges. Unploughed fields of maize were populated with drooping maize stalks with dried leaves. These were inter-spersed with stretches of sprawling savannah grassland and acacia trees. The boundaries of some of these plots were demarcated by straggly strands of barbed wire, hugged fiercely by dead thorny tree branches.

The mundane scenery carried them as far as Esigodini whose decrepit exterior did not allude to the fact that it housed Falcon College, one of the country's prestigious boys' schools, which grew from the floundering remains of the Bushtick Mine. Esigodini faded into the distance as the road led them to Mbalabala, traversing the waterless Mzingwane River. Melusi slammed on the accelerator hoping to escape the dreariness of the savannah bushland.

They stopped in Gwanda to refuel and pick up one more pas-senger; a middle-aged man whom Melusi referred to as 'Malume' settled into the car. For over a distance of 50 kilometres they were all subjected to Malume's diatribe about his ordeal of being laid off by a cement company he had served for over ten years. For the remainder of the time he regaled them with jokes. Momentarily their anxiety about the journey was forgotten.

It was close to midnight when they finally drove into Beitbridge. All Melusi's cargo was fast asleep; including Malume. Beitbridge was a small border town south-east of Bulawayo. Naked billboards and ghost road signs greeted them. Once upon a time there had been a fabulous idea to connect Beitbridge and Bulawayo by rail. It was another of those grand ideas that had lost steam; got derailed. Still Beitbridge lived on in all its noisy commotion. Night or day, the border town never closed its eyes. Its gateposts were always wide open like the thighs of a prostitute ready to receive and expel the constant stream of traffic that descended on the border town.

The Express Holiday Inn thrived by selling bed nights to the more discerning traveller. As did the prostitutes who derived an income by selling their bodies to horny truck drivers at the service stations. The commercial activity survived by virtue of those who made passage through the town. Beitbridge was nearly always enveloped by a blanket of heat. There were no seasons; it was hot 365 days a year.

That night was no different; the heat was merciless and showed no signs of abating. The air was dry; not even a breeze to gently flirt with the skin. As Melusi drove through the town, the streets were lined with men and women hustling to feed the mouths they had left at home. He left it all behind as he drove to the outskirts of Dulibadzimu Township. He would leave his cargo here for the merciless crossing and hopefully find them again on the other side. The onus was on Givemore to marshal the cargo across the mighty Limpopo, also known as the River of Death. Those deep murky waters were home to scaly, menacing crocodiles. As ominous as these creatures were, they were not a deterrent for hungry Zimbabweans who traversed the river in search of the bright lights of Egoli. The great expanse of water, that spanned a kilometre, stood between them and their dreams. A dream that had swallowed and swept away countless others only to spit out their souls into the depths of the Indian Ocean.

# FOUR

Dumisani knew from a young age that he was destined for greater things. He grew up in Mzilikazi, Bulawayo's oldest township named after the mighty King Mzilikazi, the founding father of Matabeleland. The illustrious leader had ruled till his death in 1868 and was buried in Entumbane, which was the name of yet another suburb. Most of the Western Suburbs commemorated the royal house of Khumalo and its descendants like Nkulumane and Lobengula. Dumisani was a Khumalo, a family that descended from the royal clan. He prided himself on his royal heritage and hoped to live up to the greatness of his birthright.

He was expelled from his mother's interior on a cold day in June 1976 at Mpilo Hospital. It had been the largest hospital designated to Africans before Zimbabwe attained its independence in 1980. His mother had cradled him in her hands as she had the three other siblings who preceded him. Two more followed him in a space of three years till there were seven Khumalos in their home. Their father was a teacher at Mzilikazi Primary School and their mother, when she was not giving birth, worked at the hospital as a nurse's aide.

Dumisani had sunny memories of growing up in the township playing with other children in the streets after school. Then when it grew dark they would all race into their matchbox houses jumping over the tiny vegetable gardens. Even their little home was filled with love and happiness that bounced off the walls. Like his other siblings, Dumisani went to Mzilikazi Primary School. Uniforms and clothes alike were passed down from the oldest member to the youngest member in the family. Their sister, being the only girl, was the only one who had the luxury of new uniforms.

Their father was a passionate teacher and they inherited his zeal. Failure was rewarded with lashings from the peach tree that grew in front of their tiny yard. The lashings were administered in the seclusion of their parents' bedroom. All the other children would huddle by the door in awe, listening to the anguished cries coming from within.

From a young age Dumisani vowed his body would never be a recipient of such a hiding. He worked extremely hard and was always top of his class. So he escaped his father's harsh discipline and was lavished with praise. When schools closed their father would escort them to Renkini Bus Terminal. They would go to Silobela where they spent the holidays with their grandparents. Christmas was the only holiday they spent in town.

It was also the only time they shopped for new clothes. On that day they would pile into their father's Alfa Romeo. They would have been scrubbed clean, their faces shining with a thin film of vaseline. Then they had the luxury of picking out new shoes and clothes from shops like Topics, Sales House and Edgars. Dumisani would not be able to sleep for days imagining the excitement on Christmas Day when all the other children would come out onto the street and parade their new clothes. Woe betide those kids who had no new garb to show; they would be teased and taunted.

Christmas was his best day of the year. His mother would cook rice, which would be accompanied by crispy pieces of fried chicken, coleslaw, potato salad coloured with green peas and a chunky beetroot salad. They would drink from bottles of Tarino, Sparletta and Fanta and afterwards would marvel at their luminous tongues. Only at Christmas would they have dessert in the form of greengage jelly and dollops of thick yellow custard. They would eat so much that they would be sick for days afterwards.

The next time their clothes would come out again would be for special occasions like going to church or the Independence Day celebrations held at Barbourfields Stadium every year. There would be free food and drinks for everyone. The army band would play and drum majorettes would put on a sterling performance. His sister, Buhle, on seeing the majorettes for the first time in their smart uniforms with epaulettes had declared she wanted to be one too. At that time Dumisani had no idea what he wanted to be. His older brother Nkosana wanted to be a policeman. Mandla, the one who came after him, dreamt of being a mechanic. Phumlani on the other hand wanted to be a nurse. His father wanted him to be a teacher but Dumisani had greater ambitions.

He was the only one in the family who went on to do his A Levels at St Columba's High School. He would walk back and forth from school, saving his pocket money so that he could spoil Christine. The love of his life. He dreamt of her every night and his desires would manifest themselves in a wet spot on his bed. Luckily he no longer shared a bed with any of his siblings as both his older brothers had since moved out. Nkosana now stayed at the Ross Camp police barracks with his wife and Mandla was doing his apprenticeship at a local polytechnic. A few years earlier his parents had extended their home to make a room for their sister. They were comfortable and happy and Dumisani had all he wanted. Except for Christine. He wooed her relentlessly for two years and still she would not yield to his charms.

By all accounts Dumisani was considered a catch. He was a tall, handsome man with a lithe body that came from running on the sports field. Dumisani was a natural athlete and his trophies and accolades decorated their home. He had an adoring fan club of female admirers yet his heart yearned for no one but Christine.

Every day after school he would walk her home. She lived on the grounds of Mpilo Hospital at least four blocks from his own home. However, walking the extra mile was not a deterrent. He would have walked to the moon and back for Christine. They would stroll down Old Vic Falls Road and he'd carry her satchel laden with books. It was probably just as heavy as his but he didn't mind. That was one of the things he admired about Christine; she was a brilliant student and one of the smartest girls in his class. She was also beautiful; such a potent combination. Her silky black hair was permed and he longed to run his fingers through the bouncy curls. She had an oval-shaped face with big black eyes that could never meet his intent gaze. Her eyes would crease at the corners when she laughed. She had a musical laugh that would make his heart flutter and take flight. She had full, ripe lips that he longed to kiss.

'Christine, I want you to share my life with me,' he declared, when they were a few metres away from the hospital where she lived with her mother, a stout nursing matron who was in charge of the maternity ward.

'What does that mean, Dumi?'

'I want you to be my wife.'

'I will be; the day you can afford me.'

He exhaled deeply. There was no winning with Christine.

'I have to go. See you tomorrow.'

And that was how it ended, every day. No kiss. No nothing. Even after buying her *maputi*, a crunchy local brand of popcorn sold in tiny packets on the side of the road. It always left one thirsty so he would also buy her a Superkool. Still Christine was never moved but that did not abate his determination to have her. He was in his first year of university when Christine finally agreed to be his girlfriend. She was studying nursing at a local college and they both had ambitions of becoming rich and successful. Dreams they nurtured in each other's company. Although they had graduated to kissing and canoodling, Christine would still not open her legs to him. On many nights he would furiously masturbate in the dark. Then the image of her pert breasts would come into his mind and he would spurt into his hands with unrestrained jubilation.

Temptation abounded on campus. There were young nubile women who would have willingly bedded him without batting an eyelid yet he could not bring himself to betray Christine in that way. When he graduated from NUST he immediately landed a job with a local engineering firm and with his first pay cheque paid lobola for Christine who was by then working at Mpilo Hospital. They got married in a small civil ceremony and consummated their relationship that night. Everything he was ever denied was given to him on a silver platter and Dumisani felt like a farmer with a bounty harvest. He reaped the rewards of Christine's beautiful body and sowed his seed in her deepest crevice.

Married life was everything he had dreamt it would be. They stayed at the hospital in a tiny flatlet whilst making plans to buy a home in the eastern suburbs. Their dreams came to fruition in their second year of marriage when they bought a house in Ilanda. They delighted in making love in every room, the echoes reverberating through the unfurnished home. Sipho, their first child, was conceived on those floors and he was born the following year at Mater Dei Hospital.

Life was good. Every fortnight they would socialise with other young and upcoming professionals and Sundays were reserved for church and they still attended the Methodist congregation in Mzilikazi. Afterwards they would lunch at Dumisani's parents' home. Dumisani's mom would still cook rice, chicken, coleslaw and beetroot just like she had when they were growing up. When the summer holidays came round they would spend sun-kissed days in Kariba and Victoria Falls. During winter they vacationed in the misty mountains of Nyanga and Vumba.

They were the toast of the family with a bubbly future ahead of them. Life was theirs. Until the tragic year of 2006 when the company Dumisani worked for declared they were closing down. They said that the economy was deteriorating; trading conditions were hard and they were moving into more lucrative markets. They offered him a job in their London office. Dumisani accepted the offer and woke at four a.m. one morning to queue for a passport. He found the queue already snaking around two blocks. When the sun came out so did the newspapers with huge glaring headlines: *Zimbabwe Registry Office has suspended the issuing of passports and temporary travelling documents.*

# FIVE

Givemore reached into his satchel and fished out a leather necklace with a horn pendant attached to it. Inside was a powdery mixture of crushed dried leaves mixed with crocodile's blood. A traditional healer had sold him the concoction many years ago to safeguard him from danger when crossing the Limpopo. That lucky charm around his neck had never failed him. Even under the most treacherous circumstances he always emerged from those waters unscathed. Givemore prided himself on the fact that he had a lower mortality rate for his goods than most. The last thing they wanted was to 'lose' cargo because essentially that meant no payment.

'Are you up for it?' Melusi asked Givemore, sounding concerned.

Most of the cargo was PFs (Pay Forwards). This meant they had very little cash, or what he referred to as working capital, to bribe their way through the border or past roadblocks.

'Yes. We have no choice, do we? You know each time I tell myself it's going to be the last time I'll do this I keep finding myself in that river.'

'It *is* the last time, *mfowethu*. We are not doing this shit no more.'

SUE NYATHI

Givemore exhaled noisily then disembarked from the front of the car. He slid open the doors of the main body of the Quantum and woke everyone in an authoritative voice.

'You think we are here to sleep?' he growled. *'Asizanga ukuzo lala lapha!* Let's get moving.'

Slowly the comatose bodies in the van came to life. He clapped his hands together to demonstrate urgency.

*'Hayibo!* I haven't got all night. Those who came to sleep in Beitbridge can stay behind. But if you want Egoli then you had better get moving!'

Givemore continued to address the passengers sternly.

'Leave everything. Even your brains. Where we are going there's no need for anything. No cellphones. No money. No nothing. Do you hear me? Shoes. Watches. Earrings. Money. Everything! You leave behind.'

There was shuffling and shifting as the passengers started to relieve themselves of their valuables.

'Mama, where are we going?' piped up the frightened voice of the little boy.

'Egoli mfana,' interjected Givemore. 'Joburg. That's going to be your new home boy!'

Then Givemore turned to address the cargo with a solemn face. Everyone in the car was now sitting up, listening attentively, poised to consume every word that fell from his lips.

'Two things: we move fast and everyone shurrup! No noise. One funny sound and the soldiers will spot us. I walk in front. The rest of you follow me. *I* am the leader.'

He slapped his chest for greater emphasis. The passengers nodded mutely.

'Queshions?'

No one dared to lift a hand even though a myriad questions ran through their minds.

'Good. We go. Errybody out, except for you, Lindani. You remain with Melusi.'

As each of the passengers disembarked from the safety of the van into the darkness, none of them knew what to expect. Or had any idea of what the journey ahead entailed. Like ghosts, their shadowy figures followed Givemore deep into the bush. Only when they were completely out of view did Melusi make a U-turn and head back to the border.

As they plodded through the dark they were accompanied by the sounds of chirping crickets, hooting owls and other peculiar sounds that sent shivers down Gugulethu's spine. The moon glimmered in all its brightness, casting shadows over the vast undulating landscape. The walk seemed endless. The path was rocky, littered with stones and spiky shrubs that assailed her tiny feet. No matter how great the discomfort, she bit down the urge to yelp out in pain. The intimidating voice of that man who led the way stayed with her. She followed his footsteps, knowing they would lead her to her mother. This was the reason she was on this journey, to be reunited with her mother.

Gugulethu had no recollection of her mother. All her childhood memories were painted with pictures of her huge-bosomed grandmother who wore floral aprons and a sunny smile. That was the woman who had mothered her all her life. Her heart ached at the thought of being separated from her. Huge tears stained her angelic face.

She so longed to rest her feet but the grating footsteps ahead of her assured her there would be no such luxury. The rocky outcrops that jutted from the earth scratched her soles. The stubs of hardy grass that brushed her ankles almost made her jump in the dark. The terrain changed and her toes waded through grains of sand. Her small feet made tiny imprints on the sand, which were covered by the larger feet that followed behind her. For Gugulethu, this was the most pleasant stretch of the walk. The dry sand was then replaced with mud as they approached the still body of water. The cool water washed around her ankles. The surface beneath her was uneven. She walked over a stone; it was slippery. She felt herself slide into the water. A hand gripped her arm and hoisted her up. Nevertheless her pretty yellow frock, her Sunday best, was soaking wet. She bit her tongue, fighting back the tears. Her grandmother would be so disappointed in her.

'I will hold you,' said the voice.

She nodded mutely. Afraid to open her mouth to speak. She was thankful for the hand that gripped hers as she waded through the water. It reached her waist and as they slid deeper, the water reached her neck. Her heart pounded in her chest. A hard thumping like an African drum.

'You'll be all right,' whispered the voice behind her. 'I've got you.'

It was Dumisani. His voice was decisive and reassuring. It did not rouse fear in her like the voice of the man who led them through these deep murky waters. Even when her feet could no longer touch the ground, she floated in the awareness that the strong masculine voice would keep her grounded.

Soon her feet felt the warm grains of sand at the bottom of the river. She knew they were near land. The worst was indeed over. Gugulethu was making her way to the shore of the river when a piercing scream tore through the still of the night. Her first impulse was to run. However, her feet would not cooperate. She felt like she was trapped by the reeds in the riverbed. She turned to see the source of the anguished cries.

'Help me! Help me!' screamed Malume. 'Help me!'

His hands were flailing in the air. He seemed to be fighting an unknown force. His body broke into spasms as though he was possessed by some unknown spirit. Then in a flash, his body disappeared beneath the water. Still the piercing screams resounded through the night.

Gugulethu felt something tug at her hand and she was dragged to the shores of the riverbank. What followed was a stampede as the remaining people in the water tried to wade across to safety. All were now aware of the perils which lurked in those waters, that had swallowed one of their own. The high-pitched desperate screams of the women cut through the air. Givemore, who stood on the riverbank on the other side, threw his hands up in resignation. He could not believe what was happening. This would undoubtedly rouse the attention of the soldiers who patrolled the bridge above. He held his hand to his head as if to block out the cries.

'uMalume!' gasped one as he reached the shore.

'I think we lost him,' explained another.

'He was right behind me,' sobbed a young woman. 'He was trying to hold onto me.'

All the wet bodies congregated around him. Each wanting to disclose what they had experienced. He could smell the fear. It engulfed him too. The little boy had even wet himself.

'Shurrup! Blurry shit!' sneered Givemore. 'Dammit, you want to wake up *all* the soldiers?'

His head was still spinning but he knew he had to pull himself together. He could not fall apart. He started to count his charges; everyone was present except Malume. He was just another statistic.

Givemore quickly shoved the thought to the back of his mind. Malume's journey might have been over, but theirs had just begun.

# SIX

oud banging on the door roused Portia to life. The light of a brand new morning filtered through the cracks in the door. She clasped her eyes shut. She could not face yet another day here.

'Portia! Portia!'

It was her mother-in-law's raspy voice. The person who could not even pronounce her name properly. She drew it out in her toothless mouth so that it sounded like Pour-shi-ya.

'Yebo, Mama!' she mumbled from underneath the Puma blanket whose fleece had been eroded by countless dry winters.

'*Akula manzi, wen' ulele.*' There is no water and you are fast asleep.

They had this same conversation every day, 360 days a year. In the remaining five days of the year when *her* son was kind enough to grace them with his presence the old woman let her be. Hoping that as they 'overslept' she might just conceive yet another grandson. Unbeknown to her, Portia was popping family planning pills. Bringing another child into their world was the last thing she wanted to do.

Otherwise it was business as usual in their tiny homestead in Silima School. Her mother-in- law had this irritating habit of getting up at six. She was fervent in her belief that a woman had to rise before the sun did and that women who slept beyond this time were lazy. Portia failed to see the point of getting up at the break of dawn. Especially seeing that there was nothing much to do.

Even the old woman had given up trying to till the barren land. Once upon a time when the soil yielded, they grew sweet potatoes, groundnuts, maize and sorghum. Those were the days when the heavens opened up and showered them with abundant rainfall. Now she had almost forgotten the tingling feeling of rain as it splashed against her skin and cooled her. Or that characteristic smell that lingered long after the storm had gone.

They were surrounded by stale dry air, which would not even coalesce into a single raindrop. Now all that stood between them and the cloudless sky was futility. Only the hardiest grass sprouted from the cracks in the earth. The small herd of cattle that once roamed the paddocks had succumbed to starvation and died.

Had it not been for the monthly food parcels delivered by the *umalayitsha* they too might have suffered a similar fate. The red-striped canvas bag always contained 20 kilograms of Iwisa maize meal, 5 kilograms of Selati brown sugar, 5 kilograms of Iwisa red speckled beans, three 2-litre bottles of Sunfoil cooking oil, 5 litres of Oros, 5 kilograms of Snowflake cake flour, 200 gram tablets of Lux soap and a 5 kilogram bag of Surf washing powder.

Once upon a time that bag would contain a variety of goodies like Beacon sweets, Cadbury chocolates and a 5 kilogram tin of Bakers Choice Assorted Biscuits. Those were treats she only tasted come Christmas. A lot of good things in her life were relegated to those last few days in the month of December. As if to imply that the other eleven months and twenty-five days of the year were to be spent in limbo.

Portia swung out of her bed supported on two solid bricks. She pulled on her dress from a dirty heap of clothing on the floor. She hadn't done the laundry in weeks. Portia dreaded the prospect of scrubbing the dirty clothes permanently soiled by the smoky odour of fire. She opened the door and daylight poured in; illuminating the otherwise dark interior of the hut. Her mother-in-law followed the light, charging in like an incensed bull.

'It's almost midday and *your* son hasn't eaten!'

Her face was creased with age and rage. A dirty child of four hung to her pleated brown skirt. Her son slept with his grandmother. The two were inseparable.

'I'll cook the porridge,' replied Portia.

She walked past the old woman whose gnarled hands were placed firmly on her jutting hip bones.

'There's no water! What porridge will you cook with no water?'

'I'll get the water,' replied Portia.

'And this washing? When are you going to do the washing? Nkosi and I won't have anything to wear to church on Sunday.'

Portia rolled her eyes heavenwards. 'There's no soap. Tell *your* son to send us soap.'

That threw the old woman into a long tirade about how her son was working tirelessly to support them. How she was wasteful. Portia ignored her as she picked up the buckets and piled one on her head. She made her way out the homestead, which was comprised of four round mud huts with unruly thatched straw roofs. Since her betrothal to Vusani five years before this had become her home.

Before he was her husband, he was her Geography teacher at

an old Catholic mission school about 40 kilometres away. She fell pregnant the year she was supposed to sit her O Level exams and was immediately elevated to the position of being his wife. Being a teacher's wife had its perks. They lived in staff accommodation at the mission and ate with the Catholic priests and nuns. She flourished in that environment with rounded hips and swelling breasts. Her cheeks shone with happiness. Even her mother-in-law was tolerable in those days.

It was only after the birth of their son that Vusani made a unilateral decision to try his luck in South Africa. She welcomed the move thinking they were going together. Vusani had promised he would send for her when he was settled. However, every year he came home it was the same story: Johannesburg is no place for a woman. Besides who will take care of Mama and the home?

As she made her way down the trodden path towards the river stream, the flat landscape dotted with sturdy mopani trees painted a future of futility. The sun beat down on her back. Her face and arms had been burnt black by its fierceness. She felt like she was being punished for a crime that she was not guilty of. Her feet were calloused and bruised from walking barefoot through the bush. She often begged Vusani to buy her takkies. He would respond that money was hard to come by.

The tears rolled down Portia's cheeks. She wished she had *never* fallen pregnant. At least if she had finished school she would have gone on to find a job. Her friends would write and tell her how well they were doing. One was a typist at the local municipality. The other was a trainee nurse at a government hospital. She wiped the tears from her face. There was no point in wallowing in self-pity. All the tears she cried had dried and still her situation had not changed.

By the time Portia got to the river her armpits were wet and clammy. Sweat trickled down the sides of her face. Her thighs were wet too. There were no other women by the river. This was a chore they undertook in the early hours of the morning before it got unbearably hot. She did not miss their company or the hours spent in idle gossip about absentee husbands and evil mothers-in-law.

Portia put the buckets down on the eroded riverbank. She pulled her dress over her head with one sweeping motion. Her full round breasts stood firm and proud like ripening tomatoes. Even after Nkosi had suckled on them they had not fallen. She waded into the water, which only wet her ankles. She bent over to scoop the murky brown water with her hands, splashing her face and body.

'Psst …'

The voice came from behind the trees, beyond the riverbanks. Portia looked up, her eyes searching.

'Portia!'

Her lips spread into a smile. It was the familiar voice of Thabani. He was a herdboy who lived at another homestead across the river.

'You are naked! What if someone sees you?'

'It's their fault. I have nothing to hide.'

Thabani started to take off his clothes too. Naked, he joined her in the water. They embraced and shared a long kiss. Thabani's hands immediately got lost in the untrimmed thatch of hair that grew between Portia's legs.

'I want you. I can't wait.'

Neither could she. He led her out of the water and they made love on the riverbank, the sun dappling on Thabani's strong muscled back, the wet sand cooling Portia's generous buttocks. They were oblivious to all else as they were enveloped in the heat that consumed them. Afterwards they lay in the sand, staring at the cloudless sky above them. Thabani's hands stroked Portia's belly.

'So *my* baby is growing inside you?'

'Yes. I hope you brought the money so I can go and register to give birth.'

'Portia, isn't it too early?'

'They say the earlier the better. The clinic gets full,' replied Portia.

'The money is in my trousers. Remind me before we leave.'

'I have to go now,' said Portia sitting up, 'before that witch comes after me.'

She returned to the river where she began to wash her private parts whilst Thabani looked on with deep admiration. He could have had her again and again. She was such a beautiful woman with her oval face and big black eyes. Her skin was soft and velvety like the coat of a Brahman steer. Her lips were thick, ripe and juicy like those wild berries which he ate hungrily when they were in season. He had no illusions that Portia could ever be his. However, he felt a quiet joy in his heart to know she was carrying his child. As long as that husband of hers was exiled to foreign lands he was determined to fill Portia with his seed.

'Get dressed!' spoke Portia, spraying him with water.

'Okay! Okay!'

Thabani escorted Portia back home in his scotch cart, which was pulled by two donkeys. As she sat with her legs outstretched, she felt immense joy. These were some of the few moments that took the monotony out of the drudgery of her daily life. In her hands she had two crisp R100 notes. She had no idea where Thabani got money from but every now and then he would surprise her. She already had R1 000 stashed in a corner in the roof where no one could find it. Her heart beat fast because finally she had enough money to secure her freedom.

Thabani foolishly believed that she was carrying his child. It was her way of conning him out of money which she needed to get out of this godforsaken place that had become her home. It was a shame she had to deceive a nice man but what choice did she really have?

'You look happy today,' observed Thabani.

'I am. You make me happy.'

He smiled too and kicked the donkey in the sides to make it move faster. When they arrived at the homestead he helped unload the buckets of water. Portia's mother-in-law thanked him profusely. After he had gone Portia started breaking twigs to make a fire. She dispensed with making porridge and cooked lunch instead. They ate under the shade of the gum tree, sprawled on intricately woven grass mats. The flies hovered enviously over the steaming plates of pap that accompanied the dried strips of biltong cooked in peanut butter. After a few mouthfuls Portia announced to her mother-in-law she had to go into Plumtree town.

'I got word that my aunt is not feeling well. I will be going with Nkosi.'

Her mother-in-law frowned. 'He's going to miss church!'

'My aunt really wants to see him. I cannot leave him,' Portia replied then turned to her son. 'You want to come with me to town tomorrow? We can buy Fanta and lots of sweets.'

His eyes shone radiantly. Portia had offered him bait she knew he would not refuse.

'Yes Mama, I want to go.'

Her mother-in-law pouted, annoyed.

'Just make sure you get back before it's dark, Portia! You know the dangers of travelling at night.'

'Yes Mama. We'll try get back here as early as we can.'

When Portia left the homestead early the next morning, with her son in tow, it never occurred to her mother-in-law that this was the last time they would ever see each other again.

# SEVEN

They paced purposefully through the bush; it was a familiar path that Givemore had walked many times. However, it was the first time in years someone had died under his watch. He hoped the spirit of Malume would not return to haunt him and assail him with bad luck. He shrugged the thought to the back of his mind. It would not serve him well to dwell on Malume. People died everyday on this perilous journey.

He steered them along a well-worn path, trodden by the feet of the many that had paved the way before them. They walked briskly; no one dared articulate their exhaustion to Givemore. Nothing in his stern demeanour would have entertained it. Although no one spoke the eerie night sounds around them were a constant reminder that they were not alone. Metres rolled into kilometres before they reached what was a menacing barrier of steel wire. The razor-sharp spokes that crowned the barrier's head would tear into anyone who tried to scale its heights. Givemore indicated gingerly that it was the first of four fences that they had to get under.

'Now everyone is going to crawl under this fence as fast as they can.'

Givemore held up a torn portion of the fence. The children were given the first right of passage. They manoeuvred their tiny bodies under the wiry steel easily. Then the women followed suit. Givemore's girlfriend with her lanky, sinewy body wriggled through. Chenai was next and with swift agility she was on the other side. Portia was last amongst the women. She rolled on the ground but her tangled mess of hair got caught in the spokes at the bottom of the fence.

'Move!' hissed Givemore through gritted teeth.

'I can't!' wailed Portia.

Givemore shoved her with the heel of his foot. Portia yelped in pain.

'You are hurting her!' Dumisani protested.

'Shurrup! It's this stupid hair!'

Givemore reached into his pocket. He pulled out a penknife and clicked the blade open. Portia went rigid with fear. Her son cried out in concern. The women looked aside as he cut the strands of hair. By the time he was finished with her she looked like a scarecrow. The men then made their way through the fence without ceremony and in turn held the fence for Givemore to get through. They were all standing on the other side when he addressed them with a stern voice.

'Listen here. I'm the boss. Errybody will do as I say.'

No one disputed this, or dared to answer. They stood quietly in the dark. They would not have known the intensity of Givemore's anger had a bright light not shone on it, illuminating his taut face.

'Madoda, don't lie to them. You are not in charge here.'

An authoritative voice sounded in the dark. It belonged to an equally tall man so dark that he could have easily blended in with the night. He was flanked by two shorter, squat men. The men had rifles strapped to their shoulders. The steel glinted each time a light fell on them.

'We are not here to cause trouble,' spoke Givemore in a small voice.

The bullishness in his voice had diminished a few octaves.

'Yeah, but you are in our territory. You can't just traipse through our territory without paying your dues.'

'My apologies but we have no money.'

Givemore emptied his pockets in an effort to demonstrate his poverty. The man snorted and waved his hand. His men laughed derisively but uttered no words.

'I'm not stupid! How can you not have money with all these heads?'

He used his rifle to point at the cargo for emphasis. They were all huddled together.

'If you have no cash, *lizabadala ngezibunu*, you will pay with your arses!'

Givemore exhaled deeply, 'Please *magents*. Can you just let us be?'

The man ignored his plea and commanded his men to search everyone.

'We'll start with you.'

The two men started to rifle through Givemore's pockets in complete disregard to his earlier effort. They stripped him naked and searched him a second time, probing his orifices with their stubby fingers. Convinced he had no money they shoved him aside roughly. They proceeded to accost Chamunorwa. They even ran their fingers through his thick dreadlocks thinking he might have stashed some notes in them. They found nothing and pushed him aside. The same procedure was followed with Dumisani. They

41

found a thick wad of notes in his Polo briefs, nestled beneath his balls, cushioned by the pubic hair. They surrendered the find to their boss who immediately started counting the notes.

'And you say you don't have money?'

Givemore gave Dumisani a scathing look. It communicated a thousand expletives that Givemore was unable to mete out then.

'So you lied to us?'

Givemore did not respond but stumbled back when the leader slapped him hard across the face. His men joined in the assault. They rained fists down on Givemore's body. Kicked him relentlessly. 'Stupid *basterd*. We ask for money and you tell us you have nothing! We should actually kill you! Search each one thoroughly!' he growled. Like hyaenas withdrawing from a prowl the two men retreated. They obeyed their leader's instructions and began searching the women. Like the men, they were stripped naked. Their humiliation knew no bounds as each of the men seemed to take liberties with them like fondling their breasts and squeezing their buttocks. The children were not spared either. Nkosi had again wet himself in fear. Gugulethu had to bite her lips to stave off the tears. The search yielded nothing as they had heeded Givemore's stern instructions to leave anything of value in the car.

'So we have four thousand dollars. Not bad a for a night's work,' spoke the leader. 'Now we want some female arse. Just one *nje*. We have no problems with sharing.'

Dumisani spoke up, unable to contain his rage any longer. That was what was left of his retrenchment package. Money they had spent with sober restraint as they waited for that job offer that never came. Money they had finally decided would pay for his passage into South Africa. It was supposed to buy him a new identity. His passport to a new life.

'These women have their husbands. Please. I have given you a lot of money. Let us go.'

'I don't care!' retorted the leader. 'Your money could never be enough.'

The light from the leader's torch shone in the direction of the women. Each one was brought under the scrutiny of the glaring light. The light lingered on Chenai who stood beside Gugulethu with a protective arm around the little girl. The spotlight lingered on her for a few seconds longer then bounced off to Portia whose hand was intertwined with that of her son. The light was finally cast on Thulisiwe, the lanky teenager who had arrived with Givemore. She stood alone, her eyes cast downwards. She wore a tight T-shirt with glitter on it. As it had not dried from the water escapade earlier it still clung to her perky breasts. She wore tight denim jeans, which clung to her curves.

'I'll take her. Those mothers and their milky breasts smell!'

She looked up then. The confusion and fear in her eyes was palpable. She looked to Givemore, her eyes searching his, hoping to elicit a response from him. She expected him to at least come to her defence. Instead he said nothing. He sat mutely in a heap on the ground.

'*Hazviite!*' This is not acceptable.

It was Chamunorwa's strangled voice.

'Voetsek!' spat the leader prodding him with his rifle. 'We like screamers. We'll take you too. Men or women. We are not choosy.'

That threat silenced any further objection that was lodged in anyone's throat. They watched wordlessly as the three men grabbed hold of their hostage and disappeared into the thicket of trees. When they had left, Givemore picked himself up. He spoke to no one but just assumed his position at the helm of the group and led the way. Everyone fell into line behind him and followed his steps through the bush. His shoulders hung with defeat. He no longer possessed his earlier bravado. Even his step was more subdued and measured. Unbeknown to his cargo they had just concluded an encounter with *ogumaguma*. Ruthless bandits who lurked beyond the Limpopo River; a law unto themselves.

# EIGHT

A few days earlier, Lindani had disembarked from the
bus with a suitcase filled with beautiful clothes and
broken dreams. As the bus chugged away it expelled
a haze of putrid black fumes, which enveloped her, making her
choke. She fanned herself furiously with her hands. The fumes just
merged into the dry air. She was reminded at that moment just
how hot and merciless the weather in Bulawayo could be. The sun
shone down on her smooth shaven head. She did not even pos-
sess a hat to shield her from the blazing heat. She stood with her
back to the white-washed stone wall of Grey Prison, which housed
Bulawayo's criminals at the edge of the city.

She had finally turned her back on the Sunshine City. Her last
few years there had been devoid of any sunshine; blighted by thun-
derstorms. It had been a long journey back home on Eagle Liner,
which was like an empty tin of baked beans on wheels. She had
been lucky to find a seat with a cushion intact. An old woman
whose armpits emitted an acrid odour settled down next to her, her
buttocks spilling out of the seat. The bus had barely pulled out of
the Mbare Musika Bus Terminal when the woman reached into her

bag and whipped out a red plastic lunch box. The pungent smell from her egg sandwiches was even more overpowering than that of her armpits.

'Do you want one?' asked the woman, looking her directly in the eyes.

The flecks of spit landed on Lindani's face. She wiped her skin, not masking her annoyance.

'No thanks. I'm fine,' replied Lindani crisply.

'You look like you haven't eaten in a while.'

Lindani ignored her and did not respond. She was glad when the woman sank her teeth into the sandwich. At least that would keep her silent and spare her the diatribe. However, even with her mouth full the woman continued to speak. Her words scrambled between the eggs, her voice muffled by the bread. Lindani knew she would have no peace for the next six hours. Around her, passengers spoke animatedly. A chorus of voices rose in discord with some conversations punctuated by boisterous laughter.

By the time the bus rolled into Chegutu, Lindani's senses had become impervious to the cacophony of voices around her and the repulsive smells emitted by the woman beside her. The bus made further stops in Kadoma, Kwekwe and Gweru. At every city the bus was accosted by vendors selling anything from bananas to chips, cigarettes to maize cobs, oranges to sweets. There was naked desperation in the eyes and voices of the vendors as they punted their commodities. A desperation that Lindani understood keenly. The past two years of her life in Harare had been that. A desperate fight for survival.

'So where are you going?' asked the woman whose hand was clutched around a slim bottle of Coca-Cola.

This, after she had spent the greater part of the morning narrating to Lindani how she travelled back and forth from Harare to Botswana to sell doilies and her adventures in-between.

'Home,' replied Lindani. 'My mother lives in Bulawayo.'

'And your husband? He's the one in Harare?'

'I don't have a husband,' replied Lindani.

'A beautiful woman like you? How can you *not* have a husband?'

Lindani half smiled. This was something she got told over and over again. Because of her heart-shaped face and alluring black eyes brightening her face like diamonds. Her sensual lips that looked like they had been carved with precision by a sculptor's knife. Lindani's light mocha complexion set her apart from the rest. Her bald brazen head further accentuated her features and amplified her beauty. She was indeed a picture of perfection. All her life she had tried to live off her looks. It was supposed to be her passport to a better future. The pictures of the men who had left a grubby imprint on her nubile body flashed through her head: Rhino. Tito. Farai. Jonasi. Moses. Edgar. Nhamo. Phakama. Alain. Some she had even forgotten. Blurred nameless faces. In the two decades she had lived she had probably slept with more men than some women managed in a lifetime.

'You are beautiful. Find a nice man and settle down.'

'Are *you* married?' countered Lindani.

'No,' replied the woman nonchalantly. 'I have never been married. I should have settled down when I had the chance but I never did. Now I have four kids from different men that I support on my own. I'm going to Botswana to buy stuff to sell in Harare. If I don't do this we starve. Before I would sleep with men for money. But I'm old now. You think anyone wants to sleep with me?'

She let the question linger and continued to chew on her own words.

'I don't look it but I was pretty like you once upon a time. Men used to fight for me. I lost my teeth in bar brawls. The thing is when you are young you don't think you'll age. And men age you.'

Lindani looked the old woman squarely in the eyes. Her face was lined with age, hardship and bitterness. Her face no longer held a trace of beauty but was wrinkled with wisdom.

'I was married once,' declared Lindani. 'He passed on ...'

She did not speak of her deep love for him for she had felt none, only gratitude. He had provided her with a home and a healthy income when he was alive. He had adored her and worshipped the ground she walked on. For a while that made her feel special. Like she was worth something. It was not the kind of marriage most girls dreamt of. She did not wear a fairytale white wedding dress with a tight-fitting diamanté-encrusted bodice that opened into a full skirt. There were no bridesmaids in white taffeta and ballerina shoes. There was no elaborate ceremony with a three-tier cake with figurines on top. Just a simple signing at the Harare Magistrates Court a year before her husband had succumbed to death ravished by full-blown AIDS. Then her husband's ex-wife had showed up claiming title to the house and cars. It was during the battle that ensued that she discovered her marriage was legally null and void. This had left her with no leg to stand on.

A long fight lasted over a year before she was served an eviction notice three months before by a stern-looking messenger of the court. She had tried to sell herself to him but he was unmoved. He was steadfast and unaffected by her beauty. She could barely read the fine print through the film of tears. She reached for her cellphone and called Rhino. The phone rang interminably till it went to voicemail. She called Tito. The call was answered after two rings.

'Bitch. Leave my husband alone!'

Lindani cut the call immediately. She didn't have money to waste on a vociferous confrontation with Tito's wife. She dialled Alain's number. It was no longer in use according to the operator. She tried Phakama. He answered but was curt and promised he would call her back in a few minutes. She fell into a deep troubled sleep. When she awoke it was dark outside. Lindani reached for her cellphone. There were no missed calls. She tried to call Phakama back but instead a female voice reminded her that she had insufficient funds to make a call. Exasperated she threw the phone aside. She exhaled deeply. She decided then to get dressed and make her way into town.

A two-trillion-dollar Gucci bag was strung across her shoulder with a few million dollars inside. Zimbabwe had turned them into billionaires. Poverty-stricken billionaires. She did not have enough money to fuel the cars lodged in the garage. She had tried to sell them but the deal hit a snag when she failed to produce the registration books. As she walked past the cottage, a stream of smoke curled into the air. She figured there was no electricity. She had resorted to letting out the cottage to a young couple to generate income to cover utilities and general upkeep.

She continued to prostitute herself to men using the house as a base. As the economy nosedived, penny-pinching was the order of the day. Disposable income shrank like depleted erections and lovers tightened the purse strings. Only a few could afford to keep a woman on the side. Girlfriends were now a liability for most. Lindani stood on the side of Josiah Tongogara Avenue like all the other women selling their bodies. Josiah would have turned in his grave if he'd known this was what his hard-fought liberation had resulted in. It was a particularly slow night. There were other prostitutes across the road making small talk but she didn't feel like company. She lit a joint to pass the time. It was only after an hour that a Mazda twin cab came to a screeching halt. The window rolled down to reveal a bunch of loud-mouthed, raucous men.

'We're having a bachelor party! Need some entertainment. We'll pay you well.'

Lindani did not hesitate and immediately jumped into the car. She was later delivered to a boisterous party in the burbs, which looked like it was at the peak of its madness. The host shoved some money in her hand indicating he meant business. There was no dancing out of an iced cake or sensually parading herself in front of a groom. Instead she was shown to a dishevelled bedroom and later joined by six men with glazed looks on their faces. They had their way with her … all six of them. By the time they were done with her she had urine in her hair and spunk spattered on her face. She had to crawl to the bathroom to clean herself. When she looked in the mirror she couldn't even recognise herself. There was a knock on the door. The voice of the gracious host sounded. 'Hurry, the others are waiting.'

Lindani looked at the window and decided to jump out of it.

Bruised but not broken she forced herself through the blackness of the night till she found herself outside her home. At this height of desperation she tore her weave from her head. Without hesitation she shaved her crowning glory and the thick tufts fell to the ground like freshly mown grass. She got into a shower and when the water hit her she cried. Loud racking sobs. She scrubbed her body harshly as if to erase the imprint of the men who had pawed at her body. Afterwards she crawled into bed and slept all day and all night. When she woke up she made up her mind to move back home. But her conversation with her mother did not go well.

'What are you going to do here?' asked her mother.

'I don't know yet.'

'You know I can't look after you!' screamed her mother. 'All my life, Lindani, I have been taking care of you! When will it stop? When will you take care of me?'

Lindani had bit hard on her lower lip hoping to ward off the tears that threatened to burst from her eyes.

'I'm sure I'll get a job or something.'

'You had better. Times are hard. I can't cope.'

Her mother had cut her off before she could even say goodbye. So she'd packed all her belongings into a single suitcase. The very same case she had carried when she moved to Harare a few years earlier. To think she'd set foot in this town with so much bravado but that now she was departing from it like a wounded soldier. Home would be a good respite. She needed to contemplate her future now that the king and castles had been knocked off the chessboard.

The woman squeezed her hand. 'When one door closes another one opens. You mustn't give up. Pick yourself up and keep moving.'

For the first time Lindani smiled appreciatively and her eyes misted with tears. It was not often she experienced genuine affection outside a sexual embrace. They hugged briefly before Lindani got off the bus. In a strange way she felt like that unusual woman in the bus had given her a new lease on life. No longer did she feel like she was at her wits' end; rather that she was embarking on a new path. A new chapter. She started flagging down cars that drove past. Then a white Quantum came to a screeching halt.

# NINE

The bright morning light shone, sparking some optimism in each of them. Even though it was still early morning, the heat had begun to burn in all its fierceness. The promise of a new day lay beyond the Soutpansberg mountain range. The group emerged from the bush, hastily making their way to Melusi's Quantum parked on the side of the road, the door wide open to receive them. The door closed behind the last passenger and without a second look Melusi jumped inside.

'Are we all in?' he asked as he assumed his place behind the steering wheel.

'*Sonke sikhona,*' replied Givemore with authority. 'We are all here.'

The cargo settled well into the seats. The seat once occupied by Malume was deliberately left vacant as if to accommodate his spirit. No one made mention of Thulisiwe either. The passengers' faces were etched with anxiety, their bodies exhausted and deflated from what had transpired in the last few hours. The children were the first to succumb to sleep. Deep in their slumber they were oblivious to the apprehension about the road ahead gripping the minds of the adults. No one parted their dry, cracked lips to articulate their thoughts. They were too tired. Too hungry. Some were unable to keep their weary eyelids open. The engine roared to life and the Quantum slid onto the road. The distance could only be measured by the rolling, endless stretch of tarmac. They shared the road with long haulage trucks grumbling under their heaving loads. Development replaced the straggly bushes, tall grass, tweeting birds and buzzing insects. The treacherous Limpopo River and its crocodiles and the even more menacing bandits that lurked in no man's land were all but a distant memory.

By the time they arrived in the town of Musina there were few open eyes. Most had succumbed to sleep. Messina, as the earliest twentieth-century settlers called it, was the first town to welcome you into South Africa. Unlike Johannesburg, it was not gold that had lured the early settlers but large reddish-brown copper deposits. Musina was home to a population of approximately 42 000, a quarter of whom were estimated to be Zimbabweans living either in refugee camps or spilling out onto the streets. Some came to look for employment on the nearby farms, but for others it was a transient destination before they moved onto greener pastures in the bigger cities in South Africa.

Ask anyone in Musina and they would tell you that *these* Zimbabweans were different from *those* Zimbabweans who crossed into Musina in droves in their shiny sleek sedans or 4 x 4s to do their weekend shopping along Main Road. Who shopped till the trolleys they pushed creaked in protest. Different from those Zimbabweans who inundated Spur, KFC and ate till they were bursting at the seams. Different from those Zimbabweans who spilled out of buses and almost bought out the goods from wholesalers to take back home for resale. Different from those Zimbabweans who filled the hotels, guest houses, bed-and-breakfast establishments over week-ends whilst they waited to collect their ex-Japanese Pajeros, Nissans and Toyotas, which would then be cleared over several days at the border.

Even as Melusi manoeuvred his car into a BP fuel station he had to wait behind a queue of Zimbabweans. There were trucks piled high with steel drums that would be filled with litres and litres of fuel to be transported across the border for resale. These Zimbabweans walked tall, cash bursting from their bulging wallets. Their faces did not articulate any struggle nor did their eyes convey despair. Ask any retailer in Musina and they would tell you that there were two types of Zimbabweans: the obscenely rich and the filthy poor. It was a tale of two classes.

Whilst they waited, Melusi went to buy his cargo some food. The smell of soggy fried chips smothered in vinegar accosted their nostrils and roused them. Givemore quickly distributed crispy loaves of freshly baked bread. Hungry fingers tore into the bread which was soft on the inside. The children made spongy rounds with their hands before they threw tiny morsels into their mouths. They washed the bread down their parched throats with the cold fizzy Fantas, Cokes and Sprites shared between them. Even Givemore was in high spirits as he bit into his thick, oily Russian sausage, which the others did not have the privilege of eating. Nevertheless its smell permeated the whole car, mingling with the other smells of unwashed bodies, foul breath and irrepressible relief.

'*Bekukubi!*' he explained to Melusi between bitefuls. 'It got ugly there.'

'It's over. We are doing the home stretch now,' replied Melusi stepping on the accelerator.

'Whatever happened to Thuli and Malume?' asked Lindani

who was sandwiched in the front between Givemore and Melusi. In her lap she nestled a steaming hot packet of greasy chips and crumbed pieces of fried chicken, which she shared with Melusi.

'They were left behind,' replied Givemore tersely.

'Maybe your muti doesn't work anymore,' said Melusi.

Givemore reached for his pendant and held it for a lingering second.

'It works. We are here aren't we?'

Melusi nodded and turned on the radio. The sounds of Brenda Fassie reflected the more upbeat mood in the car.

'Higher and higher,' crooned Brenda, 'Higher and higher … aint nothing stopping us!'

The Quantum glided down the polished length of the N1 toll road. The northward-bound road wound through the Soutpansberg mountain range and traversed the Tropic of Capricorn, though they were unaware of it. They stopped briefly in Louis Trichardt to refuel and use the public ablutions. Hours later they arrived in Polokwane and drove through it quickly. A few kilometres outside town they were flagged down by a police car. Melusi cussed under his breath as he brought the vehicle to a skidding halt. He swung out confidently; the paperwork for the car clutched under his arm. Givemore, who had fallen asleep, woke up. The sight of policemen scared him. He shifted nervously in his seat and almost woke up Lindani who was still asleep, her head resting on his shoulder. A policeman approached the car. He peeked in through the open window but did not bother to open the door. He returned to his car and wrote what appeared to be a little slip which he handed to Melusi.

'Speeding fine,' announced Melusi as he climbed back into the car. 'Five hundred rand gone, baba. This has been one helluva trip.'

'Tell me about it,' replied Givemore. 'And it's not even over.'

The journey continued without any further episodes. It was after three in the afternoon when they drove under a board marked Pretoria/Polokwane. Melusi exhaled deeply. Home was now in sight. He couldn't wait to park his car and rest. He stole a glance at Lindani. He forced his foot down on the accelerator thinking of the rewards that lay ahead. However, he came to a stop in Midrand when he converged with the five o'clock evening traffic snaking along the M1 South. The cars crawled at a snail's pace along the concrete highway.

When he had first arrived in Johannesburg he had been amazed to see so many cars spread across six lanes running parallel to each other. Cars of all shapes and sizes, of all makes and models and all colours of the rainbow. They were like a packet of Liquorice Allsorts. Back then he had never contemplated that one day he too would be steering his way in this traffic; manoeuvring from the slow lane to the fast lane. In bumper-to-bumper rush hour traffic tailing the rump of a sexy BMW.

In the distance he could see the tall and iconic Telkom Johannesburg tower. Egoli. The City of Gold. He smiled. A wide toothy smile that spread from ear to ear. It felt good to be back in the bosom of a city that pulsated with life. Johannesburg did that to him. It was like coming home to the arms of an unpredictable lover. He felt a rush. Every encounter was different. No one man could experience Johannesburg in the same way.

# TEN

Most children are naturally afraid of the dark. Gugulethu was not. She grew up in the dark. She was born into a Zimbabwe that was plunged in darkness. Beyond the daylight her world was pitch-black. Sometimes a lone flickering candle provided a ray of light into the dark home she shared with her grandmother. During the day she would play out on the street till she was almost unrecognisable, coated with a film of dust. However, when the sun went down she knew it was time to go home. She always played near their house. Her grandmother always cautioned against playing far away where no one could see her. There are monsters out there, she would say over and over again. Monsters that prey on little girls like you.

'Gugu! Gugu!'

'Gog!' she would respond.

She always answered on the first call because her grandmother would spank her if she had to call her a second or a third time. She ran to the gate and straight into her grandmother's apron where she was enveloped with love. They walked hand in hand into the house. That was their routine. It was always the same.

Gugulethu attended school a few metres away from her home. Her friends collected her on their way to school and she would walk back home with them. She never played along the way because her grandmother would be standing at the gate waiting for her. Once she had gotten carried away and starting playing a game of hop-scotch on the side of the road. She had no sense of the time but only realised she was late when her grandmother had descended upon them and whipped her in front of her friends. She had cried all the way home. From that day on she had learnt never to keep her grandmother waiting.

As soon as she got home she would change out of her uniform into her home clothes. These were different from her going-out clothes which she wore to church. She would eat lunch. They did not have homework so she would go out and play to her heart's content. Then when the sun set she was called in for her bath. Her grandmother would scrub her body furiously and when she was done the water would be brown and murky but she always felt spotlessly clean. She would then change into a nightdress. A different one every night. Her closet was brimming with clothes that her mother sent.

Gugulethu did not remember her mother though. Not even the pictures in the house stirred any recollection of her. They sat beside those of her grandfather, another stranger to her. Male voices had been absent for the greater part of her life. Even the little boys she played with squealed like women. All she had ever heard were high-pitched voices of the female matriarchs around her. The exception was her grandmother's voice, which was soft and melodious, music to her ears. She had been told she had a father but had never met him. There were no pictures to ever verify his existence.

'Gogo. *Ungaph' ubab' wam?* Where is my father?'

The question caught her grandmother off guard. Her brow wrinkled with apprehension.

'Well? Where is he?'prodded Gugulethu.

Her grandmother stared at her long and hard.

'He is with your mother. You will meet them soon enough.'

'When, Gogo? When?'

'Soon,' she replied.

Gogo Mkhize had never really liked her son-in-law. He had brought so much shame into her life. Patrick and Xolile had been in the same class in high school. Lovesick teenagers. Many times she had beaten her daughter trying to caution her against the dangers of playing with boys. The danger of letting boys touch you inappropriately. Then the pregnancy happened. Everyone was talking about them. She even stopped going to church that year because she could not bear those silent whispers and accusatory glances. Everyone thought she was a bad mother. That if Xolile had a father none of this would have happened.

The day Gugulethu was born the shame lifted and was replaced by an indescribable joy she had never felt. Something that had died with her husband woke up that day. She became a doting grandmother and approached her role with so much zeal. Xolile returned to school to finish her studies but her good-for-nothing boyfriend jumped his way into South Africa. Gogo Mkhize thought that was the last she would hear of him but the following year he sent for her daughter. Xolile never even said goodbye. She left home saying she was going to buy bread at the supermarket and never returned.

Gogo Mkhize had strapped baby Gugulethu on her back and had scurried through the township looking for her daughter. On the second day she filed a missing person's report at the police station. On the third day she got a call from Xolile saying she was in

Johannesburg and she was fine. They did not talk for a full year after that. Then as the groceries and money started coming, Gogo Mkhize's heart softened a little. By then Gugulethu was walking and breaking things all over the house. Nonetheless she was still the light of her granny's life. When Gugulethu turned four her father sent his uncles to pay damages to their family. The lobola followed two years later when Gugulethu started school. Then the demand for their child came shortly after.

'What are we eating today?' asked Gugulethu breaking into her thoughts.

'I made spaghetti and mince,' replied her grandmother who used to be a food and nutrition teacher. She had cooked every recipe in the green O Level Cookery Book. Gugulethu always looked forward to her colourful meals. She was not aware that sometimes her grandmother rehashed recipes because they did not have all the ingredients. But Gogo Mkhize always made a long list of things which she sent to her daughter in South Africa.

'Xoli, you didn't buy the nutmeg I asked for,' she would complain.

'Mama, is that even necessary?'

'Yes it is,' she would insist. 'My banana bread won't taste the same!'

'I will buy it next time,' Xoli would respond dismissively.

And she wouldn't, much to her mother's chagrin.

Gogo Mkhize had always prided herself on being one of the few educated women on the street. Her husband had been educated too. He had been an agricultural extension officer. They had a little garden in the back where they grew every vegetable under the sun and even after he died she continued gardening as she felt it kept her close to his spirit. Gugulethu had never known her grandfather as he had died long before she had even been formed in her mother's womb. A car accident had robbed him of his life. A truck driver had lost control and rammed mercilessly into his Mazda that careened off the road and rolled three times.

Gogo Mkhize had only been 26 when he died and was left to raise her four-year-old daughter alone. She never remarried, preferring to be faithful to the memory of her husband. Many men had made overtures but she ignored them and instead poured her soul into the church preferring to be Christ's bride. Every Sunday she would wear her red Methodist uniform and dress Gugulethu in a beautiful frock. They were a formidable pair. Now she would even be deprived of that. The thought made her push her plate aside. She looked across at Gugulethu who wolfed her food down with enjoyment.

'Your mama called again today. She says you must come to visit her in Johannesburg.'

'Johannes where?' Gugu replied, not even looking up from her plate.

'Jo-han-nes-burg,' repeated Gogo Mkhize slowly.

'I don't want to go there,' replied Gugulethu, 'I want to stay here with you Gog. I want to play outside with Nana, Basil and Lungi.'

She went on to count all her other friends on her fingers. Gogo Mkhize's heart swelled with emotion. She could not bear the thought of losing Gugulethu too. Her heart constricted painfully.

That evening after she had put Gugulethu to bed she sat by her bed and watched her sleep. It always amazed her how she would fall asleep the minute her head hit the pillow. An hour passed and Gogo Mkhize was just staring at her cherubic face. She finally reached for her cellphone and called her daughter. She rarely ever called Xolile unless there was an emergency of sorts or somebody in the family had died. Not that Xolile seemed to care; she would express her condolences and that was it. She had never returned home from the time she had left. The phone rang continuously. She hung up. A few minutes later Xolile called back. She sounded annoyed.

'*Niright*, Ma?' she asked.

'We are fine, Xoli.'

'Have you packed Gugu's things? They leave tomorrow. Don't be late, Ma, like you were last time!'

'Do you even trust this guy? Is it safe?'

Xolile snapped, 'Everybody does this, Ma! How else do you think we will get her across the border without papers?'

'You can just leave her with me. She is fine here.'

'No, Ma, she is my child. She needs her mother.'

'I have mothered her all my life, Xoli. What do you know about mothering?'

'Mama, just put my child on that Quantum. *Yezwa!*'

Gogo Mkhize was about to state her objection when the line went dead. Instead she slunk off to bed feeling defeated. That night she sought sleep and it eluded her. She tossed and turned in her bed and woke up in the morning feeling even wearier. Reluctantly she got Gugulethu ready for the trip.

They met up with Melusi at Max's Garage. Gogo Mkhize knew him from the number of times he delivered groceries to her house. He had been doing it for years but they barely spoke beyond exchanging a few pleasantries.

'Please take care of my granddaughter!' implored Gogo Mkhize.

Melusi responded with a toothy grin, 'No need to worry, Gogz.

We do this everyday.'

Gugulethu was crying, 'Gogo, don't leave me!' she wailed. 'Don't leave me!'

'*Hayi mntanami,*' she croaked, fighting back her own tears. 'You have to go to your mother.' Her voice was cracking with the weight of her breaking heart. The tears burst forth. She wiped them away quickly and looked towards the road ahead. This was for the best. Gugulethu needed her parents. Every child needed to be with their parents.

'It's okay, mama, I will watch her,' volunteered a woman who was also travelling with a young boy.

Gogo Mkhize thanked her profusely. However, Gugulethu was not comforted. Even when the Quantum's engine started up she could hear her granddaughter's cries. She banged against the window frantically.

'Gogo! Gogo! Don't leave me!'

Her tear-stained face was stuck to the window as the car pulled away. It was an image that stayed with Gogo Mkhize. One that she would carry to her own grave.

# PART TWO

**The City of Gold**

'Now the Lord had said unto Abraham, "Get thee
out of thy country, and from thy kindred, and from
thy father's house, unto a land that I will show
thee".'

*Genesis 12: Verse 1*

# ELEVEN

Hillbrow was a cluster of elevated buildings reaching towards the sky like vines trying to escape the hell that lurked below in its streets. Gutted windows with hollowed eyes looked heavenwards as if seeking salvation. Their façades were stripped naked of a much-needed coat of paint. Others with face-brick exteriors were better preserved with some outward measure of dignity. The lucky ones had recently been given a facelift and coloured pink, white or yellow; a burst of colour to otherwise grey, lifeless buildings.

As Melusi's Quantum veered onto Claim Street he jostled for position amongst the other Quantums headed towards the Noord Taxi Rank where multitudes waited in queues to be bussed home. The hooters blared noisily. Competing were equally boisterous conversations taking place along the sidewalks.

Portia was the first passenger to disembark. Melusi pointed out that Claim Towers was the address that she sought. It was the same address that had been scribbled in cursive in the last letter she had received from her husband. She and Nkosi stood awkwardly on the pavement. Throngs of people brushed past them in a mad rush and they would have easily trampled them without a care. She grabbed her son's hand tightly and walked to the entrance of the flat. Like other flats on the street, laundry was hung out to dry for all and sundry to see on tiny balconies. Claim Towers, with its bland grey exterior gave nothing away of what lay inside its walls. The entrance was almost like a prison with a barricaded wrought-iron gate. When she was through, a stern-looking uniformed guard interrogated her.

'I am here to see my husband,' she declared.

The guard was indifferent and merely asked for her ID card.

'I don't have one,' replied Portia.

'Passport?'

'I don't have one.'

The guard snorted, 'You are not going to get far in this life without any ID.'

With a cursory wave he asked her to move aside and dealt with the next set of visitors. He was rigorous. He inspected their IDs then asked them to fill out a form.

'Please understand. I don't have a passport or ID,' spoke Portia in earnest.

The guard turned to her and eyed her up and down with great circumspection.

'I can't, sisi,' replied the guard. 'We don't allow strangers here. What if you are here to kill someone?'

'*Please!* Do I look like a killer?' pleaded Portia.

The guard was unmoved, 'Mama, step aside. You are blocking the corridor.'

Portia took her son by the hand and led him outside. She sat down on the pavement between two vendors who were selling sweets, popcorn, crisps and fruit. Nkosi sat beside her and rested his head on her lap. He was exhausted. She stroked his head tenderly. To think that after all they had gone through a stubborn guard stood between their reunion with her husband. Well, she was not going to leave. Her husband was bound to come out sooner or later and he would find them sitting on the pavement like vagrants. People walked past them oblivious of their presence.

Portia's woes were temporarily forgotten as her mind focused on the well-groomed women stepping past in high heels clickety-clicking on the pavement. Some of them wore pants so tight that Portia was convinced they would split down the middle. Others wore short skirts that exposed their fleshy thighs. Some of the women had bold hairstyles that turned heads. Even the men were well dressed in tight pants and coloured shirts and pointy shoes. The fashion show continued long after the sun had gone down and the activity on the street continued unabated.

It was only when Nkosi cried for food that Portia was reminded why they were out on the street. She bought him a packet of Simba chips. She shoved the remaining notes into her bra. It was then the vendor spoke to her.

'You are from Zimbabwe, aren't you?'

It was more of a statement than a question. She nodded. Without any prompting she quickly narrated her ordeal at the hands of the guard. The vendor offered her some empathy.

'The security is just doing his job. It's not safe. You shouldn't be sitting out here! I know your husband. Let me help you. But you will need to help me with money for a cooldrink.'

Portia eyed him speculatively; not quite understanding what this man was asking of her.

'Money, sisi. I need money. There is nothing for mahala here.'

Portia reached into her bra for a note. It was crumpled and

moist. The vendor did not care. He shoved it into his pocket quickly. He escorted her back into the building. After a furtive exchange with the security guard they were granted the much-needed access. However, the thought of seeing her husband outweighed the pain of losing her R100 note.

'Your husband is on the twelfth floor. The lift is not working.'

Portia sighed heavily as she looked at the flight of stairs now standing between her and her husband. Several flights of stairs later, Portia stood at the door of number 1215 panting profusely. Her son was equally exhausted and had collapsed in a heap in the passageway. Portia knocked furtively on the door. After a while a large woman appeared at the door, a towel wrapped around her generous proportions. Portia was slightly perplexed.

'I'm looking for Vusani Sibanda,' she explained. 'He said number 1215.'

'And you are?' replied the woman flippantly.

'His wife,' replied Portia. 'I'm his wife.'

The woman eyed her from head to toe before slamming the door in her face. Portia was puzzled. She was certain she was at the right address. Or maybe her husband had moved and had forgotten to tell them. She knocked on the door again. There was no response. Yet she could hear voices on the other side of the door. Angry voices rising to a feverish crescendo. But even as she strained her ears closer to the door she was unable to hear what was being said. When the door was flung open for the second time the woman came stumbling out. She was a heaving mass of anger, now fully dressed with a bag slung across her hefty shoulders. Behind her was Portia's husband. Vusani. He was visibly distressed.

'Baba! Baba!' cried Nkosi, wrapping his tiny arms around his father's legs.

'*Mntanami!*' replied Vusani returning the embrace, yet he was stiff.

Portia's eyes met those of her husband. He was quick to look away. With a cursory nod he ushered them into the apartment. It was a huge, featureless room with few fittings except a double bed in the centre and a rickety headboard pushed against the wall. The bed was unmade and looked like it had been slept in. Portia's eyes darted to the corner of the room where a tiny cubicle served as a kitchen. A two-plate stove was hoisted on top of a drum. The sink was piled high with dirty pots and pans.

'You might want to bath whilst I look for some food downstairs,' said Vusani.

Portia nodded mutely. Vusani showed them to the bathroom. Portia could see her reflection in the cracked mirror that hung on the walls stripped of tiles. Even the bath needed re-enamelling. However, these were minor nuisances as Portia immersed herself in the tub of steaming hot water. After she had scrubbed herself clean she attended to her son.

By the time Vusani returned they had made themselves comfortable on the bed staring at the tiny television set bracketed on the wall. He had brought them cartons of fried chicken and chips which they ate in greedy mouthfuls that left no room for conversation. His attention was focused on a programme on SABC 1. Occasionally he would burst into laughter. It was only after Nkosi fell asleep that Vusani lowered the volume and started to converse with his wife.

'Portia, how did you get here?'

Portia was quick to narrate the events of the past two days since she had left home. Even though she spoke in an animated voice trying to narrate the rigours of the journey her husband merely stared at her with an insipid look on his face.

'But you still took the risk? Put my son in danger so that you could be here?'

The disappointment on his face was palpable. It left Portia feeling confused.

'I thought you would be happy to have us here!' she wailed.

'Happy? You leave my mother and the homestead to come here? For what Portia? For *what*?'

His voice had risen now above the voices on the television screen.

'I came for *you*,' replied Portia. 'I wanted us to be together. To be a family …'

She did not finish the sentence. The palm of his hand connected with Portia's cheek with a hot thunderous clap.

'Nonsense, Portia! My family stays at home. Do you hear me? This is *not* a home.'

'But it is a home for you and that *s'febe* I saw here earlier?'

Vusani backhanded her. Portia's lower lip split painfully.

'The problem is you don't listen, Portia. You don't listen!'

As he said this he loosened the belt around his trousers. He whipped it out with ease and raised it in the air. With swiftness he drew a line across Portia's face. She shrieked in pain. She buried her face in her hands to shield herself from his brutal assault.

'Portia, keep the noise down. You are going to wake the neighbours.'

As he spoke, he brought the belt down on her body. It made a whistling sound as it met her flesh.

'You are a disobedient wife! You don't *listen* to your husband! You put my son in danger! My mother is alone with no one to take care of her! You are a bad woman, Portia! A bad, *bad* woman!'

All his assertions were accompanied by the stroke of the belt. Over her head. On the bare skin of her neck. Along the length of her back. Rising and falling in a steady rhythm, the belt danced on Portia's body. When Vusani was emotionally spent he threw the belt aside and collapsed onto the bed.

'You see what you made me do, Portia? I wouldn't have to do this if *you* were not a bad woman.'

Portia did not respond. She merely stifled the cries that threatened to burst forth from within her. Vusani threw a blanket over her.

'You'll sleep on the floor. Tomorrow morning I'll escort you to the taxi rank. You are going back home, Portia. Do you hear me? I've said before I don't want you here and I meant it.'

Vusani climbed into bed beside his son who pretended to be asleep but had heard everything that had transpired. He could hear his mother crying as she lay on the floor.

# TWELVE

There was blood everywhere. It flowed in tiny rivulets painting a montage on the wall. Like used oil the blood spread over the cement floor covering every inch of the room. The soles of his feet were steeped in sticky warm blood. As he stepped away from the body he left imprints on the floor. He started to shake his head as the reality of the situation slowly sank in.

'Oh my God! What have we done?'

He did not realise how much he was shaking until Chenai grabbed him by the shoulders.

'Stop it! Stop panicking!' hissed Chenai.

The sound of her voice stunned him into silence. Ever since she had come home from the Annex, the psychiatric wing of the Parirenyatwa Hospital, no words had escaped those tightly pursed lips. She walked around in silence. The most she did was communicate with Chamunorwa using her eyes. The doctors attributed her speechlessness to the deep trauma she had obviously suffered. They said it was further compounded by the fact that she had given birth to a stillborn baby. 'Post-partum depression,' they had called it. They all had these fancy explanations for her condition but none seemed to offer a cure. They had sent her home with anti-depressants, which Chenai popped at will as she stared blankly into space.

Their aunties, from their dad's side, had a different view of Chenai's unnerving silence. They claimed Chenai had been bewitched and they skirted from one *n'anga* to another who confirmed their views and offered them bottles and bottles of muti. Chamunorwa could not attest if they worked because Chenai never drank from any of the bottles. Once the aunties had left she would throw everything into the garbage bin.

'Don't you think you should try?' Chamunorwa would plead with her.

Chenai would stare back at him with a vacant look in her eyes and steadfast silence. Yet now here she was speaking with authority like she had been vocal all along. She held a 5-litre container in her hand with a Quench Orange sticker on the side. He knew it no longer contained the syrupy juice when she splashed it generously across the room and the petrol fumes invaded the air.

Chamunorwa watched in fascination at the efficacy with which Chenai carried out her actions. She advanced towards the bulky frame huddled in the corner of the room. Blood seeped from his eyes, his mouth, and his ears. It seemed like all his orifices were pouring blood. For a long time she had considered him a bloodless, heartless fool. Her eyes met his dilated pupils. It was a sight she would never be able to completely erase from her mind. She lit a lone candle that sat at the bedside. It would only be a few minutes before the room burst into flames and consumed everything, her father included. A sardonic grin spread across her face as she pictured his fatty flesh being licked by the hot fire.

'Chamu, let's get out of here,' she spoke once more.

Her voice was strong and unfaltering. He was still stunned to hear his sister's voice. It had been years since she had said a thing. Wordlessly, he followed her out of the room. Out of the house and into the dark lonely streets covered by nightfall.

She smiled for the first time in many years. Chamunorwa was happy to see her eyes light up. They turned their backs on their smouldering childhood home.

A neighbour called the fire brigade as soon as she saw smoke billowing from the house. Help arrived three hours later. By that time the house had been razed to the ground. Only the steel frames remained intact. The police came the following morning on their bicycles to investigate what had caused the fire. It was midday when a police van came to remove the charred remains of their father. Chamunorwa and Chenai sat on the front verandah wearing forlorn expressions on their faces.

'I know this is tough,' began the first policeman, 'but I have questions that need answers.'

As he spoke flecks of spit landed on Chamunorwa's face.

'Go ahead, officer,' replied Chamunorwa.

He wanted to wipe the spray of saliva from his face but decided against it as he did not want to appear rude.

'So where were you last night? When the fire started?'

'I was at a nightclub,' stated Chamunorwa. 'I came home in the early hours of the morning to find this.'

He pointed to the charred and blackened remains of what was once their home.

'Which nightclub?'

'End Times,' replied Chamunorwa.

The policeman merely nodded and scribbled in his notebook.

'And you? Where were you sistren?' enquired the policeman

turning to Chenai.

She did not respond to any of the officer's questions. He repeated them. Louder this time.

'She can hear you, officer,' interjected Chamunorwa. 'My sister doesn't speak. She stopped talking a long time ago.'

The trauma of the abuse she had suffered under her father had almost driven her to suicide. They had been in their second year of high school when Chenai's monthly bleeding stopped suddenly. She had not been worried about it. Actually she had been relieved to be rid of the bloody irritation that came with immense pain. However, the cessation of her periods also came with an illness she was unable to explain. She was often sick, throwing up in the early hours of the morning. With time the nausea subsided and Chenai regained her well-being once more.

Over the following months she noticed that her belly was growing bigger and bigger. At first she thought that the blood that was supposed to be expelled every month was now accumulating inside her belly. That it would explode in a bloody mess. However, it eventually dawned on her that she was pregnant. This was a common occurrence with other girls at school. The realisation hit her with a gruesome force that almost caused her to faint. With the comprehension came the shame. How was she going to deal with the stigma and being ostracised by other students? She could not even bring herself to confide in Chamunorwa but he felt her anguish every day. Felt it keenly as if the pregnancy was his.

It was not long before the school authorities unearthed Chenai's pregnancy hidden underneath her blue jersey that never came off. Even through the burning heat of October Chenai clung to that jersey. However, when she fainted during physical education her secret was exposed. In the headmaster's office she had been asked to name the boy responsible for her state. Chenai had burst into tears because there was no way she could blurt out that it was not a boy but her father who had done this to her.

As much as the female teachers were moved by her plight there was little they could do to save her from expulsion. The school rules were clear. Pregnant girls were not allowed to continue with their schooling. When her father learnt of the news he shrugged without much care. As far as he was concerned women were better off without an education. It was just money down the drain as women would go on to marry and have children.

'You will just stay at home and raise the child,' he said with nonchalance.

It did not occur to him that she was still a child herself. That it was he who was responsible for this abomination that was growing inside of her. The following day when he had gone to work, and Chamunorwa had gone to school, Chenai went to the dustbin and fished out an empty bottle of Don Juan Sherry that her father had drunk the night before. She broke the body of the bottle against the wall and used the serrated edge to cut deep grooves in her wrists. Eyes tightly shut, she bit down on her lip as she drove the jagged edge deeper into her flesh. The pain pulsated through her entire body. It was like no pain she had ever experienced. She opened her eyes and was awed at the sight of the blood that painted her hands a brilliant red. It pumped from her like a crimson spring.

'Oh God!' she gasped before she keeled over and fell to the floor.

That was how Chamunorwa found her. Comatose on the floor. He grabbed her by the shoulders and shook her furiously.

'So you are the one who found your sister?' probed the policeman bringing him back to the present.

Chamunorwa nodded.

'Okay, we will leave your sister for now. I will get her to write down her responses. You don't know where your sister was?'

'She had gone to visit a friend. I am not sure which one.'

'All night? What kind of friend is this?'

Chamunorwa shrugged his shoulders, 'I am sure she will explain.'

'And you say when you left home your father was drinking?'

'Yes, he was drinking.'

'So you think he was drunk? Knocked the candle and the house caught fire?'

'Maybe. I'm not sure. It's possible.'

'*Oro mebbe* that would explain why he didn't run for cover. Most people will try to escape a burning house. He did not even cry for help.'

'Like I said I don't know. I can only speculate. Our father is, or was, a heavy drinker. He would drink until he passed out.'

'What did your father drink?'

'Beer.'

'What kind of beer? Clear? Opaque? Homebrew?'

'Lion. He loved his Lion Lager.'

The policeman's pen danced across his notebook once again.

'But he only drank that when he had money. When he was broke he drank tototo. Lots of it.'

No one could tell you with precision the ingredients nor the exact quantities used to brew this bootleg alcohol. However, many would tell you of its potent effect. Some men walked around with damaged livers, impaired vision and in the worst instances had suffered mild heart attacks.

'I have no more queshions for now. Let's talk after the funeral.'

Chamunorwa's face rumpled with concern. 'Why officer? Is there something else?'

'You are still confused. I am *shuwa* that after the funeral you will remember other things.'

The policeman turned to look at Chenai who had tears streaming down her face. She looked vulnerable.

'So where will you sleep tonight?'

'We have an aunt in Mabvuku,' explained Chamunorwa.

The policeman promptly shut his notebook and wished them well. He swung a leg over his bicycle and cycled off.

'He was asking too many questions,' said Chenai.

Chamunorwa scratched his head.

'Do you think he suspects something?' he asked.

'I'm not sure, hey.'

'Do you think they'll ever know it was us?' asked Chamunorwa.

'No,' replied Chenai. 'Only we'll ever know. It's our secret.'

He put a protective arm around his sister. Once they had buried their father they would put all this behind them.

# THIRTEEN

The day had broken and the promise of a new day lingered with the rising sun. Even though it was only six a.m., the streets of Hillbrow had already come alive, teeming with people. It was a melting pot of African cultures, creeds and languages stewing in the heart of Johannesburg. People came from as far north as the Democratic Republic of Congo. From as far west as Ghana and Nigeria to the eastern shores of Mozambique. From Africa's bleeding centre of the war-torn countries of Somalia and Sudan down to the southern enclaves of Zambia and Zimbabwe. They spilled into the inner-city residential neighbourhood till they were overflowing onto the sidewalks paved with crime and grime. The hustle and bustle of foot traffic swept the dirty pavements.

Portia and her son were part of that traffic. They trailed behind Vusani, failing to keep up with his swift pace. Portia's eyes were curious to absorb every building, every sight that lined Claim Street. The current inhabitants would not have believed that once upon a time in the seventies, Hillbrow was the New York of Johannesburg with its vibrant nightlife and luxurious apartment living. Back then it had been the sole enclave of the white population. Over time the colours got blurred as ethnicities from different racial groups began to infiltrate. By the mid-eighties there was a visible exodus of middle-class residents. By the time the nineties rolled around Hillbrow was showing signs of decay and disintegration coupled with lawlessness. Shattered windows, cracked walls and peeling paint interfaced with the Johannesburg skyline.

You could buy almost anything on those streets. From something as innocent as a packet of sweets to something illicit like a gram of cocaine or a backstreet abortion. Posters were pasted on the walls and on poles punting services from spiritual healing to penis enlargement. One huge poster read: Prophet Moyo from Binga. 0798421234. Below his name and number in tiny print the poster promised that the prophet would cure ills ranging from low sexual libido to financial problems, marital problems and joblessness.

Vusani marched further down Claim Street making a sharp turn into Wolmarans Street. A huge synagogue sat on the corner. A man stood outside screaming that salvation lay beyond those doors. Portia made a mental note of the place. It would be a place of safety if she and Nkosi needed it. Vusani led them down King George Street, which was choked with blaring taxis. A putrid smell invaded the air but as people jostled for space along the street they seemed unaware of it. Portia tugged at her son fearing he would get run over by a taxi. The sidewalks where people were supposed to walk were populated by vendor stalls almost concealing the greenery of Joubert Park behind it. It was Nkosi who spotted the themed Simba Park, a children's playground. Adults nearby found refuge amongst the park benches and grass.

'Mama, look!' came Nkosi's shrill voice as he pointed out a yellow tunnel with Disney characters painted on it.

'Yes, my child,' she replied.

'Can I go and play there?'

'There's no time to play,' responded his father.

Portia promised herself she would bring him back there to play. She memorised the street. King George. He would play all day if he wanted to. She would sit with the other adults on the park benches or on the grass and watch him play. She vowed he was going to have a better life than she had ever had; a life that did not exist in Plumtree. More vendors with their stalls sprouted like weeds covering every inch of available space. It was almost impossible to walk without brushing shoulders with the next person. Bodies collided without the personal warmth that accompanied such proximity. People disappeared into the milieu of black faces, typical of the mad morning rush in Johannesburg as masses moved from Noord Taxi Rank to the CBD where many were employed at the numerous retail enterprises and high-rise office buildings.

They finally stopped at a noisy taxi rank outside the Park Station transit terminal. Without much conversation her husband thrust them into a taxi headed to Zimbabwe. He shoved some clean crisp notes into Portia's hands assuring her it was enough to cover her passage safely. He shook hands with his son and gave a cursory nod to Portia.

Without any further banter he turned his back on them and was gone. He too disappeared into the throng of dark faces until he was no longer visible to them. The taxi was only a quarter full. Even the driver seemed oblivious to them as his face was buried inside the *Sowetan*. Portia informed him that she wanted to get some food and would return soon. He grunted something inaudible. Portia and her son forged their way through the crowds. Nothing in her bones would make her return to that taxi. She had found freedom at last and was not about to give it up.

She made a stop outside the many food stalls lining the entrance to Park Station. Even though it was still early morning; the aroma of braaied steak, spicy boerewors and barbecue chicken filled her nostrils. Portia bought some sausage and *amagwinya,* a local delicacy of dough deep fried in smouldering fat. From another vendor they bought cold cans of Lemon Twist and Fanta Orange. Together, they sat under a tented eating area and devoured the food with much relish.

'I like it here,' declared Nkosi.

'So do I,' replied Portia, wiping his oily face with her hand.

'Why is uBaba sending us back?'

Portia shrugged. 'Because he is selfish. He wants to enjoy the good life for himself. Well, you know what, my boy, we are not going back home, do you hear me? We will make this *our* home.'

Nkosi nodded with conviction, 'I hear you, Mama.'

She rubbed his bald head affectionately, smearing it with the oil residue from her hands.

'But before we get too comfortable I must look for a job.'

'Okay Mama, but before you start your new job can you take me back to that park to play?'

Portia nodded.

Even Portia had no way of knowing how to go about that but she was determined to find work of any kind. They had over R1 000, which was safely tucked into her bra, however, she had no idea how long it would last and did not want to deplete her stash too soon or they would be penniless. Armed with confidence and a false sense of boldness, Portia too disappeared into the swarms of people and the madness of the morning rush hour.

# FOURTEEN

Lindani leaned against the balustrade of their tiny balcony overlooking busy Pretoria Street below. She sought much-needed respite from their overcrowded apartment. When Melusi had told her he had a place of his own in Johannesburg she had envisaged some plush penthouse in the middle of Sandton. Much to her chagrin he had led her to a dilapidated six-storey walk-up nameless building, dashing all her expectations of grandeur.

The rather roomy and spacious two-bedroomed flat was shared with a host of other people. There was a couple with a one-year-old son in the one bedroom whose distressed cries competed with the noisy Hillbrow nightlife. The couple paid Melusi R2 500 a month. The living room was occupied by three Congolese men who conversed in French. Each one paid Melusi R500 a month and slept on spongy foam mattresses. During the day these were piled into a corner giving free passage to everyone to traverse their room on their way to the kitchen, which was a communal hub with dissonant smells as everyone rustled up something to eat. They also all shared one bathroom, which was constantly occupied in the evenings, especially when the Congolese had female visitors.

On some nights that living room could be transformed into an orgy as the men engaged in coital activities. Melusi prided himself that all his tenants combined contributed to his mortgage. He had casually informed her that he had bought the place for a mere R150 000 when the market had bottomed out and property in the area was going for a song. He gloated that his place was almost paid up and that soon he would have the title deeds. She had to give him credit for having ambition. Even if it meant taking ownership of a hovel. She, Melusi and Givemore occupied the second bedroom. As Gugulethu's mum had not collected her she also became part of the equation. In the beginning Givemore had insisted they all sleep together, their two single beds joined.

'This is what we often do,' he said pointedly.

Melusi had excused himself and led his friend outside onto the balcony. Lindani had stood against the window trying to get an earful of their conversation.

'Hands off Lindani!' declared Melusi.

'*Hawu ndoda?* But we always share.'

'This is different,'replied Melusi. 'Lindani is special. No sharing.'

Givemore smirked, 'Special how? *Liwule!* She's a whore!'

'Mind your language,' warned Melusi.

Lindani's mouth curved into a smile. Melusi did not know her from a bar of soap yet he was out there defending her. She had already made up her mind that Melusi would be her meal ticket until her future looked more certain. That first night Givemore had slept in his own bed, which he'd pushed against the wall. She and Melusi had slept on the other bed at the extreme end of the room. Gugulethu had slept on the floor, in the sea of space between them.

Nothing had transpired that first night. They had collapsed into each other's arms in exhaustion.

On the second night Lindani had climbed into bed and collided with Melusi's aroused member. She knew then what was expected of her and without much ceremony she parted her legs. However, she had not expected to be bedded with such skill and precision. It was a shock to her system to be reminded how poetic and soulful lovemaking could be. In the dark Melusi strummed her body like he was playing a guitar. Her hips swayed to the musical symphony. Every night their bodies danced together in cohesion. If there was anything Lindani began to look forward to it was their coupling. Her days might have been long and boring but her nights had become electric and exciting. Unbeknown to them Givemore keenly watched their spirited union.

Every morning Lindani woke up famished. So did her little ward.

'I'm hungry!' declared Gugulethu.

Lindani pulled the girl into her arms and squeezed her tiny body. She had taken it upon herself to take the kid under her wing. With her innocent eyes and sunny smile Gugulethu had to be the cutest little girl she had ever seen. In a strange way Gugulethu reminded her of herself at that age.

'Are you my mother?' asked Gugulethu.

This was not the first time she had posed this question.

Lindani laughed, 'I wish I was, darling. Now what do you want to eat today?'

Once you got past the shy exterior, Gugulethu was a delightful child with a sunny disposition.

'Chips, chips and more chips,' replied Gugulethu.

To which Lindani threw her head back and laughed. They were

both junkies living on fast food. They never cooked for the simple reason that Melusi did not own a pot or any cutlery. They ate take-aways every day; whether it was fish and chips or pap and wors. You could pretty much find anything on the streets of Hillbrow, even pap and tripe when the occasion called for it. Not that Lindani minded, it was a convenient and fuss-free way of living.

They descended downstairs to Shoprite, which was almost concealed behind the vendor stalls that lined Pretoria Street. Had it not been for the bold red signage asserting 'Lower prices you can trust', you could almost overlook its presence. Opposite it was PriceRite supermarket; price was everything on these streets. They bought some bread, Russian sausages and hot chips. When they returned to the flat they sat down to eat the spread before them.

Melusi had left early in the morning to do his pick-up as he was preparing for the trip to Bulawayo over the weekend. And his trusty lieutenant Givemore had gone with him. Lindani was glad to be rid of him. The way he ogled her made her very uncomfortable. His eyes were like lasers, stripping her naked even in a room filled with people.

'What are we doing today?' asked Gugulethu after she had finished the last soggy chip smothered with tomato sauce.

'I will take you to the salon. They will fix your hair.'

'My grandmother fixes my hair. But I want to go to the salon with you.'

She was unsure of the word even as she said it. The only place her grandmother took her was to church. She had frequented more places in Jo-han-nes-burg than she had in her entire lifetime.

'How come you don't have hair, auntie?'

Lindani smiled wryly, 'It's a long story but it doesn't matter. I like not having hair.'

Mornings in the flat were subdued as all the men invariably left to earn their daily bread. Lindani was able to take a leisurely uninterrupted bath. When she came out she exchanged small talk with the mother and her child. On many occasions Lindani had tried to engage her fully in conversation but the woman was aloof so in the end Lindani had decided to let her be. She cleaned Gugulethu up and they took off as they did every morning. She took her to a hair salon on Kotze Street. If there was anything that was in abundance in Hillbrow it had to be hair salons. Like wild flowers in an open field they grew on every street corner. Names like Paradise Hair, Make Me Beautiful, Black Beauty and Turning Heads shouted from large posters picturing black women with long flowing tresses. Hairdressers stood out on the street promising to transform even the ugliest ducklings into princesses. For R40 Lindani was able to get Gugu's hair washed and plaited.

While a dextrous hairdresser called Margret manipulated Gugulethu's hair into cornrows, Lindani sat in the reception reading one of the outdated magazines on the table. She was lost in the glossy pages of *True Love* when a deep silky voice resonated through her thoughts. She looked up and her eyes met those of a tall dark man whose pearly eyes were set deep in a face with fine-chiselled features. His dark, velvety complexion evoked memories of chocolate liqueur.

'How you dey?' he said.

Lindani winced and strained closer to him, 'What?'

'I say how you dey? I dey fine. Wetin dey happen?'

Lindani looked around as if searching for someone to translate what this man was saying to her. Everything about him was nice until he spoke. She could not understand the gibberish. He extended a friendly hand to her. She accepted it. His hands were warm and he held onto her hand longer than was necessary.

'My name is Kayin Frank Abota.'

Kayin? Such an unusual name. He was obviously foreign. He handed her a business card. It stated his credentials. Chief Executive Officer. Abota Properties. Hillbrow and Berea. There were five cellphone numbers listed on the card. There was a head office in Abuja along with several other numbers.

'Chickito, you must call me. Like you very much!'

As he walked away, Lindani was baffled. She shoved his card in her purse and thought nothing much of it. He went on to confer with the cashier/receptionist in a language she did not understand. Although she could not make out what they were saying she suspected they were angry because their voices were rising. He left the shop but returned minutes later with some refreshments, which he handed to Lindani.

'Thank you,' said Lindani, 'but this is not necessary.'

'Don't mention. Enjoy dear!'

Gugulethu, who was shrieking with pain as the hairdresser tugged tightly at the roots of hair, was silenced by the packet of Jelly Babies that landed in her lap. Lindani sipped on her Coke and continued leafing through the magazine.

'So what did Kayin promise you?'

It was Margret, the hairdresser. She had finished plaiting the little girl's hair and secured it in a little ponytail atop her head. Lindani eyed her up and down.

'What's it to you?' she replied.

She lowered her voice and almost whispered in Lindani's ear.

'Kayin is a dangerous man. Stay away from him.'

'Thanks for the advice, sweetheart, but in life I like to make my own mistakes.'

Lindani handed the hairdresser a crisp red R50 note, 'And keep the change, sisi.'

Lindani stood up, took Gugulethu by the hand and they walked out of the salon. She was actually annoyed by the hairdresser's presumptuousness. She could barely make out what Kayin was saying; what could possibly drive her to want to know him better?

# FIFTEEN

Sibongile woke up at five every day without prompting. Even on weekends when she did not work she still woke up at the same time. Then she would sit on her bed waiting for the sun to rise. Sometimes she would flip through her Bible, reading words but not really understanding the meaning behind them. At other times, she would switch on the television, which was Chamunorwa's wake-up call. He would immediately go and shower in the tiny cubicle that served as their bathroom. Chenai, on the other hand, would pull the blankets up over her.

This annoyed Sibongile no end. Women were not supposed to sleep in; her mother had taught her that. She had no idea how to impart that to Chenai without being abrasive. She still had not found a way to communicate with her children. They spoke to each other but often excluded her. The conversations she shared with them were stilted and awkward. If she had not been their mother they could have easily been strangers sharing a home in Hurlingham.

Even when she had gone to collect them at Park Station she had failed to recognise them. In her mind they were still the four-year-olds she had left behind. She had not expected Chamunorwa to be a tall, sinewy man with a mop of hair on his head. Neither had she expected Chenai to have blossomed into a pretty young woman with perky breasts. Seeing them made her realise how much time had gone by. How much she too had aged without being aware of it. She was still at loss as to how to fill the gap between them. They had grown without her and apart from her and she didn't know how to minimise that distance.

After Chamunorwa dressed he said goodbye.

'Don't forget your lunch!' she reminded him.

She had made him lunch; he smiled appreciatively.

'Thank you, Mama.'

The sound of the word 'mama' warmed her heart. Chamunorwa was always polite but Chenai was aloof, almost aggressive and Sibongile could not understand the root of her anger. As she got ready for work Sibongile wondered when relations between them would thaw. She slipped into a crisply ironed pink uniform. She had a uniform for every day of the week. Blue for Monday. Green for Tuesday. Orange for Wednesday. Pink for Thursday. Red for Friday. In winter she wore a polo neck underneath and matching tights. She fastened the doek onto her head which matched the tiny white apron she wore in the front.

When she had started her first job as a maid ten years before with the Kroners, she had been kitted out in a starched blue uniform. Back then the range was limited but now they had them in all sorts of colours and prints from floral to animal print. When she started working for the Molefes they had her kitted out in uniforms made of Shweshwe fabric. The Molefes came after the Kroners sold their house and decided to relocate to a retirement village in Durban after their children left home. So the deal was that the Molefes would inherit her as a maid. They were an affluent black family. There were lots of those now in Sandton.

When she had first moved to the leafy suburb of Hurlingham, with its tree-lined boulevards, the only blacks who roamed the leafy streets were the hired help. Now, in their street alone, there were three black families. She never wanted to work for a black family ever again. The hours had been long. She started work at six a.m. by getting the children ready for school and she knocked off at five but was often called in during the evenings to do the dishes. The Molefes had a chef, Philemon, who lived in the servants' quarters with her. Mrs M did not allow visitors (she attributed the rising number of house break-ins to domestic workers). So inevitably she and Philemon ended up keeping each other company well into the early hours of the morning. Philemon was a retired sous-chef who had a wife and ten kids in Limpopo who he only saw during holidays. Even his family were not allowed to visit him on the job.

Sibongile discovered just how paranoid Mrs M was about security when she showed her footage of herself as she dug into a tub of low-fat pistachio nut ice cream. Sibongile was hot with embarrassment as she watched herself on camera delve into the tub with the exuberance of a child. This was after Mrs M had repeatedly asked who had eaten the ice cream and Sibongile had merely shrugged her shoulders and said, 'I don't know. Ask the kids.'

'I don't pay you to eat ice cream,' she had spoken in her low, even voice.

One thing about Mrs M was that she never raised her voice. When she admonished the children she maintained a steady, even voice. And her confrontations with Mr M were equally subdued. He would be the one shouting the house down and she would maintain her cool. Though without raising her voice she had the ability to diminish you into feeling smaller than an ant.

'You can take the ice cream, Sibongile. Eat your heart out. '

Sibongile never ate ice cream again.

However, it was not the ice-cream incident that made her loathe her black employers. It was the merciless authority with which Mrs M ran her household. She was a full-time housewife so she was always there to supervise her and oversee her work and made sure Sibongile earned every generous cent she was paid.

'You earn more than the minimum wage,' she would remind Sibongile as she asked her to wash Mr M's underwear. Some of which was often stained with skid marks. When Sibongile had articulated her disgust, Mrs M had merely shrugged her shoulders and said, 'You would have no problem doing it for Mrs Jones.'

When the job opening with the Hirsches came up Sibongile was happy to hand in her resignation. The only regret was leaving Philemon and their shared nights of passion. Of course Mrs M was unmoved by her departure. She was paid her last wages and before she knocked off for the final time that day Mrs M had the security guard search her from head to toe just in case she had decided to steal something.

She had been with the Hirsch family for three years now. When she had first joined them they had two children: Aaron and David. Now there was Gila, a green-eyed, red-haired little girl with an equally feisty character. Mrs H did not work either. Well, not in the conventional way that Sibongile understood work. She had a huge studio in the attic of the house where she painted pictures. She always had a glass of wine by her side, insisting she needed inspiration. Mr H was the one who worked. He always left early in the morning and came back late at night.

The minute Sibongile walked through the door in the morning

Mrs H immediately shoved Gila into her hands. The little girl began to gurgle happily. 'We didn't get an ounce of sleep!' complained Mrs H. 'She refused to sleep in her room. Don't disturb me. I'm going back to bed. Take her out. Take her anywhere. Just keep her out of my hair.'

Gila started giggling. She had an infectious laugh that made Sibongile laugh too.

'Who's been a naughty, naughty girl?' admonished Sibongile with mock sternness.

Gila shook her head, her springy red locks bouncing. Sibongile put her down on the floor and threw some toys at her feet and got busy with the chores of the day. She started with the laundry, loading clothes into the washing machine. As the cycle began, she fed Gila some oatmeal porridge, which the little girl spat out after a few mouthfuls. After hanging out the clothes to dry she decided to take Gila to the park. She could not hoover the house as it would undoubtedly disturb Mrs H.

Perched in her stroller, Gila keenly pointed out everything they passed. Birds. Cars. Grass. It was not even midday yet but the park was already filling up with uniformed maids attending to little children. They all knew each other and began chatting amongst themselves whilst the children ran amok on the field. The ones who had no mobility were strapped securely onto the backs of their nannies.

'I'm here but the piles of washing I have!' complained Connie. She stayed one block away from the Hirsches and had feisty two-year-old twin boys in her care.

'I'm glad my boys are in school,' replied Sibongile. 'They used to drain me!'

'I tell my madam to send them to crèche but the boss says it's too expensive. He says that's why they hire me. But they don't pay me enough. I still have to cook and clean!' moaned Milly.

'*Abelungu* are stingy!'moaned Patricia as she joined in the conversation. 'Each time I ask for a raise, boss says I must ask Mbeki!'

Patricia stopped mid-sentence as she paused to scream.

'Andrew get off that swing. Get off. Now. Andrew!'

Seeing the child's unresponsiveness Patricia marched off towards him.

'I am tired of these kids. Tired of cleaning houses, *shem*!' complained Rue who was perched on a park bench. She took a swig from a silver hip flask that she had inherited from her boss. It was no secret that she drank on the job. It was the thin line between sanity and complete insanity.

Connie. Milly. Patricia. Rue. Those were not their real names. Those were the identities they assumed during the week with the exception of Rue who also worked on weekends. Their madams had struggled to wrap their tongues around names like Kananelo (Connie), Milusuthando (Milly), Patiswa (Patricia), Ruveneko (Rue). Those names made them sound young and girlish yet they were all well into their fifties although Connie insisted she was forty. She had a rich daughter, Poloko (Polo), who had been put through school by her generous former employer. Now Connie worked for the daughter of the same employer.

Connie's daughter lived in a fancy duplex in Sandton and drove a fancy Mercedes. They were often regaled with stories of how Polo had taken Connie out to eat at a fine restaurant in Mandela Square. How on the weekends she shopped in Hyde Park. Connie always came to work dolled up with make-up and her nails done, bathed in expensive perfume. When she knocked off over the weekends, with her hand-me-down weave cascading down her shoulders no one would suspect she was the hired help.

'What's the point of shopping at Hyde Park when you live in a shack!' remarked Rue.

'Polo should do more for her mother. You should see what my kids have done for me,' boasted Patricia.

Patricia said her children had bought her a house in Cosmo City. Sibongile and other maids in the area had been invited to her housewarming party where they had the iconic seven-colour lunch. Each dish served represented at least one colour of the rainbow which implied diversity in the spread. Patricia made a heartwarming beef stew served with yellow rice. There was bright red beetroot salad which stained their lips and creamy mashed yellow butternut and a colourful green salad. For dessert they had custard and blackberry jelly. They ate till their stomachs were stretched taut. In the taxi on the way home they had gossiped about how tiny the house was.

'She's lying. Her kids didn't buy it. The govanment gives out those houses for free!' said Connie with authority.

'The govanment would have to pay me to live in a house like that! *Angeke shem.* Never!' voiced Milly.

They had all laughed and clapped their hands together animatedly, drawing the attention of other passengers in the taxi.

Rue, like Sibongile, was also from Zimbabwe. But for a long time Sibongile withheld the truth, preferring to be synonymous with her South African friends, but a sense of shared kinship got the best of her and she shocked Rue one day by responding to her in Shona as they sat alone in the playground. Rue's eyes had widened in disbelief.

'You *taura*?'

'I was once married to a Shona,' confided Sibongile. 'His sisters interfered in our marriage so much I was forced to leave.'

Rue quickly divulged that her husband had left her for another woman and she was left to fend for their three children. A former history teacher at a mission school, she had been forced to give up her job and seek work in South Africa so that they would not lose their home in Budiriro. When Sibongile had narrated the story to the other maids none of them had bought into it.

'Teachers are sitting in their own homes, not cleaning after white people!' reasoned Connie.

'Things are tough in Zim,' Sibongile had replied coming to her friend's defence.

'*Mxm … amaZimba niyachoma*,' replied Patricia. 'You are proud people.'

'There are no poor people in Zimbabwe yet you are all here!' added Milly.

Sibongile was certain when she was not around they also discussed her, especially with the arrival of her children two months ago. That morning Sibongile lamented to the group that her daughter had still not found a job. They all expressed their sympathies. It was only when Patricia returned to the conversation that she declared she knew of a job opening.

'My madam's friend of a friend in Bryanston is looking. Apparently her maid went to Zim-bakwe and never came back.'

'Zi-mba-bwe,' corrected Rue.

Patricia ignored her and continued talking, 'She can start today even. *U*desperate. Des-pe-rate!'

Sibongile's eyes perked up with excitement. She decided to inform Chenai immediately. She searched the playground for Gila who was now covered in dust with leaves in her hair and bade them all goodbye. As soon as she turned her back the other maids began to complain bitterly in Sesotho about how their own children could not get jobs because of all the Zimbabweans who were now living illegally in their country. Rue did not understand a word of what was being said. She was slowly getting too inebriated to care. She merely laughed when they did, not knowing they were laughing at her and not with her.

# SIXTEEN

If the Quantum had been able to speak it would have spewed a stream of expletives at its owners. A trailer was attached to its rear and was piled high with goods ranging from television sets, fridges, headboards and beds to other forms of furniture destined for Zimbabwe. The interior of the car was also packed with cartons of groceries ranging from Sunfoil cooking oil to Colgate toothpaste. Goods that had not been able to fit inside the vehicle sat on the floor of the basement garage. Melusi folded his arms in resignation.

'We need to get another car. That way we'll be able to do more trips and double our profits.'

Givemore nodded. 'Yeah, this one-car situation isn't working anymore.'

Lindani stood by the car, awed by the volume of goods that had been delivered over the past few days. Even basic food items like eggs and potatoes found their way onto the trailer. Some families would starve to death if they did not receive their black, blue or red-striped Shangaan bags filled with provisions for the month.

Gugulethu hung onto Lindani's arm, a finger stuck in her

mouth. They were parting ways as Melusi had informed her he was going to return Gugulethu to her grandmother since they had failed to locate her mother.

Melusi exhaled noisily. 'Anyway we need to hit the road. It's a long journey to Bulawayo.'

Lindani sighed. 'It is indeed.'

'Behave yourself,' said Melusi stroking her cheek tenderly.

He kissed her lovingly before shoving a few rand into her gaping cleavage. She was starting to fill out nicely. The fast food they lived on was quickly finding its way to her hips and thighs. He loved her fuller figure. He was not the only one. Givemore also found himself staring at her lustfully.

'Go shopping. Buy yourself some nice clothes and look pretty.'

'I will,' replied Lindani.

Lindani turned to kiss Gugulethu goodbye. Then drew her in her arms and squeezed her so hard the little girl flinched. She could feel Gugulethu's heart beating through the flimsy material of her dress. Melusi had to wrestle the child from her arms. Then he packed Gugulethu into the car amongst the groceries. As they pulled out of the basement garage Lindani felt slightly melancholy.

Not long after, the Quantum pulled up in front of a decrepit-looking building which gave a hint of its past as a hotel with its naked poles that once hoisted the flags of America, England and South Africa. Hillbrow had its fair share of hotels. Each with a story to tell. The Hotel Quirinale hogged the headlines when Brenda Fassie's lover was found dead in one of its dingy rooms in 1995. The Landdrost Hotel, once a glamorous five-star hotel on Plein Street, was the first to be converted into residential apartments overlooking the congested and filthy Noord Taxi Rank. The Dorchester Hotel was one of the better-kept establishments. Back in the day it had catered to Hillbrow's early immigrant population from eastern and central Europe. It still catered to an immigrant population but faces had changed from European to African. Claim Street could easily be the red-light district of Hillbrow with its notorious establishments like the Ambassador Hotel, Europa, Moulin Rouge and the Summit Club.

In the seedier establishments one could easily buy a beer for R15 and a blowjob for R50. The classier establishments like the Summit, with a more discerning clientele, had much higher fees where R145 could get you a night's worth of fun. Not that Melusi was looking for a cheap thrill. He had figured out a long time ago that you could get a roll in the hay without having to fork out a dime for it. Besides, prostitutes left a bitter taste in his mouth.

'Make it quick,' he instructed Givemore as he disembarked from the car.

He opened the door so that Gugulethu could also get out and they then disappeared into the squalid-looking building. The billboard that once carried its name was now perforated and destroyed by wind and water. Walking into the lobby they were met by an indelible stench of urine. After a furtive exchange with the cagey-looking guard, they waited for the old Schindler lift to reach the ground floor. It elevated them to their destination on the sixth floor. They knocked on the door and a Chinese man opened. He eyed Givemore warily.

'Can I help you?'

'I phoned you about the girl child,' replied Givemore.

The Chinese man ushered them in with a swift wave of his hand.

He lingered in the hallway to check there was no one lurking in the shadows. The room was sparsely furnished with a lone settee

103

backed up against the wall and a small TV screen mounted on the wall. A tall lithe woman lay outstretched on the couch half asleep. The Chinese man quickly settled into a chair behind a desk leaving Givemore to stand awkwardly in the middle of the room with the child.

'How much you want? I give one thousand.'

Givemore shook his head in disdain.

'I want ten thousand rand. Girls are in high demand. She young *and* beautiful.'

He cupped Gugulethu by the chin and tilted her head upwards. She was undoubtedly a beauty and he knew for certain if she was sold into child prostitution that money could easily be recovered in a day. Givemore could not understand the allure of having sex with flat-chested shapeless little girls with spindly legs. But who was he to judge?

'Innocent too. Never been touched. She's cheap.'

'Ten thousand too much,' protested the Chinese man. 'I buy three boys with ten thousand.'

'Take it or leave it. Good bargain.'

The Chinese man barked to the young woman lying on the couch. She rose immediately. He spoke quickly in Mandarin and immediately the woman responded by taking Gugulethu by the hand. They disappeared into the bathroom. When she returned the little girl looked pained and visibly distraught. A tear rolled down her cheek.

'She fine,' spoke the woman. 'Virgin meat.'

The Chinese man exhaled deeply and started pulling out notes from his desk. The crisp wads of money flipped through his hands. Givemore counted with him in his head. He was almost salivating when they were done. He stuffed the wad of notes in his pocket.

'Now this is your mama,' he explained to Gugulethu. 'Listen to everything she speaks.'

Gugulethu's face was hot with tears. Givemore was not moved. All he could think of was the bulging wad of cash lining his pockets. He thanked the Chinese man profusely. The Chinese did not reciprocate with equal graciousness but instead looked pissed off for having paid so much. He grumbled a few words before seeing Givemore out.

By the time Givemore returned to the car Melusi was restless.

'What took you so long?'

'Stingy Chinese *basterd*. He gave me five thousand. What can five thousand buy?'

'It will get us another car. You follow this evening.'

Melusi revved the engine. 'If that mother ever shows up looking for the kid we'll say she died in the river. That's our story.'

'Stupid woman. Sends for a child then doesn't claim her. We are not a storage company!'

And just like that, Gugulethu's fate was sealed. Melusi dropped Givemore off at the flat then faced the northward journey with the wind in his sails.

Givemore did not bother looking for a car to hire. Instead he went to The Base, a pub on Twist Street and ordered a steaming hot plate of pap and braaied chicken. He washed the food down with a cold beer. Then he had three more in succession. Givemore was tired of being treated like a child by Melusi. They had started this thing together but now Melusi was lording over him. Givemore was sitting alone when an obese oily looking man invited himself to his table. He had a gold chain around his thick neck and wore a thick gold Rolex watch. Both looked obscenely out of place. Givemore welcomed the company nonetheless. After the fifth drink he knew his companion to be Malume Jackson. Said he ran all sorts of businesses. He even pointed to his gleaming Mercedes parked down the street.

'I am always looking for men to work.'

'What kind of work? I don't want to be somebody's garden boy.'

Malume Jackson roared with laughter. A deep belly laugh that made his entire body vibrate.

'It's big money. You won't regret it.'

Givemore was sold. He took Malume Jackson's number and promised he'd be in touch.

Many hours later he staggered back to the flat. Lindani was fast asleep when he stumbled into bed beside her. She woke up with a start.

'Where is Melusi?'

'He is probably hitting Polokwane now. Don't worry. We are safe.'

He pulled out a wad of notes from his pockets and threw them on her lap.

'I can lurve you better. Better than he can.'

Givemore sounded like he had lifted those lyrics from an R Kelly album.

'Voetsek,' replied Lindani.

'*S'febe!*' he said.

Lindani was about to get up but he grabbed her and pinned her to the bed. She tried to wrestle free but he was too strong for her. Instead he laughed in her face.

'I will eat you till the sun comes out.'

'If Melusi hears about this!'

'Who do you think he will believe? Me or you?'

He was already naked; she could feel his hardened member pressing against her belly. His bloodshot eyes were consumed with lust. She would not let him take her without a fight. She kicked him in the groin with all the strength she could muster. He yelped in pain like a wounded dog recoiling from his position of attack. She rolled off the bed and fell onto the floor with a crashing thud. He was onto her, settling his entire weight on her back. She could feel his hardened penis against her buttocks. She tried to wrestle free from his grasp but instead he held onto her with a fierce determination. He started biting into the side of her neck. She squealed in pain. He was unyielding in his resolve to have his way with her.

# SEVENTEEN

The bright morning light shone into Garth Mansions, the humble abode that had become Dumisani's home. It was a modest six-storey apartment block that looked out onto busy Twist Street. He slept on a foam mattress on the hard cement floor of his uncle's enclosed balcony. Every night he dreamt of his double bed with its Luxaire mattress. Every morning he woke up with severe backache but he dared not complain.

Below their flat was a cellphone and stationery shop where he made copies of his CV. Now that he was on friendly terms with the Pakistani cashier they usually allowed him to photocopy for free. He had arrived in Johannesburg without a cent to his name and a cellphone. One of the passengers had given him R20 which he had used to call his uncle, who had tried to accommodate him the best way he could. Malume Jackson was his mother's younger brother. Jackson had come to Johannesburg way back in the eighties and still sported a curly Pat Shange perm like the music legend who had ruled the airwaves during that time. He had fully integrated into the South African way of life from his mannerisms to the way he spoke.

He was proud to have finally moved his family into this apartment building, which had a veneer of respectability. The place might have looked more homely had Malume's wife bothered to clean up once in a while. She was a whale-shaped orange-coloured Motswana woman who spent her days stretched out on a red velvet couch watching soapies on SABC. The only time she moved off the couch was to use the toilet and to retire to bed at night. They had three beautiful daughters who wandered around the flat in a state of semi-undress. Just like their mother, they did very little cleaning but pranced around preening and grooming themselves.

'You'll sleep here,' Malume Jackson had declared, pointing to the enclosed balcony that housed all the junk there was no longer room for inside the main house. Dumisani had sorted through the rubble and carved a little niche for himself behind an old fridge and some empty Polvin paint containers. He placed the framed picture of his wife and son on top of an old Windhoek beer crate. That picture spurred him on when he felt at his lowest, which was often. For the first few nights he struggled to sleep. There was always noise from downstairs.

On nights when sleep completely eluded him he would watch the activity down below. It was like watching a movie in real time. There were high-speed car chases. Gunshots that rang through the night. Piercing screams that could wake up the dead. He saw drugs being peddled in the street below with unashamedly rich white men driving up in their fancy BMWs and Porsches. Windows would roll down. Money and neat little white packages would change hands in a split second. Prostitutes plied their trade on the streets without fear. Punting a breast and shaking an arse cheek. Selling the little that was left of their souls. It was a story that played itself out every night.

Dumisani soon got tired of it and managed to sleep through it all. That morning he woke up to Malume Jackson fighting with his wife. Apparently Malume had waltzed in at five in the morning and could not account for his whereabouts and his wife was demanding to know where he had slept. Malume had responded acidly that it was none of her business. That was when his wife started screaming expletives amongst which the word 'kwere-kwere' came up often.

As he washed his face in the basin Dumisani could not wait to be out of earshot of the argument, the volume of which had increased to unbearable levels. He dressed quickly in a black T-shirt and blue jeans. It was the mandatory dress code at the restaurant where he had found a job. Malume Jackson had assured him it was the quickest job he would get with no valid work papers and he had been right; he'd been hired on the spot.

However, Malume Jackson had not told him it was also a demeaning and often thankless profession especially when the clients he served did not give him a voluntary tip. The hours were gruelling, the pay was meagre and not commensurate with the effort. Dumisani grabbed his apron and made his way out of the apartment. The entrance to the building was almost obscured by the unsightly Telkom public phone cubicle. It was here that Dumisani made furtive calls home with the tips he had garnered from waiting tables. He had figured out it was cheaper than calling on a cellphone that used his airtime and cut him off just as he was about to articulate endearments to his wife. They texted each other every day but it could never surpass the feeling of hearing Sipho mumble 'Daddy, I love you,' into the mouthpiece. Hearing Christine's effervescent voice always cheered him up immensely.

'Sweetie, I miss you *so* much.'

'I miss you too,' replied Dumisani. 'You have no idea how much.'

He often woke up in the middle of the night yearning to return home but he knew that was an option he did not have.

'Everything is going to work out all right. Once you get your permit, you'll see.'

Dumisani had not told her about the robbery that had occurred in the bush that not only robbed him of his dignity but his life savings too. Without that money he would not be able to purchase an identity. Malume Jackson had hinted several times that for the right price he was willing to facilitate the move. Dumisani had tried calling some guys he knew from school but as soon as he started narrating his ordeal their tone would change. The next time he called they would not take his calls. He was working in earnest trying to save enough money as Malume had hinted that he would need at least R10 000 to grease a few palms at home affairs. At this rate he doubted that would even be feasible. On most nights he pocketed R200 or if it was an extremely good night he could walk home with R400.

'The baby is kicking now. So playful …'

Dumisani's heart sank even further. Christine was five months along. The original idea was that Christine would join him after their second child was born. He would have been settled in a nice two-bedroomed apartment had things gone according to their original plan. But as things stood he was nowhere near to achieving his goals.

'How is uBaba?' he asked.

'He's getting better,' replied Christine. 'I was with your parents yesterday. Phumlani's wife gave birth to a baby girl. Buhle got accepted into university …'

In the distance Dumisani could hear the beeping sound warning him that his money was about to run out.

'Sweetie, I have to go. I promise I'll talk to you soon. I love you.'

'I love you too,' replied Christine.

Then the line went dead. He hadn't even said goodbye. He felt as if his insides had been momentarily gouged out. Dumisani reached deep into his pockets for that lone R5 coin so that he could call back but his pockets were empty. With a heavy heart he crossed the tree-lined avenue and started the long journey to work. He often walked past a pawn shop and it was here that he often contemplated pawning his gold wedding band but his better judgement normally prevailed. He eventually emerged onto Empire Road where he sometimes flagged down a taxi but today decided to save the ten rand. He continued along Louis Botha, then cut through Orange Grove before he reached his destination in Norwood. It was a leafy neighbourhood with pretty houses with box-sized gardens. He worked on Grant Avenue, a street lined with outdoor cafés, restaurants, hair salons and supermarkets.

When he had made enough money he hoped to settle down in Norwood with his family. It was a fairly safe and secure neighbourhood and he could imagine playing in the park with his children on the weekend. They would eat at restaurants like Shai Karma, Europa and Schwarma, just as the many families he served. He would also buy his wife a nice SUV and he would drive a fancy Mercedes. These dreams kept him going; fuelled the ambition that bubbled beneath his calm façade.

He wore a sunny smile the minute he walked into Café Dolce Vita. It was an Italian restaurant serving authentic Italian food. On his first day on the job he had been forced to memorise the menu and then take a test, which he passed. He'd always had a photo-graphic memory. Dumisani was usually the first to arrive at work and helped the proprietor open every morning. The breakfast run was light and Dumisani had his regulars. His favourite was a mid-dle-aged Jewish man called Solomon Kaufman. He came in every morning to have his cappuccino as he perused the *Business Day* and the *Financial Times*. As Solomon drank his cappuccino he lamented how the world markets were in crisis. What Dumisani liked about Solomon was that he was one of the few customers who took a few minutes to chat to him. Who would ask about his life, wife and family. And Solomon always left him a tip. That morning was no different and after he had left, Dumisani started to go through the papers. He hoped by doing this he would have more to contribute to their conversations in future.

'Ey, Dumi, I don't pay you to read the papers!' lamented his boss. 'On your own time!'

Dumisani folded the papers promising himself he would return to them after hours.

Another long day ended and he was walking up towards Louis Botha when a familiar voice called out his name. Dumisani looked up and saw Chamunorwa. They had sat next to each other on their unlawful journey into South Africa. Dumisani was pleas-antly surprised to see him. It was Chamunorwa who had loaned him the R20 to call his uncle. After they had parted ways he had never entertained the possibility that they would meet again. The two young men embraced enthusiastically. This was as familiar as it got in this sea of strangers. After an exchange of pleasantries Chamunorwa revealed he was working at a fast-food joint.

'Seems like we're all in that business,' replied Dumisani. 'I'm a waiter.'

'At least you're waiting tables. I'm the guy who cleans the floors and toilets,' replied Chamunorwa.

'Where are you staying?'

'Hillbrow. With an uncle.'

'Well, let's walk together. I catch my taxis at Noord. I live with my mother. It's comfortable but not the best of situations.'

Chamunorwa did not have to elaborate further. Dumisani immediately understood.

So the two men walked back to Hillbrow commiserating about their experiences since they had arrived in Johannesburg but more importantly they spoke of their aspirations for the future. Walking in tandem it felt like the journey had been halved. Dumisani even waited at the busy taxi rank for Chamunorwa to board his taxi. They swapped numbers and promised to keep in touch. As he walked home Dumisani felt like a boulder had been lifted from his shoulders. He was comforted to know he was not alone in his drudgery. Comforted to meet a familiar person from home familiar with his struggles. They had, in all sincerity, come a long way together.

# EIGHTEEN

Majestic palaces where kings and queens lived in royal luxury were things relegated to Chenai's imagination. An imagination stoked by the storybooks she had devoured as a child where sleeping beauties waited to be rescued by princes. However, those palatial images finally came to life the day she was dropped outside the Van Tonders' home in Bryanston.

She stood in the driveway, in awe of its sheer size. The double-storey home was set on rolling acres of lush green gardens coloured with blossoming hyacinths and chrysanthemums. Standing in the spacious reception area for the first time she was mesmerised by the glittering chandelier. On the walls were gold-framed mirrors that reflected back her image. She felt extremely self-conscious. A sweeping staircase with a gold balustrade led upstairs. Large gold-framed portraits of each of the family members hung on the wall. Portraits of shiny, happy people.

However, her amazement quickly diminished when she realised she would be the one responsible for cleaning this monstrosity of a home from top to bottom. Her mother had assured her the money was good and she would have her own living quarters at the bottom of the garden. The living quarters were small but adequate. She had her own room with a little television set attached to the wall. There was a small kitchenette and a tiny bathroom. It was slightly bigger than the flatlet they had shared with their mother. However, these were tiny luxuries compared to the grandeur of the Van Tonder home.

By midday Chenai was often about to keel over in exhaustion just from cleaning the downstairs area. She wondered how someone could commit to doing this kind of work for the rest of their lives. Maybe it got easier with each passing year. Her mother had been working for her *mlungus* for years. Had raised their kids and was now looking forward to raising their grandkids. As Chenai dusted the vases in the living room she thought about the mess that awaited her upstairs where she had to contend with five spacious en-suite bedrooms and a pyjama lounge.

The Van Tonders had three messy children ranging in age from eight to fifteen. Chenai still could not get over how it was possible for anyone to have so much wealth. Walking into the madam's bedroom she almost tripped over clothes scattered all over the floor of her spacious dressing room. The madam had gone to some function the night before and had tried on several silky chiffon gowns with exotic names like Dolce & Gabbana, Gavin Rajah, Thula Sindi, David Tlale and Marion & Lindie.

As she picked up an emerald organza gown Chenai held it against her body. She fingered the fabric; the material was so soft and silky. She decided to try it on. Just for a few minutes she wanted to feel what it was like to be a princess. She stepped out of her flowery print cotton uniform, stood in front of the full-length mirror and slid into the gown. It fitted perfectly and clung to her svelte frame. Chenai did a pirouette. For a moment in time she felt so pretty and feminine. She discarded it and tried on a yellow dress with a tight-fitting bodice and a full skirt. One would think the dresses were made for her. They clung perfectly and the colour was a beautiful contrast to her sleek black complexion. She decided to slip on a pair of the madam's shoes. They sat in poised dignity, row upon row. Boots, strappy sandals, pumps, pointy stilettos, slippers, sneakers and wedges.

All colours of the rainbow were represented from amber, beige to neon greens and nudes. The shoes had names and surnames; names she could not even pronounce. Christian Louboutin, Jimmy Choo, Manolo Blahniks, Miu Miu, Nine West and Steve Madden. Chenai felt like a little girl in a candy store surrounded by guilty pleasures. She finally reached out for silver strappy sandals covered with sparkling diamantés. Standing in them she was unsteady and almost toppled over.

She laughed at herself. She had seen the madam prance around the house in even higher heels and she walked with such poise and grace. She decided to make a point of watching her more closely. She threw her head back like she had often seen her madam do but her thick curly Afro would not cooperate. She turned to the side, admiring her figure. The woman in the full-length gilt-lined mirror smiled back at her. It dawned on her at that moment that she was really beautiful. Until then she had never felt that way. She felt ugly inside and out but in that moment she felt like she was the most beautiful girl in the world.

There was measured applause, which broke her reverie. Chenai gasped on realising she was not alone.

'Quite a show you've put on here!'

It was Danie. The madam's husband. Chenai's skin prickled

with panic. She wanted to quickly tear the dress from her body. Erase this whole moment.

'I'm so sorry!' she apologised profusely, reaching for the zip.

'Don't worry. I won't tell if you won't tell.'

He said it with a naughty glint in his eye.

Chenai's hands were shaking as she reached for the zip.

'Calm down now,' he said. 'Let me help you. Imagine how much more trouble you'll be in if you tear madam's dress.'

He was calm and collected as he stood behind her. His thick hands reached to the side and with one sweeping movement he pulled the zipper down. His hand lingered on her hip for what seemed an eternity. He pushed the dress down till it fell in a circle around Chenai's legs. Standing in front of the mirror, Chenai felt vulnerable. She had no bra on. Had never worn a bra in her life but still her breasts stood pert and pointed. They had never been big. Only that one time in her life when she had been bursting with life. But soon after her baby had died they had shrunk to their normal size. Danie cupped them in his hands. His white skin on her was a shocking contrast to her dark skin. As he pressed into her she could feel the hard organ which immediately evoked the memory of her father.

'You are *so* beautiful. Has anyone ever told you how beautiful you are?'

Tears began to roll down Chenai's cheeks.

'Please sir. *Please.*'

She felt his beard scratch the side of her neck.

'I promise you I won't hurt you. It will be over before you know it.'

'Please sir. I will never do this again.'

With his other hand Danie loosened his trousers.

'I'll be quick. Madam will only be home after three. No one will know. I won't even tell her about you trying to steal her clothes ...'

'I wasn't stealing!'

'*Shhhh* now. How do you think it would look? Who do you think she would believe?'

He pulled her panties down and Chenai knew the fate that lay before her. He prised her legs apart and shifted his member between her thighs. Chenai clasped her eyes shut. She was no longer a princess but the dirty ugly child she used to be. No longer was she in a palace. Instead she was transformed back to that time in her father's house. As he tore into her she yelped out in pain.

'*Shhh*,' he cajoled, putting his hand over her mouth.

He continued to thrust wildly into her. Chenai bit down on her tongue smothering her pained cries. It was over quickly. Danie's sperm spewed all over her buttocks and down her legs in a sticky stream.

'Good girl,' he said slapping her pert buttocks. 'Now go and clean yourself up!'

Chenai picked up her clothes and ran out of the dressing room without turning back.

As she immersed her hands in the soapy water in the sink her mind drifted beyond the dirty dishes. She could still not believe what had just transpired. Had she imagined it? She knew she couldn't have, not when the pain was still within her. A searing pain that burnt through her womanhood. She reached for a porcelain plate. Although the kitchen was equipped with a Smeg dishwasher the madam never allowed her to use it. Not that she minded; some of the gadgets in the house were overwhelming and complicated. Just like the situation that had played itself out earlier.

She knew what would happen now. Danie would probably

try to have his way with her whenever he wanted, whenever he could. The workload she could handle but that part she could not. Perfectly formed droplets fell from her face into the soapy water. As she tackled each piece of cutlery she did so with mounting resentment. Life was so unfair.

Why her? Why did things like this happen to her? She knew they did not happen to every woman. In school she had confided to a friend about how her father raped her. Her friend had looked at her like she was a pariah. That there was something wrong with *her*. She recalled the horror on Chipo's face. 'Daddy don't do that!' Then from the soapy water in the sink her father's face emerged. He had a lopsided grin on his face. He started to laugh at her. His eyes filled with mockery. Chenai reached for a porcelain plate and slammed it against the sink.

'Damn it!' she swore.

He laughed harder instead. Chenai hurled the dishes at him. One after the other they broke in protest. Splintered with anger. Her rage abated only when she could no longer see her father's face, when his image had dissipated with the bubbles in the sink. There was broken crockery everywhere. Chenai looked around in horror. There was no way she could conceal this evidence. It was then that Mrs Van Tonder walked in; Woolies bags in her hands. The bags dropped to the floor when she caught sight of the broken pieces of crockery.

'Chenai?'

Chenai shrugged and immediately launched into an apology.

'I'm sorry ma'am. I don't know what happened.'

'What do you mean you don't know what happened? You stupid *kaffir*!'

The madam slapped her hard across the face. Chenai hung her

head.

'You are fired!' she screamed. 'Who does this? You can't do a simple thing like dishes! Damn you! And you know what, I'm not going to pay you a cent, do you hear me?'

Chenai nodded mutely.

'Get your bags and get off my property before I call the police.'

Chenai's heart galloped at the mention of police. The reason she was here was that she was running away from the police. She gathered her belongings and made a hasty exit.

# NINETEEN

Every morning Portia paraded down Pritchard Street to the offices where she worked on the corner of Market Street and Von Brandis Street. Even though her shoes squashed her corns and made her feet swell she bit down the pain and soldiered on. She practised walking in her heels diligently in her apartment. Many times before she had fallen flat on her face leaving her son reeling with laughter. However, Portia was determined to master the art of walking in high heels like her work colleagues at Hulisani, Hirsch, Hlomani and Associates.

They occupied the seventh floor which they shared with some accountants and consulting engineers. Portia sat in reception greeting clients with a sunny smile and answering telephones with practised efficacy. She had not always been in the foreground. Instead she had lingered in the background; cleaning toilets, making tea and sweeping the office floors. Beyond these chores she was often sent to run the personal errands of her bosses.

Advocate Hirsch loved a particular brand of Colombian coffee, which she bought at a café at the corner of De Korte and Juta Streets. Advocate Hulisani often sent her to pick up his dry cleaning from a laundromat on Eloff Street. When lunch time came, she would go and buy Advocate Hlomani his chesa nyama lunch on Commissioner Street. He thrived on his staple of pap and braaied meat and never deviated from the set menu. Sometimes when the messenger was out running errands and there was an urgent delivery to be made they sent Portia.

It was for this reason that Portia had made a habit of memorising street names. Kotze. Loveday. Kerk. Plein. She had a map of the CBD etched in her head. It was the only way she could navigate the city of Johannesburg without getting lost. Even if she got lost, which she had on many occasions, if she could find a familiar street name she would easily find her bearings once again. With the passage of time Johannesburg became less intimidating and more accommodating.

She had no idea how the city actually came to be christened 'Johannesburg', which to her seemed like an odd name. The origins of the name 'Johannesburg' were contentious but most accounts seemed to allude to the fact that the city was named after Johannes Joubert and Johannes Rissik, men who had both been responsible for land surveying and mapping of the town. The combination of their first names led to the coining of 'Johannes-burg'. The suffix being an Afrikaans word meaning 'town'. But whatever you wanted to call her. Egoli. Joni. Jozi. Joburg. Johannesburg was undeniably one of Africa's economic powerhouses and it is for this reason that she was able to lure people from all over the continent. All of them were gold-diggers seeking fame or fortune. Or both.

Portia had found her gold nestled amongst the long overgrown grass in Joubert Park. For the first few weeks in the city she and Nkosi had slept on the vacant seats in the busy transit terminal. They slept in good company with other passengers who were transiting from one city to another. Every morning they showered in the public ablutions. When they were clean they would spend the day roaming the city with Portia knocking on doors for a job. Any job. Doors were slammed in her face. Exhausted and dejected they'd spend the rest of the afternoon at Joubert Park. Nkosi had even made friends with children who had finished school. Portia would watch him from the park bench, trying not to feel sorry for herself. Her optimism was wearing thin and so was their money. She spent her every penny sparingly but two months of sleeping on the streets was enough to get her worried. She contemplated catching a taxi back to Plumtree with the little money they had left.

Her husband had been right; Johannesburg was no place for a woman. But then Nkosi had kicked a soccer ball under the park bench where Portia was seated. When she bent over to retrieve it she stumbled across a handbag which looked like it had been thrown hurriedly under the bench. Curiosity got the better of her. The bag had already been ransacked, it seemed. However, the real treasure was the green ID booklet. She took possession of it and threw the bag aside. She quickly shoved the booklet into her bra. The next day Portia assumed her new identity as Phakama Hlophe. After a visit to Harrison Street she was able to get a passport-sized picture which she superimposed on Phakama's picture. Armed with her new ID, Portia went about trying to enrol Nkosi into a crèche. Little Angels Daycare Centre was happy to take him. She paid the enrol-ment fee and left him there as she went about her job-hunt. By the end of the week she had landed herself a position as a cleaner with Hulisani, Hirsch, Hlomani and Associates.

Portia and her son continued to sleep at Park Station. They ate the leftovers that she cleaned off the plates from the staff at work. She would walk Nkosi to crèche every morning before racing off to work. She was the first person in the office but never the last to leave. The advocates were always in the office. Sometimes when she arrived in the morning she would find Advocate Hulisani still in his office looking ruffled and exhausted with bloodshot eyes. Of all the advocates he was the most vocal and often succumbed to fits of rage. It was not unusual to see interns or legal assistants running out of his office followed by law journals and anything else he could throw at them. Often after such incidents Advocate Hirsch would go into his office to calm him down.

Clifford, the messenger, had told Portia countless times that Advocate Hulisani was good at his job, which is why his name appeared first. His reasoning however could not be substantiated and Portia never questioned it. Clifford maintained that Advocate Hulisani insisted that the practice would die if he ever left. Portia was fearful of him and tiptoed around him lest he unleash his rage on her.

When month-end came Portia was excited to receive her first salary. That night she and Nkosi did not eat leftovers but instead ate from one of the fast-food restaurants at Park Station. When they went to sleep on one of the benches Portia assured her son they would be doing it for the last time. The following day they went hunting for a place to live. They managed to find a one-bedroomed apartment on Edith Cavell Street. It was a threadbare apartment with the cupboards almost coming off the hinges. The landlord said that was the reason he only wanted R1 000 for it. They slept on the parquet floor on their sponge mattress which they had purchased for R600. Portia assured her son that things would be better.

'Next month I will buy you a bed.'

Nkosi threw his tiny arms around her and hugged her.

'I know you will, Mama.'

At night Portia dreamt of all the things she would do once she got her second pay cheque. The new stove. The new sofa. The new television set. She fell asleep dreaming about the new bed.

One afternoon at work, as she was washing cups in the kitchen, she heard Advocate Hulisani shout that he needed some documents typed. Portia went to the front to hear what the commotion was about.

'Where is everyone?' he screamed. 'Where are the interns?'

'At court,' replied Portia.

'Kopano? Where is she?'

'Still at lunch,' replied Portia.

Hulisani kicked the plant in the reception knocking it over. Portia quickly rushed to catch it but it was too late.

'I need this document typed *now*!' he screamed.

'I will call her,' replied Portia shrinking away and heading towards the switchboard. At times she did hold the fort for Kopano when she wanted to take an extended lunch. Kopano's phone just rang. Portia hung up feeling disconcerted.

'I can't get hold of her,' she replied. 'But I can type.'

He eyed her circumspectly. 'Are you sure?'

Portia had taken a typing course at school. She could type 80 words a minute so when her fingers hit the keyboard she was not in totally unfamiliar territory. The computer keyboard was much softer than the typewriter and her fingers slid across the keys. She typed whilst Advocate Hulisani paced the room as he dictated to her. He often came round to look over her shoulder to see if she was actually typing.

By the time Kopano came back Portia was editing the document, checking it for errors. Advocate Hulisani was so impressed with Portia that Advocate Hirsch and Advocate Hlomani soon got wind of it. They started saying her talent was being underutilised in the kitchen as a cleaner and that was how Portia got promoted to front office. She now sat with Kopano and helped with other office duties. Her promotion came with a pay increase which Portia welcomed.

The following month she and Nkosi moved from the grimy apartment to a beautiful high-rise apartment on Kerk Street in the heart of the Johannesburg CBD. It was clean and secure with controlled access. She could sleep at night without fear in her heart. She could now afford to shop at the department stores like Edgars, Foschini, Spitz and Truworths. She had bought her furniture from Russells and Morkels. For the first time she felt like she was living the life she deserved. A life she was determined to live to the fullest.

As much as possible Portia tried to emulate the ladies at work. She looked at the way they dressed and would improvise slightly and come up with her own look. She listened to how Kopano and the other ladies spoke and would imitate them. She would practise religiously at night, imitating the intonation and mannerisms. Gradually the old Portia began to disappear, making way for Phakama.

Portia always enjoyed the brisk walk to work through the CBD. The town was always full of life and joie de vivre. The only time it took a sojourn was on Sundays. On those days she went to church at the Methodist Church on Delvers Street. She could have easily attended the central Methodist Church on the corner of Small and Pritchard but it was overflowing with Zimbabwean refugees who poured into Johannesburg like heavy rain. The church sheltered thousands who slept on its floors. Portia preferred to distance herself from her kith and kin. Phakama had no place being there. She felt no allegiance to or kindred spirit with them. She had a new life now. A new beginning.

# TWENTY

When the thirtieth of each month came around it only served to remind Dumisani how much time had passed and how much further he was from achieving his dreams. The only good thing was the receipt of his wages. He was also immensely cheered by the hefty commission he received. His boss tapped him on the back proclaiming him to be the best waiter they had ever had. Dumisani had half smiled. If only his boss knew he had bigger ambitions than working in a restaurant all his life.

Nonetheless he went about his job with his usual cheerfulness. He even engaged Mr Kaufman in a lengthy debate about the mortgage crisis that had led to the collapse of many European banks and eventually precipitated the global debt crisis. The financial markets were in a precarious position and always dominated the business headlines. Dumisani read the newspaper from cover to cover as he had nothing better to do with his evenings; he preferred to be out on the balcony alone. He surprised Mr Kaufman with his profound knowledge.

'Tell me Dumi, did you study finance? You seem to have an

excellent grasp of the subject.'

'No, I'm actually an engineering student. Civils. I came here thinking I would get a great job but *eish* things haven't worked out as I had planned.'

'Hmm, that's tough,' replied Mr Kaufman who seemed to be deep in thought.

'I own an investment management company. We are actually looking for someone who could trade. They need to be mathematically inclined. Look, I know it's off the beaten track but is it something you could consider?'

Dumisani nodded. 'Most definitely. I'll be honest it's never crossed my mind but I could give it a try.'

'We would sort out all your paperwork and I'm willing to give you on-the-job training. Six months and then we'll see if there's a future for you in the markets.'

Dumisani could not suppress his smile. He wanted to reach out and hug the elderly white man with greying hair but restrained himself. Mr Kaufman pulled out his business card and handed it over to Dumisani.

'Be at my offices first thing Monday morning and we'll take it from there.'

'I will be.'

Mr Kaufman paid for his usual cappuccino and tipped Dumisani generously as usual. Dumisani could not believe his good fortune. He couldn't wait to call his wife and share the good news. Suddenly the prospect of being reunited was not some event in the distant future.

That evening he shared his good news with Chamunorwa as they made their daily walk back to Hillbrow. Chamunorwa had good news of his own to share. He had finally been promoted from cleaning assistant to peeling potato chips. They laughed about it but both men agreed they were indeed making strides in their lives.

'I want to move out this weekend,' declared Chamunorwa. 'I have found a back room in Alexandra. The rent is only one hundred and fifty rand. I can't continue living with my sister and mother.'

'I feel you there. I also need to think about moving out. Staying with my malume is becoming problematic.'

Walking into the flat that evening he walked right into another fight between Malume Jackson and his wife. He thought of going back downstairs to hang out in the street until the noise died down but their fights could go on all night. Besides he was tired and wanted to lie down after a long day on his feet. He was about to shove some money into the spongy pillow he slept on when Malume Jackson walked out onto the balcony. No one ever bothered to knock; robbing him of his last thread of privacy.

'Yeesus,' he lamented. 'Women talk too much and half the time they talk through their arses.'

Dumisani did not respond. He could not relate. His mother was soft-spoken, so was his wife.

'I need a drink. Come with me.'

'Malume, you know I don't drink.'

Malume Jackson smirked, 'Okay you can come and watch me drink then. Yeesus! Which planet are you from?'

So he accompanied Malume Jackson to The Base Night Club. They were greeted by the stench of urine and unwashed floors. Nonetheless this did not deter the crowd which was slowly filling up the premises. Dumisani had never been a clubber. He disapproved of the young women who walked around half naked. He felt like he had entered Sin City which his pastor had often described during feverish sermons.

Malume Jackson was a regular and was quickly ushered to his table on the balcony overlooking the streets of Hillbrow. Loud music blared from the stereo drowning any attempt at any meaningful conversation. Malume Jackson called for his Castle Lager, which came in a brown bottle with cold droplets on its glassy body. Dumisani opted for his usual Fanta Orange.

'You are too sober for your own good,' chastised Malume Jackson. 'You need to learn to live a little.'

'I will live when my family is finally here with me.'

'*Mxm*,' snorted Malume Jackson. 'You need to stop living in the past and live in the present. Forget about Zimbabwe and everything you left there. Start a new life here. There are beautiful women here.'

As he said that Malume Jackson beckoned to two light-skinned women clad in black bustiers and matching shorts. They were very familiar with him and wet his face with syrupy kisses before finding refuge on one of his thick thighs; he was a hefty man and could easily accommodate them both. Malume Jackson started to paw their showy breasts.

'Don't you want one of my women?' he coaxed Dumisani.

'No, Malume,' he replied emphatically.

The sight of their luscious thighs stirred life into Dumisani's loins but he would not allow himself to yield to the temptation. He would not only be defiling himself but Christine too. He imagined her in her advanced stage of pregnancy, her burgeoning belly spilling onto her lap. He could not dishonour her by having a mindless shag with some Hillbrow whores.

'If you change your mind they're always here,' responded Malume Jackson reaching for his beer.

He dismissed both girls with the wave of his hand. They

almost spat in his face.

'*Usimoshel'iqesha mkhulu*. You are wasting our time, Grandpa!' hissed one.

'Voetsek,' replied Malume Jackson.

'Fuck you,' replied the other one acidly.

'*S'febe sothuvi*,' countered Malume Jackson with equal venom.

Malume Jackson reached for his drink and gulped it down while signalling for another with his free hand. He had three drinks in succession whilst Dumisani was still lingering on his Fanta Orange.

'So mfana, you don't drink. You don't fuck. What do you do?'

'Malume, I am faithful to my wife.'

'*Hayibo. Suka mani!* You think your wife is being faithful? Women are such cunning creatures. Full of shit.'

Dumisani decided to finish his drink and head back home. He was getting tired of Malume Jackson who was now inebriated and becoming more unbearable with each passing minute.

'You know Malume, I have to go. I have an early morning shift tomorrow morning.'

'You are going to work yourself to death at that stupid job of yours. You should come and work for me. Do you know, mfana, that I own Garth Mansions? This nonsense of working in restaurants. You will never get far.'

Dumisani wanted to tell him that he had landed a better job but decided against it. The enormity of it would probably be lost on Malume Jackson.

'With me you would work on commission. Whatever I make you get a percentage.'

'Malume, what exactly do you do?'

Malume Jackson lowered his voice and moved closer to

Dumisani.

'Come work with me and you'll find out.'

'I think I'll take my chances in the restaurant business,' replied Dumisani. 'I have to go home now.'

'Well, leave a hundred rand for the drinks, mfana. Don't be stingy.'

Grudgingly Dumisani pulled out a R100 note. As he was about to rise out of his seat Malume Jackson stopped him mid-movement and asked for the rent. Dumisani's eyes almost popped out of his sockets.

'Rent?' he gasped.

'*Hawu*, mfana,' replied Malume Jackson. 'You thought you were going to live for free? It's eight hundred rand.'

'*Hawu*, Malume? For that little corner?'

'You go around Hillbrow knocking from door to door and see if you can get rent that cheap. If you can't afford better *odula ko lokshini koAlex or Thembisa.*'

Dumisani swallowed hard and reached into his pockets for a few more notes. He made up his mind then and there that he would move out of Malume Jackson's home that weekend. He was sure Chamunorwa could guide him in looking for a cheaper place in Alexandra.

'*Uyabonake* mfana,' said Malume Jackson taking the crisp fresh notes and shoving them into his leather jacket, 'And *irent yami* goes up every month. Next month it's a thousand rand.'

With a sullen face Dumisani bade his uncle goodnight. He could feel the onslaught of a headache as he realised he was now R1 000 poorer. Money he could have sent to his wife and family was now languishing in his uncle's hands. As he walked across the street he cursed.

When he got home he found Malume's wife lolling in front of the television with a sullen face. She was nursing a black eye, which she had acquired the night before. Malume's daughters were nowhere in sight. Come to think of it, they spent very little time at home. He didn't blame them. Home could be a battlefield with landmines waiting to explode any minute. Dumisani greeted her perfunctorily before heading out to the balcony. He was getting undressed when the door opened. It was Malume's wife.

'Where did you leave that bastard?' she asked.

'He's still drinking,' replied Dumisani.

'I guess that gives us ample time,' she replied sidling up to him and gently stroking his hard back.

'*Hayi* mama! What are you doing?'

'Don't be scared,' she replied reaching for the front zipper of his trousers. 'I know you're hungry.'

Before Dumisani knew what was happening her tongue was all over his face, licking him like an excited puppy. Except because of her size it was more appropriate to liken her to a baby elephant. She pushed him onto the floor and Dumisani felt the wind escape his body as she collapsed on top of him with all her weight.

'Mama, *please*,' he implored. 'Stop this!'

She covered his mouth with another slobbering kiss while her other hand attempted to stroke his genitals through his jeans. Dumisani tried to muster the strength to heave her off his body. He did not stand a chance. Even her breasts, the size of overripe watermelons, weighed him down.

'Gawd!' he cried out over and over again as her gargantuan body began to gyrate eagerly above him.

Against his will he spurted into his pants; the load of pent-up desire exploding in one furious orgasm. He screamed out. He could not hold it back and regretted it immediately. Loathed his very being for giving in to this sinful act with his uncle's wife. That was how Jackson found them. His wife writhing on top of him fully clothed.

'*Heeeee!*' Malume Jackson screamed. '*Niyenzani*? What are you doing?'

Like a tsunami, his wife removed herself off Dumisani and sped off the balcony into the flat. With equal efficacy Malume Jackson lunged towards him. Dumisani expected to be assailed by a flurry of feisty fists in quick succession but Malume Jackson merely picked him up off the bed with ease and threw him over the balcony.

'*Heeeee … udl'umfazi wam'*? You want to have your way with my wife?'

Those were the words that followed Dumisani to the ground where he landed with a thundering thud.

# PART THREE

**Gold Mining**

'For the love of money is a root of all kinds of evil.
Some people, eager for money, have wandered from
the faith and pierced themselves with many griefs.'

*1 Timothy 6: Verse 10*

# TWENTY-ONE

Nightfall had cast dark and sinewy shadows on the streets of Alexandra Township, yet hundreds lingered on the streets outside their homes. Street lights, where they could be found, illuminated the dusty roads where many children continued to play. Alex, as it is fondly known, was nestled on the banks of the Jukskei River. It was a bit like the poor relative that lives next door to the more affluent neighbour of Sandton.

From a distance it might have looked like a chaotic mess but the intricate road network housed a vibrant economy in the midst of the housing. Spazas, hair salons, tuck shops, day-care centres, pubs, lounges and car washes all existed to serve the local community. Chamunorwa had soon come to learn the mixed character of the neighbourhood. He did not live in a walled and gated home or a four-storey walk-up. His home was a tiny shack made from asbestos and other scrap material. He was a few streets from his home when he witnessed a young woman being thrown out of a tavern. Two guys were hot on her heels and began to boot her rump like she was a soccer ball. Chamunorwa watched in horror as they

SUE NYATHI

both kicked her.

'Leave her alone,' he called out.

'Mind your own business,' replied the man.

Something in his conscience would not leave it alone. He thought of his own sister. The abuse she had suffered at his father's hands. How he had not done anything about it because he was helpless. He was not that helpless young boy anymore. He was in a position to help.

'I said leave her alone!'

'Voetsek!' hissed the other man defensively. 'This is none of your business.'

The woman lay on the ground whimpering as the two young men attacked her with brutal kicks with their shiny patent leather Carvela shoes.

'Go ahead and hit me,' challenged Chamunorwa throwing himself in their faces.

He held his hands up in resignation. He was willing to take the blows on behalf of this woman. The two men eyed him circumspectly then they decided to let it go. They disappeared back into the tavern. Chamunorwa helped the young woman to her feet. Blood was trickling from her mouth.

'Are you all right?' he asked.

She nodded. 'I think so.'

She could barely stand up and had to hold onto Chamunorwa's shoulder.

'Where's home? Let me take you home.'

The woman started to cry. 'Home is with them. That's my boyfriend.'

Chamunorwa felt the anger creep up his throat like bile. How was it possible for a boyfriend to treat his lover like that?

'I have nowhere to go,' she sobbed.

'It's okay, you can come home with me. We'll make a plan tomorrow.'

She did not respond but merely succumbed to the tears she'd been holding back. All her pent-up emotions burst forth like a bubbly spring. Chamunorwa merely put a comforting arm around her. He welcomed her into his one-roomed shack. Many might not have considered it worthy of being called a home but Chamunorwa was proud to have a place he could finally call his own. A single bed was backed up against the wall. He had bought it on sale at Bed and Mattress. There was a solitary armchair whose floral façade had almost faded. But he'd picked it up for almost nothing at a Hospice shop on Louis Botha. The table that was backed up against the wall came from there too. On it sat a two-plate stove with a tiny oven. He had electricity to his place through some illegal Eskom connection. He also had a tiny second-hand television set that sometimes failed to pick up the SABC signal. There was a stand-alone toilet outside which he shared with the other residents. It also doubled up as a bathroom.

His landlady was a widow in her fifties who lived in her two-roomed house with her nine children. As long as he paid his rent on time she never bothered him.

'You can call me Chamu,' he said by way of introduction. 'What's your name?'

'Lerato,' she replied.

'Just make yourself comfortable on the bed.'

She shifted on it nervously. He could see her eyes darting around, taking in the sparse details of his existence.

'I'm going to start cooking,' he explained to her, putting a pan on the stove.

He had bought a small packet of stewing beef which had more fat than meat. He went out onto the street to buy spinach, a tomato and an onion from a nearby vendor. Wanting to be hospitable he decided to get a bottle of Coca-Cola for his visitor. He was so used to living alone that he had almost forgotten what it was like to have company. Though Lerato was not the most communicative person, he asked questions and she answered curtly.

By the time supper was cooked he had gleaned that she was originally from Maseru but had lived with her aunt in Soweto for a while. She had come to Johannesburg to study but had dropped out of college when she met Kgosi, her boyfriend. They lived in the council flats just off London Road. Kgosi had a good job at some manufacturing concern in Kew. He drove a Golf GTI and was basically doing well for himself.

'So do you want to go back to him?' asked Chamunorwa.

Lerato shook her head. 'I have wanted to leave him for a long time now. My aunt won't let me back into her home. I left her on bad terms. And now I'm pregnant.'

She started to cry again.

'You are welcome to stay here. I don't have much.'

He was almost apologetic about this fact. He wished he had more; to make his home comfortable for this broken flower. His heart went out to her. Her vulnerability reminded him of his own sister. She sat with her head buried in her lap. She did not seem too keen to talk so Chamunorwa busied himself with the supper. He soon served up the piping hot pap with spinach and beef and tomato gravy. Lerato marvelled at his culinary skills.

'We grew up without a mother. I had no choice but to learn how to cook.'

'Sorry to hear that. I also grew up without a mother. She died when I was three.'

Between mouthfuls she went on to narrate to Chamunorwa a harrowing childhood in Lesotho with her grandparents. It was only when the last morsel of meat was eaten that Lerato stopped telling her story and volunteered to wash the dishes whilst Chamunorwa sat in the armchair until he dozed off. It was Lerato who woke him up later.

'Why don't you go to sleep? I will sleep on the floor.'

'No,' replied Chamunorwa. 'Sleep on the bed. I will sleep here on the chair.'

'Oh no. I feel bad. This is your home!'

'And you are my guest. Sleep on the bed. I insist.'

The following day Chamunorwa accompanied Lerato to Kgosi's flat so that she could collect her belongings. Chamunorwa waited outside the flat pacing anxiously. The incident unfolded with much drama. He could hear the spirited shouting coming from inside. The door flung open and Kgosi threw Lerato's clothes out on the doorstep. Lerato bent over to pick them up but Kgosi kicked her in the rear making her tumble over.

'Leave her!' barked Chamunorwa.

'*Hawu.* What's with this dude of yours? *Ke lekgowa?* Is he white? He only speaks English.'

'Leave him alone,' shouted Lerato. 'He's not from here.'

Kgosi snorted. 'What is he? A kwerekwere?'

Lerato did not respond. Kgosi grabbed her roughly by the hand and spun her around.

'Don't tell me you are leaving me for some low-life kwere-kwere!'

This was when Chamunorwa barged into the conversation.

'Don't ever call me that!' he hissed.

143

'Kwerekwere!' jeered Kgosi. 'You come here and take our jobs, now you want to take our women! *Tsek!* Go back to where you came from! This is not your country!'

Chamunorwa grabbed Kgosi by the collar and shoved him against the wall.

'Lay a finger on me, *monna*, and you'll spend the rest of your life in jail. Who do you think the police will believe? You or me? *Ngiyekele.* Leave me alone!'

'Leave him,' yelled Lerato.

Grudgingly Chamunorwa loosened his grip on Kgosi, who dusted the spot where Chamunorwa had touched him. He then spat in his face.

'Piece of shit. You come into our country and disrespect us. I will teach you a lesson, kwerekwere.'

Chamunorwa wanted to lunge at him but restrained himself. Kgosi was right. He did not want to incite him because if the police were called onto the scene he was clearly the disadvantaged one. Instead he motioned to Lerato and they left. Kgosi stood on the balcony watching them in deep contemplation.

# TWENTY-TWO

The good news that Dumisani's daughter had made a screaming debut into the world reached him in his hospital bed. He had been lying prostrate for the past two months in the infamous Joburg Gen, which he now called home. Christmas had come and gone without ceremony, paving the way for a new year, yet nothing had changed in his circumstances. He was still stuck in the 2007 rut.

Flying from the fourth-floor balcony of Garth Mansions had broken his arm and shattered his thigh. Both limbs were suspended in a white cast. With limited mobility all he could do was stare at the sterile walls and inhale the strong smell of disinfectant that permeated the air. The nurses suspected he had suicidal tendencies as he had not been able to provide a satisfactory explanation as to how he had jumped from such a dizzying height.

He had not wanted to implicate Malume Jackson. As much as he loathed the man he was still family, though Malume Jackson had not been as conciliatory. He had not hesitated to contact Dumisani's mother to tell her how her son had been trying to seduce Malume Jackson's wife. His mother had contacted him, visibly distressed.

'*Mntanami*, my child, this is not how I raised you.'

'It's not true, Mama. That's not what happened.'

'I don't even know what to say to your father. Much less your wife. Her blood pressure shot through the roof when she heard you were in hospital.'

'Mama, the less you say the better,' he had replied.

His mother had discreetly kept the accusations to herself. She merely lied and said the banister on the balcony had weakened and Dumisani had accidentally fallen over. Christine took the news extremely badly, crying that she wanted to be with him. But she couldn't be. She was sequestered in hospital with strict orders of bed rest for the remainder of her pregnancy until their child was safely delivered into the world. It wrenched Dumisani's heart that he was not by her side during that time. What was even more heartbreaking was that he could not alleviate her suffering with some money.

Christine had been forced to deliver at Mpilo Hospital. Under the tutelage of her mother, things had gone well but the fact that she had to give birth in a government hospital without any of the comforts and luxuries she had previously been used to, reminded Dumisani that he had failed as a husband. During one of their snatched conversations Christine told him she had been stitched up without any pethidine. She told him how she had cried till her voice was dry and parched and her body was numb from pain.

It was no longer the same Mpilo Hospital they were accustomed to, she had explained. The standards had deteriorated together with the quality of service.

'I'm feeling better now. Much better.'

He could hear the cooing sounds of the baby in the background.

'I'm on the mend. Getting better every day. Damn it, Christine!

I should be with you and the kids!'

'Well there's not much you can do about it, is there?' replied Christine.

He thought she sounded offish and distant.

'Is everything all right, Christine?'

'No, it isn't, but I have to go. I need to bath Sipho and get supper ready.'

'I love you, Christine!'

She did not respond. She had already hung up. Their conversations once cheered him. Now he felt an empty hollowness that he could not fill.

It was the first time in their married life they had been apart. It was also the most challenging. That regretful feeling of moving to Johannesburg resurfaced. He wished he had just stayed in Bulawayo to slog it out. He might have found another job there. It might not have paid as much but at least he would have been with his family. What value was he adding by lying in a hospital bed in a foreign land? He flirted with the idea of returning home. However, the feeling of failure gnawed at him. Until this juncture he had never failed at anything. He had always authored a narrative of success. Thinking of returning home, and telling everyone that he had failed to strike it rich in the City of Gold, was more humiliating than he could fathom. It was this crushing shame that always lingered in his mind before he dozed off and the first thing to confront him when he woke up.

Half the time he was drugged with painkillers and he liked it like that. The more time he spent asleep the less time he spent awake feeling guilty. When he woke up a few hours later Chamunorwa was at his bedside. His presence cheered Dumisani immensely. Since being admitted to the hospital Chamunorwa had been his only constant and reliable visitor. He was there every day at the tail end of the four to six p.m. visiting time.

'How are you feeling today?' he asked, settling into the empty chair beside him.

'The same way I was feeling yesterday and the day before that.'

'I was speaking to Sister Karabo. She says the leg is healing well.'

Dumisani smiled weakly. 'The nurses have been kind to me. Otherwise I would have killed myself!'

'Don't talk like that,' chastised Chamunorwa. 'You have everything to live for.'

'Did they say when they are going to discharge me?'

'No. Not that there's any rush,' replied Chamunorwa. 'Even if they did, you can't work in a cast. You'll be out for at least another three months.'

Dumisani's face crumpled.

'You might as well pack me in a bus and send me home. What's the point of me being here?'

'I'll look after you when you come out. You can stay with me as long as you need. My place isn't much but we'll get by. We will. '

'And *my* family? What happens to *my* family? What will they survive on? Chamu, it's okay for you because you only have yourself to worry about. I have two young kids and Christine is all by herself and that eats me up ...'

His voice broke as Dumisani started to choke on his own sobs. Chamunorwa let him weep till his anguished cries degenerated into mere sniffles.

'I'm sorry,' apologised Dumisani.

'Don't be,' replied Chamunorwa patting him gently on the back. 'I know you don't want to hear this right now but it's going to be all right. I've been there.'

Dumisani nodded meekly. He had no choice but to believe it. 'Otherwise how is your work going?'

'It's fine. I've been promoted tó cutting potatoes for chips. I'm the chip man. You think your life is bad?'

Dumisani smiled wryly. 'How many potatoes did you cut today?'

'Don't be cheeky man! I might just bring you a sack of potatoes to keep you busy. Actually maybe I should bring potatoes for the whole ward. How about it? Ten one-kilogram bags each and I collect them every evening?'

'Remember I have one arm that works and that won't cut it!' said Dumisani.

They both erupted into a fit of laughter. In the background the siren sounded to signal the end of visiting hours. Dumisani was sad to see his friend leave. He was about to turn onto his side to sleep when Nurse Nomonde arrived. He could smell her from miles away. She wore this overpowering flowery scent that wafted into a room long before she did and lingered long after she'd gone. She was an attractive nurse with a heart-shaped face and big brown eyes. Her silky black hair was always worn in a ponytail swept away from her face. She wore no make-up but never needed to because she was a flawless beauty with full strawberry-coloured lips. Her nurse's uniform fitted her slender frame like it was tailor-made for her. It was cut short above the knees leaving her stockinged legs in full view. She always wore silky stockings.

'*Molweni* Dumisani!' she greeted him airily.

'Sis Nomonde. How are you?'

'I'm good now,' she replied, pulling the curtain around his bed. 'How is my favourite patient?'

'I'm okay, Sis Nomonde.'

He hoped his eyes weren't red from crying. He did not want to expose his vulnerability to this young woman.

'You'll be far more than okay after your bath,' she replied with a salacious smile and a naughty wink.

To move him into a bath at this stage was cumbersome and would also jeopardise the healing process. He was only able to take bed baths where the nurses wiped him down with a wet towel.

'You see. I told you that you are healing well,' cooed Nurse Nomonde as his member sprang to life.

Dumisani was embarrassed at the countless number of times his own body betrayed him.

'Nurse *please*, you shouldn't do this to me.'

Nomonde pouted sheepishly, 'I'm only trying to make you feel better. Doesn't it feel better already?'

Her manicured hands exerted gentle ministrations on his penis. Dumisani groaned as she began to rub him up and down.

'Ssshh,' she whispered. 'You don't want the senior nurse to think there's anything wrong, do you now?'

'No,' croaked Dumisani but it was almost a growl.

Nomonde leaned over and kissed him. Her tongue danced in his mouth, teasing and taunting his. He felt his whole body break into a sweat before jerking into spasms as he spewed into her hand.

'Good boy,' she whispered in his ear after he was physically spent.

'This is so wrong,' he replied, panting profusely.

He said this yet he was flushed with pleasure and overcome with guilt.

'No shame in feeling good,'she replied as she wiped his genitals with a towel.

Afterwards she fed him the food Chamunorwa had brought for him. He felt like a spoiled little child. When he was done she brushed his teeth and he spat into the plastic cup she provided.

'I will see you later,' she mouthed before leaving.

Dumisani's thighs tingled as he lay in anticipation of what awaited him later. When all the lights were turned off Nurse Nomonde would climb into his bed and straddle him. His face flushed with heat as he thought of their after-hour shenanigans. It was cheap comfort, he reasoned. Nothing more was going to come from it. He loved his wife and family.

# TWENTY-THREE

Chenai woke up with a start as her mother pulled the linen from beneath her. Had her mother tugged with more force Chenai would have rolled off the bed.

'All you ever do is sleep!' hissed Sibongile.

Chenai sat up and stared at her mother, trying hard to stifle the rising tide of irritation.

'Some of us have to work,' continued Sibongile with indignation.

'I am looking for a job, you know. Don't think I'm not.'

'I hope you find one since you are too special to clean houses.'

Chenai exhaled deeply. She had not revealed to her mother what had really transpired at the Van Tonders. She had been unable to find the words to articulate the real reason behind her abrupt dismissal. Instead she had let her mother continue to believe that it was her ineptitude and clumsiness that had gotten her fired. Every day Chenai went out scouting for work and when she returned home desolate and unemployed her mother would give her a scathing look as if to say 'I told you so'. It was almost like she rejoiced in her daughter's failure.

That morning Chenai decided to walk to the Sandton CBD. As she was making her way out so was madam Hirsch, who stopped to offer her a lift. Chenai's first impulse was to refuse but she swallowed her pride and slid into the sleek Mercedes Benz.

'I'm rushing for my mani and pedi. Hope traffic isn't too heavy on Rivonia!'

Chenai smiled nervously. She had no idea what a mani and pedi were and did not want to expose her ignorance by asking.

'So how is the job hunt going?' She did not even wait to hear Chenai's response but carried on talking. 'If I hear anything I will let you know. Jobs are hard to come by. There are so many Zimbub-weyans here now. Thousands come in every day. I don't know how this country is supposed to cope!'

The statement lingered uncomfortably in the air. As they pulled up to a robot, a blind woman led by a child no older than seven, came to the window holding out a bowl.

'You see what I mean,' continued the madam, 'every street corner. If *they* are not fighting to clean your windscreen *they* want to sell you something!'

Chenai shrivelled in her seat in embarrassment. She wanted so badly to tell the madam that 'they', Zimbabweans, came from a place of desperation.

'Even our own people can't get jobs!' continued the madam. 'This country is going to the dogs!' She enumerated all the negatives from crime to poor service delivery. 'There is no future for us here. We are thinking of emigrating. For the kids' sake.'

Chenai was quiet. She had no idea how to respond to the madam's little rant but she was glad when the madam pulled up into a vacant spot on Maude Street.

'Be safe,' she called out to Chenai, 'they rape women here!'

Chenai went from shop to shop in the Village Walk Shopping Centre cold-calling at places like Europa, Pick n Pay and Planet Fitness. Even though her mother had organised papers for her and Chamu it didn't make the hunt any easier. She always encountered the same responses: we are not hiring; sorry, that position has been filled; South African citizens only.

Even when she implored she was willing to do anything her pleas were met with annoyance. Encounters with despairing jobseekers were the norm. They often gave off a rabid scent of desperation. The manicured madams who managed exclusive boutiques and posh beauty salons were quick to fend her off with a dismissive wave of the hand. She walked with her head hung low in shame. She did not bother stopping at the large corporate offices whose glassy exteriors looked intimidating. She attempted to sell her mediocre skills at the hotels but the uniformed doormen were quick to chase her away.

Out on the tree-lined boulevard the morning heat was gaining momentum, burning her into a dramatic shade of black. She was aware that she was starting to sweat, obliterating the freshness that had come with her early morning shower. She walked into Gwen Lane and almost walked past a poster: Wanted: Waitresses for a busy bar/nightclub. Chenai decided to try her luck but with each step towards the establishment her confidence waned. She finally presented herself at a trendy bar lounge called Sparklers.

The interview, if it could be called that, was pretty simple. The manager, a white rugged male, took one look at her and decided she fitted the bill. He threw an apron in her direction and told her she could get started. She was employed in the kitchen with the unenviable task of washing a mountain of dishes. Chenai washed each dish with the efficacy of a machine, taking extreme care not to break one. She worked tirelessly; sometimes working back-to-back shifts. Even on her 'off' days she showed up at work. Her diligence impressed her manager and she went from being a temporary staff member to a permanent one. Soon she was promoted to trainee waitress. She was kitted out in a short black skirt and a crisp white shirt serving patrons out front.

She earned a basic salary but it was through tips where the bulk of her money was made. The men did tip generously but when they had women on their arms, tips seemed to be reduced drastically. Some men seemed to take advantage of the waitresses' scant dressing and on several occasions Chenai had to put up with a grubby hand pawing at her legs.

'Just relax,' said Tryfina walking past her, carrying an empty tray.

Tryfina, also a waitress, encouraged the men and openly flirted with them. Something Chenai could not bring herself to do. She feared men. There was one in particular who came in almost every other night who kept begging for her number. His name was Antonio and he had long black hair like those antiquated pictures of Jesus she had often confronted in her childhood. It was another thing Chenai failed to understand. Why was Jesus not black like them? Maybe that's why he often failed to answer their prayers. Maybe he did not understand their language or their struggles. In her eyes white people appeared more blessed. They certainly had more money. They lived in big beautiful homes. Their plates overflowed. They were never in want.

'I just want you to come to my studio. I want to take pictures of you. For a magazine.'

What Chenai heard was: I want you to come to my studio so I can rape you.

155

'No,' replied Chenai. 'I don't do pictures.'

'I promise you, I do this for a living. You have the kind of look that will make it in modelling.'

'I'm not a model. I'm a waitress,' replied Chenai staunchly.

However, Antonio was persistent. He came in every day and tipped her generously. Still Chenai was unmoved. In the end, Antonio appealed to Tryfina to speak to Chenai and try to convince her he was a legitimate photographer. He even left his portfolio of work and a list of references. Tryfina was more successful in winning Chenai over.

'I'll come with you on your next day off. How does that sound? If he tries anything I've got your back.'

Chenai was mollified. 'Okay fine, I'll do it.'

Her boss was most surprised when Chenai declared she was actually going to take her 'off' day. He even suggested she take two days. She and Tryfina set out for Rosebank. Getting there was in itself a mission. They had to catch a taxi from Sandton to Illovo and Illovo to Rosebank. Chenai was grateful for Tryfina's company as she would never have known where to begin in this maze of a city.

Rosebank was a cosmopolitan enclave of corporate offices, residential apartments, upmarket hotels, popular restaurants and a smorgasbord of retail outlets. During the day it bustled with life. You could bump into a young suited executive rushing into a meeting or a fashionista out on a shopping spree. Then there were the men and women of leisure who seemed to be a permanent fixture at the fashionable outdoor cafés.

At night the suburb came alive, patronised by revellers who came out to enjoy the vibrant nightlife in the hip clubs like Capital Café, The Bank, Latinova and Moloko, Tryfina deftly pointed out a number of restaurants where she had waitressed before moving on to Sandton. However, looking at her now no one would guess she was a mere waitress. She could have easily been one of those girls that just hung out at the mall tottering in high-heeled shoes dressed to the nines. Those girls never seemed to be in a rush or have a job to go to. The only business they appeared to have was looking pretty and well put together. Chenai paled in comparison in a lilac maxi dress that she had bought from Mr Price with her first set of wages.

'You need to step up, girl! With legs like yours I would show them off.'

Chenai caught a glimpse of her own reflection in the glass mirrors. She hated flaunting any part of her body and attracting any unnecessary attention. However, every woman they walked past called to be noticed; to be seen. Those elegant, well-dressed women exuded confidence with each step.

Antonio's studio was located in the Mutual Mews. A tall, slender woman ushered them into the cool interior. His offices were decorated with portraits of beautiful women and ad campaigns for Guess Jeans, Mercedes Benz and Hilton Weiner. The waiting room was filled with stylish young women sitting pertly as they held their portfolios in their laps. They were all so well-groomed, with perfectly made-up faces, that they almost looked like the mannequins in shop windows.

Antonio came out to greet them and thanked them profusely for coming. He then asked his receptionist to direct Chenai to the make-up department. Tryfina was right behind her, insisting she was her manager. A woman who introduced herself as Bernadette immediately started prepping Chenai's face. As she worked she remarked what beautiful cheekbones Chenai had. With her well-practised hand Bernadette transformed Chenai from an ordinary-looking plain Jane into a glamorous eye-catching Susie. As she worked she spoke continuously, quizzing Chenai about her life. The bracelets on her arms clanked together each time she moved her hand. She worked on Chenai's face with an assurance that Chenai admired.

'Wow, is that really me?'

'Even I can't believe it,' enthused Tryfina.

Bernadette smiled, pleased at her own effort.

'I told you before that you have a beautiful face,' remarked Bernadette.

Antonio finally saw them after an hour. He was apologetic, explaining how they were running behind time.

'You say you haven't modelled before?'

Chenai nodded, 'I haven't.'

He looked her over again with one sweeping gaze then spoke.

'You have the kind of look that we want. We are going for ethereal and fairy-tale innocence. A client is launching a new perfume. But we need to do a portfolio for you. Run a couple of test shoots.'

Chenai was tremendously excited and nervous about the whole affair. She hoped she would be good enough. What could be so hard about smiling at a camera?

She was soon to discover how exacting a photo shoot could be. After two hours of changing into ten different outfits and posing in more than a hundred different stances, Chenai was exhausted. Nonetheless she never complained and smiled at the camera like her life depended on it. She loved it. When the camera clicked she came alive. In that moment she felt so beautiful, so happy and it shone through her big brown eyes.

When they wrapped up the shoot, Antonio gave them R300 for a taxi home, which Chenai promptly shared with Tryfina. They decided to trawl through the mall. However, the price tags on some of the clothes made Chenai's heart sink.

'If you win that contract you'll be able to afford these dresses,' declared Tryfina holding up a chiffon sheath.

Chenai shrugged her shoulders. 'You think I will? There are so many beautiful girls out there.'

Tryfina jabbed her in the ribs with her elbow. 'I don't get you at times. You have everything but you don't see it. I *know* you'll win that contract.'

Tryfina threw her arm around her. 'I can't wait to see you in a magazine!'

After a futile shopping trip they walked back to the taxi rank listing the things they would buy when they were rich. When the taxi veered onto the highway, with it's billboards of beautiful women, Chenai wondered if it would be possible that her face could be up there too. Was she reaching for the impossible? Could she dream that big?

# TWENTY-FOUR

The atmosphere was charged with tension as Zimbabwe prepared for the March 2008 elections. Newspaper headlines screamed of violent skirmishes between the opposition party and the ruling party. For the first time in Zimbabwean history, Morgan Tsvangirai challenged Robert Mugabe's stronghold on power. It was called that because for the first time in Zimbabwean history there was a credible opposition party. Christine had never been one to follow politics. It was considered an unladylike pursuit. Politics was always something for the men to debate whilst women were meant to preoccupy themselves with being better lovers, better wives and better mothers. For the longest time Christine had been apolitical. She had never even voted in an election. However, something now appealed to her to take a stand because for the first time in her life she realised that politics played a big role in the way they lived.

She had seen how their fortunes had changed as the economy nosedived into an an abyss due to bad political decisions. She looked at her daughter, Silindile, who was plugged at her breast and realised that if the political landscape did not change there might not be a future for her children. Every night they went to sleep, unsure what they would wake up to. Newspaper headlines screamed of violent skirmishes between the opposition party and the ruling party.

She tried to explain to Dumisani that the economic situation had deteriorated significantly since he had left. He didn't understand, which annoyed Christine. She could barely make ends meet and Dumisani's absence was doing little to alleviate the situation. Her forehead was lined with worry. Oblivious to his mother's anxiety, Sipho played at her feet with a broken toy truck. It now moved on its belly, with Sipho giving accompanying sound effects.

'Vroom vroom,' hooted Sipho. 'We are leaving for South Africa. We are going to fetch Daddy in South Africa.'

'Do you have enough petrol?' responded his grandmother in a sarcastic voice.

She sat on a chair by the window, absorbing the early morning sun as she knitted a jersey for her granddaughter.

'I do, Gogo,' replied Sipho. 'We've been queuing for fuel for the past ten days.'

Although his grandmother laughed the sound was tinged with sadness.

'I'm surprised he actually remembers he has a father.'

'Mama, it hasn't been that long!' replied Christine.

'It's been over a year, Christine, and there's no sign from him that he's actually doing anything there. *Usedliwe yiGoli.* He's been swallowed by the City of Gold.'

'Mama, he's been in hospital for the past few months,' replied Christine.

'Yeah, but who has actually *seen* him?'

Christine exhaled deeply; she did not want to lose heart and hope in her husband even though her mother continued to sow the seeds of doubt in her mind every single day.

'If I were you,' continued her mother, 'I would just go to the UK. This is your chance to make something of yourself.'

A few months earlier, Christine's cousin, Busisiwe, had sent her an Air Zimbabwe return ticket. The same ticket she had used to secure a visa to the United Kingdom. Even as she had filled out the forms she'd not been confident of her success. So many people were being denied visas to live and work overseas. Deep down she also hoped the same fate awaited her and had prayed fervently that her visa application would be denied. It was not. Her passport was returned with a sticker that granted her a single entry into the United Kingdom for the duration of one year. It stipulated that she was not to undertake any work or seek recourse to public funds.

Her cousin had urged her not to worry about the terms and conditions and that gaining entry into the country was the key issue; once inside they would find a way around the rules and regulations. Busisiwe had made the exodus to the United Kingdom in the late nineties before visas were an issue. Well before the mad scramble to the Queendom. She had lived there for over ten years and had since acquired British citizenship. She now boasted a British accent and three equally British kids with accents. All trace of her Zimbabwean-ness had been wiped away. Only her name was a reminder of where she came from. Every month she sent her mother an envelope of pounds, which she promptly changed on the black market becoming an instant millionaire.

Her mother, whom they called Mam'dala, had built herself a beautiful house in Mahatshula with her daughter's hard-earned pounds. While others struggled to put bread on the table, Busisiwe's mom drove to Francistown in her Nissan X Trail to do her monthly groceries. Mam'dala continued to bail Christine and her mother out financially but she was getting tired of giving handouts.

'My child is out there working two shifts! Why should my daughter suffer whilst yours sits on her arse all day!' complained Mam'dala.

'The sooner you leave the better,' her mother would often tell Christine. 'What are you still waiting for?'

Christine looked at her daughter who was now sound asleep in her arms. She was barely six months old and the thought of leaving her behind tore her apart.

'I will look after the kids,' said her mother as if reading her mind. 'Once you're settled you can send for them and *that* husband of yours.'

Christine exhaled deeply. Her mother was right. They could barely make it from one day to the next and there was nothing Dumisani could say or do to help them. There were million-dollar bills stacked on the coffee table. Next to them sat final letters of demand from CABS, the Central African Building Society, for the overdue mortgage, which they had failed to service three months in a row. She had tried to put their other car on the market but there were no buyers. Her liabilities continued to grow like cancerous tumours. There was no doubt in her mind that her mother would take care of the children. Still, this thought would not abate the numbing pain of being separated from them. It hurt even more than being separated from Dumisani.

She called him again that evening with money that was supposed to buy them a packet of ration meat. That would have been an assortment of bones and chunks of meat from the shin, threaded with sinew. It would have been so tough she would've had to boil it for hours. But without it they would just have to eat a piping hot plate of *isitshwala*, a maize staple with boiled kale, which grew in the back garden. Sipho would complain incessantly that there was no meat. Not even a whiff of meat amongst the gravy or bones he could suck on. She hated to deprive her son but this was their life now. Sometimes they would just eat *isitshwala* accompanied by sour milk from a packet that often reminded her of her daughter's reflux. She ate for sustenance because as a lactating mother her daughter constantly drained her. She looked deflated, her body emaciated. Even her voice was devoid of enthusiasm.

'Hi Dumi. How are you?'

'I'm much better,' he replied. 'I'm getting discharged this week.'

Dumisani sounded upbeat on the other end. It was a welcome change from his depressive state.

'That's good news indeed,' she replied. 'I also have good news myself. Sis Busi helped me apply for a visa to go to the UK. It was approved. I'm planning to go there to look for a nursing job–'

Dumisani cut her off abruptly. 'Are you *asking* me or are you *telling* me?'

His voice was abrasive and harsh. It was the tone of voice Dumisani assumed when he was irate or agitated or both.

'I'm telling you,' she replied in a softer voice. 'Things haven't exactly worked out there for you.'

'Whoa! So now you are calling me a failure?'

'No, Dumi. All I'm saying is that this opportunity has presented itself and I'd be a fool to let it go.'

'So you've decided what to do? You didn't even consult me? I thought we were a team? I thought we did things together, Christine? Now you're making decisions on your own?'

Christine remained mute on the other end. Tears rolled down her gaunt cheeks.

'So what happens to the kids? Huh? Who's going to take care of *my* children whilst you are busy gallivanting in Europe?'

'My mother will take care of them until I'm settled. The plan is that you and the kids will join me once I'm settled.'

'*Akulant'enjalo.* Nothing like that is going to happen, Christine! If you go ahead with that plan you are on your own! Do you hear me?'

'Dumi, you are being unreasonable!'

'I'm being unreasonable? Who wants to abandon the kids and go to the UK? Listen to yourself, Christine! If you get on that plane know that you are turning your back on our marriage and the kids.'

Christine started sobbing loudly, 'You're not being fair.'

'I'm fair, Christine. Just know what you stand to lose.'

The line went dead. Dumisani was tempted to fling his cellphone into the wall. He restrained himself and punched into the air instead.

When the time came for Dumisani to be discharged from hospital, Chamunorwa and Lerato were the first ones at his side. They looked like peas in a pod with Chamunorwa in his work uniform and Lerato in hers. There had been an opening at the fast-food outlet where Chamunorwa worked and he had ensured Lerato got the job. Dumisani doubted she would have been able to secure the job herself. She was shy and reserved and diminutive in stature. Chamunorwa probably said more about her than she said about herself; she barely opened her mouth and merely smiled good-naturedly. Just as Chamunorwa had described her, she was very pretty with a cute pert body but her belly was distended showing the telltale signs of a baby growing inside.

'You didn't waste time, did you?' chuckled Dumisani.

It was one of those rare moments when Lerato had left Chamunorwa's side and disappeared into the bathroom.

Chamunorwa chuckled but did not reveal the child was not his. The same way he claimed the child as his own when he introduced Lerato to his mother. It made his mother more accepting of his urgency in wanting to marry the girl.

'I am so in love!'enthused Chamunorwa patting his chest for emphasis.

Dumisani felt a momentary stab of jealousy. He was so out of love. How he wished he too could be as happy as his friend.

'She seems like an amazing girl,' he conceded.

Lerato returned, cutting their conversation short. She offered to pack Dumisani's things but he was quick to point out that Nurse Nomonde would do that.

'She has offered me her home until I get back on my feet.'

Chamunorwa eyed him quizzically. 'Is that a good idea? Would your wife approve?'

Dumisani did not care what Christine thought. Not after she chose to go ahead with her plan to go to the UK. For him, her decision was the biggest betrayal. He felt as if she had undermined his authority as a man. It felt like she had taken a knife and cut his balls off and thrown them out the window. The one person who was supposed to stand by his side for better or for worse had abandoned him.

'She is dumping the kids and going overseas. Who does that? I told her I was going to get things together but she doesn't have faith in me. Women don't have faith. Things get a bit rough and she decides to leave.'

Chamunorwa didn't comment. The tone of his friend's voice

conveyed a lot of anguish. He wanted to point out that maybe he was being unreasonable but decided not to.

'You and Lerato need your privacy. I'll be fine with Nomonde. I want to show Christine that I can make it and I *will* make it.'

'Well, if you need a place to stay or anything, we are here. Lerato and I are here.'

'I'll be fine,' replied Dumisani. 'Don't worry about me.'

Dumisani was now more determined than ever to make it. He wanted to prove to Christine that she had made a grave mistake by leaving him. She would rue the day she got on that plane and turned her back on their family.

# TWENTY-FIVE

She woke up in 200-count percale Egyptian sheets. She no longer woke up to the hustle and bustle of Hillbrow life. She now slept in the quiet serenity of suburban life. However, the transition had come with a big price tag. She was about to climb off the bed but Kayin clutched her hand and pulled her towards him.

'We not finish here!'

Lindani wanted to cry. They had been at it so much she was raw down there. Nonetheless she clamped her eyes shut and turned to kiss Kayin like her life depended on it, because it did. After Givemore had raped her she had run from him into Kayin's arms. He was the only other person she knew in Johannesburg. She had retrieved his card from her wallet and called him. He had been quick to respond and offered her a place to stay in one of his many apartment blocks. However, his help came with terms and conditions. She had not been privy to these when she signed on the dotted line. Even though she now shared his lavish penthouse in the Michelangelo overlooking the glorious Sandton Square, she felt no joy.

She just felt trapped. His home was decorated in pristine white. They lounged on velvety couches. They drank Cristal from crystal goblets. Feasted in his gilt-lined dining room whilst his personal chef waited on them. Even now she watched the crystal chandelier above them while Kayin pummelled vigorously into her. When he finally came she pretended to share his jubilation by screaming out in fake pleasure. He collapsed on top of her, marvelling at how delicious she was. Sometimes she could barely understand what Kayin was saying and would merely nod agreeably.

'We going to London next week,' he announced casually.

Lindani eyed him warily. She had come to know that money was not an issue for him.

'London?'

'Oh yes, my dahling. I take you to Buckingham Palace. Take you on a ride on the London Eye. We go clubbing in London. You will love it! My little Zimbabwe rose,' he mused. 'I teach you the world, my dahling.' He slapped her buttocks playfully. 'Wash up now; I take you out for dinner later.'

Lindani jumped off the bed before he had a chance to change his mind.

It was Kayin who had introduced her to the fun, frivolous and fancy side of Johannesburg. The vibrant energetic Johannesburg that never went to sleep at night. He wined and dined her at the city's finest restaurants introducing her palate to Chinese, Greek, French, Portuguese, Indian and Mediterranean food. When international artists like Joe Thomas and Usher performed, they would occupy the VIP suites at the giant stadiums.

Kayin had a penchant for gambling and so they frequented the city's glittering casinos. They danced till the wee hours of the morning at swanky nightclubs in Rosebank and Sandton. Lindani hung onto his strong arm as he steered her through the social cacophony. She made for the perfect accessory. He also kitted her out in the most expensive jewellery. Pure gold diamanté earrings hung from her ears. A diamanté gold chain with a heart-shaped pendant rested in her bosom. Whenever they went out Kayin would be equally suave in a white shirt and white-fitted pants. He wore a gold cravat that picked up the colour in her dress. They looked like a 'his and hers' advert in a glossy magazine.

That night they walked into a dimly lit bar lounge and were quickly ushered to the VIP section, which was cordoned off with a velvet rope. They settled onto a velvet settee and Kayin immediately motioned to the waitress. He ordered a bottle of Moët & Chandon for her and Hennessy for him. They always ordered by the bottle. Even if it cost more than R1 000 a bottle. Kayin never winced when he saw the price of things. He always carried cash in a small Louis Vuitton bag. Lindani drank like she was drinking water. Looking at her life through inebriated eyes made her life seem much happier than it actually was. They would party until the early hours of the morning and she would only wake up at midday. Kayin always woke up earlier because there was always business to take care of. Always.

Their trip to London was their first overseas trip together. They had travelled to Cape Town together but never abroad. Lindani was quite anxious, having never left the continent. They boarded at about ten in the evening and landed in Heathrow the following morning. The sun was just rising but as they shuffled from the aeroplane into the airport terminal they barely got a glimpse of the outside world. There was the usual scuffle to retrieve their luggage. It didn't take long for Lindani to identify her Gucci bags, which she had bought a few days earlier. Kayin had insisted she get herself proper travel bags. It seemed another woman had the same luggage as her and they almost had a scrap at the conveyor belt.

'My apologies,' she said, flicking back a long mane of Brazilian hair.

'No problem,' replied Lindani. 'These things happen.'

The woman retrieved the rest of her luggage paying more astute attention to the labels on the bags. Lindani did the same. Kayin told her he had to dash to the gents but told her to go ahead despite Lindani's insistence on waiting for him.

He kissed her hurriedly, pulled his single bag off the conveyor belt and headed off. Lindani proceeded on her own to immigration. The queue moved along swiftly. When her turn came the immigration official eyed her with a bland expression.

'Passport please,' she said through pursed lips.

Lindani promptly handed over her South African passport.

Kayin had bought her citizenship. She was paying him back for it in flesh.

'Is this your first trip to the United Kingdom?'

Lindani nodded.

'What's the purpose of your visit?'

'Holiday,' replied Lindani.

The immigration official flipped through her passport then stood up and went to the back office. When she returned she asked Lindani to kindly step aside. Lindani's brow furrowed with worry.

'Is there anything wrong?'

'Routine inspection ma'am. Just follow me.'

After a lengthy interrogation in a tiny room with two female immigration officials she was asked to strip naked. Her eyes widened in horror but she complied. A female officer was tasked with searching her from head to toe. A scanner was beamed the length of her entire body but nothing showed up. After a profuse apology from the officers, she was allowed to dress and proceed through immigration. Kayin was waiting for her on the other side. He looked calm and collected.

'What was the hold-up?' he asked.

'I was literally searched inside and out,' replied Lindani. 'I think they thought I was carrying drugs.'

Kayin wore an outraged expression on his face. 'What? They can't do that. Let me have a word with them. It's a violation of human rights.'

'Kayin, it's okay,' replied Lindani. 'It's over.'

She didn't want to have another confrontation with those non-smiling immigration officials. Even though she felt thoroughly violated she didn't want to irk them further.

'It's not all right,' he insisted. 'Just because you black. Did you see them do this to anyone else?'

Lindani stroked his elbow, hoping to calm him down. She was genuinely touched by his concern. They made their way out of the airport walking hand in hand. Kayin hailed a taxi, which deposited them outside the twentieth-century-built Waldorf Hilton Hotel in the West End. Located in the heart of London it provided easy access to the theatres, Covent Garden, the London Eye and other iconic places of interest. Kayin pointed them all out, promising to take her after he had completed his round of meetings.

Standing out on the pavement of the Aldwych, Lindani was awed by the sterile and immaculate look to the area. Nothing appeared out of place. Even the branches on the trees had a manicured look to them. The cars parked on the side of the road were pristine and posh. Red double-decker buses glided along the streets. They didn't even emit an offensive cloud of smoke.

They entered the hotel which was elegant with understated glamour. A staff member checked them in with an enthusiastic smile. They made their way to a luxurious suite on the fourth floor. Lindani's eyes darted around the room making a mental note of every detail. Kayin reclined on the sofa with a remote control flicking through the channels on television.

'What a beautiful hotel!' remarked Lindani.

She threw herself onto the bed, landing on its downy softness.

'It's all right,' replied Kayin flippantly. 'I have slept in better places.'

'Well I have slept in worse places,' remarked Lindani.

She laughed at her own joke, which was lost on Kayin who suggested she freshen up so that they could go and get something to eat. Lindani was running her bath when she went back into the room to retrieve her toiletry bag. Kayin was on the phone and stopped speaking mid-sentence when he saw her. He covered the mouthpiece with one hand.

'What's the problem?'

'No problem,' replied Lindani waving her toiletry bag.

He didn't start talking again until she was back in the bathroom. It made Lindani suspicious about who he was talking to. Kayin could be overly secretive at times. Even when there was no need to be. She figured he was seeing other women; it didn't bother her. She was immersed in the water when Kayin peered around the door. At first she assumed he was going to join her. However, he said he had to rush off to an urgent meeting.

'I'm not sure how long I'll be but order room service. Anything. See you later.'

He blew her a kiss and left. After her bath Lindani decided to take a nap. When she woke up it was dark outside. She looked at her watch lying on the pedestal next to the bed. She had been asleep for a good nine hours. She decided to order in and watch some television. She fell asleep again until well after midnight and Kayin had still not returned.

Lindani woke up the next morning with a strong sense of apprehension. Her stomach churned. Something in her subconscious stirred sinister thoughts. Four days later and Kayin had still not returned. He hadn't even called to say he was all right. Or to find out if she was. Panicked thoughts began to race through her head. In one scene she imagined Kayin lying dead in a mortuary, his unidentified body waiting to be claimed. In another he was lying in a hospital bed clinging to life. She could not even bring herself to go downstairs for the buffet breakfast. Her body was taut with anxiety.

She sat by the window ledge looking out onto the street counting nameless passers-by, hoping that the next one would be Kayin. She was afraid to venture out beyond the confines of the hotel. The cold was even more reason to keep her in her room. What bothered her even more was that she did not have any money. Kayin had the airline tickets. She knew no one in London. She was totally alone. Totally. Alone.

The doorbell rang. Her heart jumped. Relief washed over her. She jumped to her feet and ran to answer the door. All she could think of was Kayin and that he had finally found his way back to her. She opened the door and two bulky men stood there. The disappointment quickly registered on Lindani's face. They did not wait for her to speak but entered the room, pushing past her. They were both tall beefy men in black coats worn over pristine suits. One was Caucasian with a shock of blonde hair secured in a ponytail and the other was African with a bald shiny head.

'Kayin sent us,' said the Caucasian. 'My name is Bond. James Bond. And this is Mr T.'

He laughed out loud but the humour evaded Lindani and she stared back at him with a blank look on her face.

'Your friend Kayin owes us a favour,' said Mr T in a steely voice.

'He isn't–,' replied Lindani.

James Bond cut her off. 'We're not here for him. We just want our cash.'

Lindani was confused. What did they need payment for? What had Kayin done? Maybe there was a mistake. Maybe they had the wrong room.

'There must be some mistake!' she wailed.

'There's no mistake, young lady,' replied Mr T throwing her passport onto the bed.

She knew then that these men had made contact with Kayin somehow. She collapsed onto the bed feeling light-headed.

'We can make this easy for you. All you have to do is carry a parcel to Johannesburg.'

Lindani looked up at the James Bond like he was extending a lifeline to her. That seemed like a simple enough task. It was something she could do easily.

'Where's the parcel?' she asked.

James Bond whipped out a bag of cocaine from his jacket. He threw it onto the bed.

'It's only a hundred grams of coke. You'll manage,' spoke the Mr T with nonchalance.

'Cocaine?' croaked Lindani.

'You carry the coke and we settle your hotel bill. Then you put this whole thing behind you.'

Lindani shook her head. She was adamant. She was not going to do this. She raised her hands to the side of her head. She started muttering and then screamed: 'Where is Kayin? What did you do to him?'

Mr T laughed; very much aware of Lindani's growing hysteria but unaffected by it.

James Bond drew a gun from his jacket and started waving it menacingly in her direction. Lindani felt the warm urine run down between her shaking thighs.

'Just swallow each pellet,' explained Mr T. 'Don't make this any harder than it needs to be.'

Lindani's eyes widened in disbelief, 'I thought you said *carry*?'

'Yes, carry in your stomach, you stupid cow. How else did you expect to carry the coke?' hissed James Bond.

'We don't want to hurt you. Don't make us hurt you,' continued Mr T as he grabbed her by the hair and tugged at the roots until Lindani winced in pain. With his other hand he shoved a pellet into her mouth.

'Make sure you keep each one down, you little bitch. If you so much as shit one, make sure you wash it and swallow it again.'

Lindani nodded mutely as a pellet slid down her throat, scraping her oesophagus as it did. How she wished her tears could provide the much-needed lubrication but she had always struggled taking pills.

# TWENTY-SIX

When the call finally came many weeks later Chenai had long stopped daydreaming about the grandeur and glamour that awaited her if she won the modelling contract. She had fully immersed herself in the drudgery and monotony of her job. She was changing in the bathroom one night after a long shift when her cellphone rang. It hardly ever rang so she was completely surprised to see Antonio's name flashing across the screen.

'I've got good news!'

His voice was frantic. Chenai stiffened with nervousness.

'We're going to sign you up. The client *loves* you!' continued Antonio.

'What?'

'Yes! The client loves you!'

After she hung up, Chenai danced up and down and then went to tell Tryfina.

'So did he say how much they are going to pay you?' asked Tryfina.

'I didn't ask,' replied Chenai.

'When do you start?'

Chenai bit her lower lip. In all her excitement it had not occurred to her to enquire about the finer details. Tryfina took it upon herself to call Antonio to find out exactly what the job entailed. When she got home Chenai told her mother her exciting news. In contrast to Tryfina, her mother received the news with less euphoria and more misgivings.

'Are you sure it's not one of those magazines where people come out naked?'

'No, Mama. It's a perfume ad. It will be in *all* the magazines in South Africa.'

Sibongile was sceptical. 'Of all the girls in South Africa they chose you? *Wena? Umafikizolo?*'

Chenai ignored her mother's scathing sarcasm. She was determined not to let her mother's negativity dampen her excitement.

'We're doing the shoot in Cape Town. We fly out on Friday night and we're back on Sunday evening. They are putting me on a plane.'

'And your job? Or have you forgotten you still have to earn a living?'

'I've taken some days off. I haven't taken time off since I started so my boss understood.'

Sibongile clapped her hands together and then held them up in the air.

'This I will wait to see! Johannesburg is filled with crooks. I have lived here longer. I see them in Santin all the time. Those white men with black girls. They are prostitutes those girls.'

Chenai climbed into bed and pulled the blankets tightly around her. It was her polite way of communicating that she no longer wanted to take part in the conversation. She even feigned snoring to give the impression of being fast asleep. But she was wide awake imagining what lay ahead. Nothing could dampen Chenai's spirits. Not even her mother's pessimism.

Friday seemed like an eternity away. Had it been possible, Chenai would have rearranged the calendar and swapped Tuesday with Friday. By the time Wednesday rolled into Thursday she knew she was closer to her destiny. Antonio had organised a taxi to pick her up and chauffeur her to OR Tambo. After some confusion Chenai finally located her check-in terminal. She met Antonio and the rest of the crew in the queue. They were welcoming, calling her the star of the show. She felt at ease, dressed in new pair of blue denim jeans and a white T-shirt. It was all Tryfina's doing. Her dear friend had marched her off to Foschini to do some shopping. Every item in her bag was brand spanking new. Even her toothbrush. Before they boarded, Chenai observed all the activity at the airport with keen interest. Were they all flying to Cape Town too, she wondered.

But when she finally boarded the plane she realised it wasn't big enough to fit all those people. The two-hour flight was uneventful for most frequent flyers but for Chenai being in the air for the first time was the most nerve-racking experience. As the plane took off she felt as if the contents of her stomach were being vacuumed upwards. She desperately wanted to go to the loo but was afraid to leave her seat after a cherub-faced air hostess had buckled her in. Thirty minutes into the flight, the beautifully preened flight attendants pushing carts down the aisle were quick to offer her something to eat and drink. She declined their offers as she feared there would be an additional cost. When they landed in Cape Town she was ravenous.

The city of Cape Town was nothing she had ever imagined.

SUE NYATHI

Set against the majestic backdrop of a mountainous landscape and sweeping seascapes, even the air that brushed against her face felt cleaner than Johannesburg, less polluted. However, it was not all beautiful as they drove past the glaring poverty of Gugulethu and the Cape Flats, which was in stark contrast to the beauty of the V&A Waterfront where they were booked to spend the weekend staying at one of the luxury hotels.

Antonio and the crew agreed to get an early supper as they had a long day ahead of them the next day. After they had checked in they met for dinner at an outdoor restaurant on the wharf. The cool breeze blowing from the Atlantic Ocean gently fanned their faces. A waiter approached them with huge menus and introduced himself as Lovemore. That name revealed his origins and Chenai instantly befriended him. They were soon having a side conversation in Shona.

'Please help me,' she entreated. 'I have no idea what to order.'

The seafood menu was entirely alien to Chenai and she didn't want to appear to be a novice in front of the team. The waiter suggested the grilled sole and calamari with chips for her.

'You want to lay off the fries,' cautioned Antonio when the order arrived. 'The camera adds more pounds to you.'

'Don't listen to him,' said Bernadette dismissively. 'You have such a tiny body!'

'I'm sure you did too,' replied Antonio pointedly. 'Trust me Chenai, in this business less is more.'

Nervously Chenai pushed the chips aside and concentrated on her fish. The other team members had ordered a bottle of wine but Chenai stuck to her Coca-Cola. She had never tasted wine in her life. The only alcohol she knew was that overpowering smell of beer that always permeated her father's skin.

180

'You really should try a glass of wine,' insisted Antonio as he turned to Chenai. 'The Cape has some of the best wines. I will take you to the winelands if we have time.'

'It would be great if we get the time but you know how hectic our schedule gets,' said Corinne.

'We can't come all this way and not at least make it to the vineyards,' moaned Darryl.

Chenai was not sure what all their roles were but accepted them as part of Antonio's entourage. They were an eclectic bunch, Darryl with his green spiked hair and Corrine with red curly hair that cascaded down her shoulders. Bernadette had long blonde hair like a unicorn and sea-blue eyes that Chenai found fascinating. After dinner they all headed back to the hotel. Antonio walked her to her room.

'See you at six a.m.!'

'Okay Antonio,' replied Chenai. 'And thank you once again.'

He smiled, 'Please. Just call me Tony.'

He leaned forward and kissed her on the cheek. First the left and then the right. After the door had closed behind her, Chenai wiped her face. He was really big on kisses and it made her uncomfortable but she could not bring herself to tell him lest it offended him. She threw herself on the queen-sized bed with crisp white linen. The room was spacious with an expansive view of the ocean. Too keyed up to sleep she turned on the TV and flipped from one channel to the other. She finally succumbed and was roused by Bernadette's incessant knocking the next morning.

They did the shoot on a stretch of beach in Camps Bay. Except for a few surfers and joggers, the beach was pretty deserted that early in the morning. Corinne was the stylist and she picked a gold swimsuit for Chenai to wear whilst Bernadette painted her face.

Darryl assisted Antonio with all things technical as they set up the cameras for the shoot. Two more unfamiliar faces joined them and Chenai figured they were from the fragrance company because they placed oversized gold jars of perfume on the sand to integrate with the shoot. A young black girl also joined them on set; apparently she was an intern. She basically ran around getting coffee for the team and was also the girl who was sent to buy a razor after Corinne came face-to-face with Chenai's full bush.

'Oh my gawd dahling! How can you not shave?'

As Corinne expressed her shock to Bernadette, Chenai stood awkwardly willing the ground to open up and swallow her. Bernadette said something to Corinne under her breath and they both laughed, adding to Chenai's discomfort. When the shoot finally started, Chenai was on edge and it showed.

'Relax honey!' coaxed Antonio trying to tease a smile out of her.

There was a genuine warmth and sincerity in his eyes. It melted away Chenai's anxiety.

After the first couple of shots they stopped and Corinne had a look at the images and exchanged a few hurried words with Antonio. Bernadette was called to dust Chenai's face with more powder. The shoot resumed and Chenai continued to roll around in the sand with gold jewellery draped around her neck. In the second round of shots she wore a white bikini which looked amazing against her black shiny skin. Just those two shots took them till midday with all the pauses in-between rearranging the perfume.

Despite being exhausted, Chenai continued to smile for the camera. In the final shot she would be styled in a shimmering gold dress. However, Antonio wanted to wait till sunset for that one so they decided to have a long lunch on the patio of one of the many beachfront restaurants. Chenai loved the ambience and the relaxed atmosphere. As they ate, the team agreed that they had done a great job and kept praising Chenai for her good work. Afterwards they took a stroll on the beach and Antonio and Chenai walked side by side while the others hung back at a slower pace.

'You are such a natural. I'm so glad I discovered you!'

'Thank you for giving me the opportunity, Tony,' replied Chenai.

He stroked her face gently. 'You are so beautiful and the beauty of it is that you are not even aware of it.'

Chenai looked down at her toes. She was uncomfortable looking him in the eye. She felt awkward and nervous and she was relieved when the others joined them, almost forming a half circle around them. They relocated to a more isolated beach and began the set-up for the sunset shoot. It was only after nine when Antonio called it a day, satisfied with his shots. They got back to their hotel later that evening and Darryl insisted they go clubbing on Long Street. They moved from one club to another but Chenai's stiff demeanour and awkwardness carried on through the night.

'Loosen up, Chenai,' insisted Corinne.

'Yes, don't be a bore,' said Darryl, as they shoved a pink cocktail with an umbrella in it in her hand.

She lost count of the number of coloured drinks she had. Some had cherries floating on top and others had mint leaves floating in them. All she knew was that the night continued in a beautiful bubble of laughter and light-headedness with her newfound friends. She had no idea how and when they got back to the hotel. All she knew was that when she woke up the next day she was naked in the crisp white linen with a splitting headache. Bernadette was knocking frantically on her door once more.

'Sleeping beauty!' she called out. 'We have a flight to catch.'

As Chenai stumbled into the bathroom she vowed she would never ever drink again. When she looked at her wretched self in the mirror her father was staring back at her laughing. Her body stiffened in shock. She sobered up in that moment. She reached for a glass at the sink and without thinking threw it at him. She covered her face as if trying to block the image of it smashing into smithereens. When she finally opened her eyes he was gone.

# TWENTY-SEVEN

She had often heard many lies being repeated. One of them was that *all* babies were cute. It certainly didn't apply to the one she was staring at. The baby lay in her crib swathed in a pink blanket. Black curls of hair peeped through from the beanie covering her tiny head. Her eyes were shut tightly almost as if her eyelids were glued together. Her skin was dull and waxy with none of the newborn newness. Her lips were drawn together and her tiny fingers curled in a tight fist. Her face did not crinkle up into a smile. Nor did her mouth twitch nervously before breaking into a loud cry. Nothing in the baby's appearance endeared Lindani to it.

'Where did you get such an ugly baby?' she asked.

Even Kayin's taut lips gave way to a sardonic grin.

'Don't say that about my baby,' replied Kayin dismissively. 'She's just jaundiced.'

'So what do you want me to do with a jaundiced baby?' replied Lindani flippantly.

'My girlfriend delivered last week. She doesn't want it. Neither do I.'

Lindani's eyes widened with disbelief. 'So now you want me to raise it?'

'We have a client in Malaysia who wants a baby. You *will* deliver it.'

Lindani held her hands up in resignation.

'No, Kayin! First you have me delivering drugs, now babies? Come on now!'

'This is your *last* assignment and then you can walk free.'

The thought of freedom placated Lindani, ironing out her wrinkled forehead.

Then he added gently, 'Don't forget you *still* owe me fifty thousand rand.'

Lindani shot him a look filled with intense loathing. Her debt to Kayin was like a bottomless pit. Just when she thought she had settled it, he would remind her of something else she owed him for. She rued the day she'd ever met him. How she wished she'd listened to that interfering busybody at the hair salon! If she had she would have known that Kayin's intent had always been to use her and abuse her.

This she discovered after landing at OR Tambo, her gut laden with drugs. He'd been there to meet her after she made it through immigration. She had known then that his disappearance from their suite in London had been carefully orchestrated. Of course he professed ignorance but had been ruthless when he asked her to shit every pellet of cocaine. For all his charm, the flip side of Kayin was ugly and cruel. He insisted Lindani would transport drugs for him until she repaid all the money he had spent on her. He did it with all his women. Lured them into his life with expensive gifts and clothes, got them accustomed to a fancy lifestyle and then told them they owed him for the Gucci bags and gold earrings.

Each time they did a run he would 'deduct' cash to cover whatever money he had spent on them in the past. As unfair as it was no one dared argue with Kayin. She soon discovered there were many other beautiful women transporting drugs for Kayin. He had a stable of well-groomed mules to do his bidding and had carnal knowledge of all of them too. The other girls insisted that if you were 'nice' Kayin could pay generously for the service. He would give them R30 000 a trip; R50 000 if he was feeling generous.

Lindani knew it was peanuts as Kayin was making so much more money. It was not the cash she was after though. It was her freedom. She was well aware of the dangers in what they were doing with some of Kayin's girls languishing in jails in countries as far-flung as Brazil and Thailand. Others who had not complied had mysteriously fallen to their deaths from hijacked buildings in Hillbrow.

Often Lindani lay awake thinking how she could plot her escape. She sometimes thought of calling Melusi and asking him to smuggle her back across the border but after what had transpired with Givemore, it was likely she had earned herself Melusi's disdain. There was no way he would take her side over Givemore's. He would probably kill her first before he smuggled her anywhere. She exhaled deeply. Her only choice was to repay Kayin and start her life over again. She would simply disappear into obscurity in Bulawayo and he would have no idea where to find her.

'Everything is here,' said Kayin handing her two passports.

One for her. One for her daughter. Stolen identities. Of course.

'Your name is Lesedi and your daughter is Zipho. Everything is packed; even her milk is in there. She's not a problem kid. Doesn't cry. Just don't forget to act motherly. Her parents will meet you at the airport. They will have a banner with your name on it. '

The brief was pretty simple and at least she wasn't carrying drugs. It could have been a lot worse.

'Now be on your way. The flight departs at midnight.'

Lindani loathed those midnight flights. Hated that long wait with nothing to fill the hours. Even duty-free shopping held no allure, especially when the uncertainty of your trip weighed down on you. Sometimes when she transited at airports, Lindani would make up stories about the interesting people she saw. She'd become so lost in her thoughts that she could block out the flight announcements on the intercom.

She decided to avoid the noisy food court that night and the competing aromas of crispy chicken, beefy burgers and fried fish and instead found refuge at a corner table in a secluded pub. She ordered grilled halloumi to start and a sirloin steak with mushroom sauce and chips for her main. As she waited for her food to arrive she drank two glasses of Jack Daniels on ice in quick succession. Then she wolfed down her food. She skipped dessert and ordered a shot of crème liqueur instead. Normally she was not one to eat before her trips. It was close to impossible to eat with a gut bloated with drugs and the accompanying anxiety.

None of which she was experiencing this time! She stole a glance at the baby. Not an eyelid fluttered. Lindani signalled to the waiter to bring her the last whiskey and the bill. Even the waiter remarked how well behaved the baby was as he presented Lindani with the bill. She tipped him generously and could still feel the warmth of his smile as he walked away. She decided to get moving before she missed her flight. Kayin would certainly skin her alive if that ever happened. She was almost out the door when the waiter came running after her. She wondered why he was calling her so frantically after the enormous tip she left him.

'Ma'am! You forgot your baby!'

Lindani was not used to lugging around a baby carrier. She normally travelled light without any baby baggage.

'Oh *my*! How silly of me!'

Lindani was flushed with embarrassment and the other customers were eyeing her quizzically when she returned to retrieve the baby. She proceeded to the departures terminal, walking amongst the thousands of passengers thronging the airport. It was an eclectic mix of Arabs, Asians, Africans, Americans, Europeans, Latinos and Orientals. All jostling past each other on a journey somewhere. All the seats in the departure lounge were taken but a man with a generous face stood up for her. She realised it was because she was carrying a baby. As she sat down she contemplated waking up the baby but decided against it, afraid she might not be able to quiet her once she was roused. She had no experience with babies. To think how tirelessly she had tried to have one during her short-lived marriage yet all their efforts had yielded nothing but spontaneous miscarriages.

She thought of Gugulethu then and figured she would have made a pretty good mother. Melusi had often joked that she would be the mother of his kids. That was now just another episode from her past and one she tried not to think about. Her thoughts were drawn back to the present when standing just a few metres before her was someone she used to know well. A woman called Joyce. They once shared a husband. As ludicrous as that sounded. Instinctively she almost called out to her but the words remained lodged in her throat. To think they had once loved the same man. That they had been bitter arch-rivals. She studied Joyce. She was standing beside a tall man and they were chatting amicably. The man reached out for her hand and brought it to his lips. She laughed, throwing her perfectly coiffed head back. She was always elegant. Always graceful.

Lindani looked away. She knew she had been staring for too long and looked down at her feet. What were the chances? Confronting your past in a busy airport terminal. Before she could dwell on it any further, a chirpy hostess announced the boarding call for Flight MH230 to Malaysia. This time she made sure she picked up the baby carrier as she made her way towards the boarding gate. The flight attendant casually remarked that she had a pretty baby and helped Lindani to her seat. There were other babies on the flight but they were more boisterous than Zipho. After she was strapped into her seat, Lindani decided to pick her up and cradle her on her lap. It seemed more natural that way. Still the baby did not twitch or warm to her in any way. She wondered if Kayin had drugged the poor baby. She would not put it past him.

On the seat in front of her a television screen was playing an advert over and over again about how drugs were outlawed in Malaysia and drug trafficking was an offence punishable by death. After the advert came the flight safety regulations. An efficient, slender-looking flight attendant stood in the aisle demonstrating what was being said on the video. After that Lindani dozed off. It was only hours later she was roused by a rather concerned-looking flight attendant.

'Ma'am, is everything okay?'

Lindani nodded, feeling rather flustered.

'Is your baby okay?'

The baby was still lifeless in her arms.

'She sleeps through the night,' replied Lindani. 'She's a good baby.'

The flight attendant left her and Lindani stared at the baby, who was as unresponsive as it had been thus far. Lindani eventually fell asleep. A sleep so deep she dropped the baby without even being aware of it. The passenger next to her picked up the baby from the floor. Even after landing with a loud thud on the floor, the baby did not break into a loud wail or even make a murmur. The passenger woke Lindani up.

'Ma'am! Your baby!'

'What baby?' replied Lindani flustered.

'This baby,' replied the passenger shoving the baby back into her lap. Lindani shifted nervously in her seat. She knew then that there was something horribly wrong with baby Zipho.

She decided to take the baby to the toilet to change her nappy, drawing curious stares as she did so. It was only when she laid the baby flat and undressed her that she unveiled a row of ugly stitches from her neck down to her groin. Her tiny stomach was bloated, reminding her of malnourished babies that suffered from kwashiorkor. A silent scream escaped from Lindani's lips.

'Fucking sonofabitch,' she swore.

She cussed him over and over again. Again she wet herself. There were no parents waiting to adopt the baby. This dead baby had her insides filled with drugs. Lindani's body convulsed in fear. What was she to do now? It's not like she could throw the baby out of the window.

There was a knock on the door and she knew she had to come out of the cubicle before drawing further attention to herself. She dragged herself and the baby back to her seat and held baby Zipho close. She was certain passengers around her suspected something sinister. Any mother would be able to tell that there was something unnatural about her situation. Other mothers fussed through the night either trying to quell their babies' restlessness or calm their bouts of crying. They were eight hours into the flight and not once had baby Zipho even squealed, let alone woken up to feed. She lay noiselessly.

Lindani sat. Sleep escaped her, even the alcohol evaporated and left her stone-cold sober. She tried to watch the movie but 30 minutes into it another advert was flighted issuing a warning that trafficking drugs into Malaysia carried with it the death penalty. Lindani felt her bowels loosen and all the food she had consumed earlier filled her underwear. She started to pray. Feverish disjointed words strung together as she pleaded for mercy. Up until that moment God had not existed in her life. She had often heard of Him and His mercy. Many had testified to His goodness. She needed Him now. She didn't know it then but the Lord would indeed keep her company as she was going to spend the rest of her life in a Malaysian prison before being hanged.

# TWENTY-EIGHT

The perfume launch was held in the centre court of Hyde Park against a backdrop of fine art and imposing sculpture. There were huge canvases with 'Jewel', the name of the perfume inscribed boldly on them. Chenai was lying on the sand, the bottle of perfume cradled in her bosom. Her face was iconic; her beauty more mesmerising than the figurines in the centre.

Like its namesake in London, Hyde Park was synonymous with prestige and elegance. Hyde Park Shopping Centre made history by becoming the first decentralised shopping centre when suburban malls were in vogue back in the fifties. The centre was still patronised by fifty-year-old madams with perfectly coiffed hair and flawless faces with all the wrinkles ironed out. Perfect Botox smiles and painted red lips blew air kisses that floated in the sparkling surroundings. The centre also drew the city's nouveau riche who wanted to be part of the pizzazz. That night was no different. The crème de la crème of Johannesburg's high society and fashionistas had turned up for the glittering affair to launch the new fragrance. Despite the fact that Chenai was kitted out in designer garb she still felt out of her element amongst all the pomp and finesse of the occasion.

Antonio had decked her out in a beautiful sequinned ballgown that swept along the floor. It was backless with a plunging neckline. She had spent the greater part of the afternoon in a hair salon and the kinky tight black curls that had hugged her scalp had been straightened by a no-lye relaxer. Indian hair extensions had been woven in to give her hair some length so that it cascaded down her back in a glorious mane. Her eyebrows had been plucked and primed. The bright red lipstick she wore made her entire face come alive. A whore's lipstick, her mother called it.

Sibongile had refused to come to the launch and insisted she would feel out of place even when Chenai had said she would buy her a dress for the occasion. But her mother did go on to show all the maids in the neighbourhood the magazine with Chenai's picture in it. For Chenai that was all the approval she needed.

Everyone kept reassuring her that she looked amazing but she rushed to the bathroom to give herself another once-over. She wasn't aware of it but Antonio followed her. When she looked in the mirror she was amazed at the woman who looked back at her.

'Just relax and enjoy the moment,' said Antonio, reassuringly placing his hands on her naked shoulders.

'What if people ask me questions?'

Antonio exhaled deeply. 'We've rehearsed this over and over again. You are a clever girl. You *know* what to say.'

Still Chenai was not convinced. She feared the clever words would leave her once the cameras descended on her and started clicking away. Afraid her words would not be sophisticated and fluid enough to impress the mighty crowd that had formed.

'Look, I have something that will take care of your nerves. Just do a line and you'll be fine.'

He led her into a cubicle and kicked the door shut to give them privacy. He reached for a tiny packet from the pocket of his form-fitting trousers. He emptied the powder onto the toilet cistern and drew a white line with his finger. He then snorted the white powder with practised ease and inhaled deeply. He drew one for Chenai and egged her on to do the same. She followed his example. As she inhaled the white powder she felt a tingling feeling that spread through her entire body. An exhilarating rush.

'It will make you feel good,' said Antonio softly. 'It will give you the confidence you need.'

He stroked her exposed back. Chenai felt the tension inside her dissolve along with any other anxiety she had been feeling. She closed her eyes and gave in to the electric sensation that spread through her entire body until it settled into the apex at her groin. It was such a good feeling; like nothing she had ever experienced before. Antonio could see the yearning in her eyes. Even her bright inviting lips beckoned to him. He edged closer, his warm breath fanning her face. She inhaled the woody muskiness of his cologne. His heady aroma and proximity were an intoxicating combination. Their lips touched slightly; teasing and taunting. The kisses were light and airy like a butterfly. His wet tongue gently prised her full lips apart. There was no roughness, only tenderness, and the utmost sensuousness as his lips caressed hers. Their tongues danced together like flames fanning a passion deep in their loins. A fire that could not be subdued.

Then there was a loud knock on the door. It was Bernadette's commanding voice.

'Chenai? Are you in here? People are waiting outside,' said Bernadette.

SUE NYATHI

There was sharpness in her voice. A reprimand. Chenai felt like a little child who had been caught stealing sweets.

She quickly extricated herself from Antonio's embrace but felt heady and breathless and a little unsteady on her feet.

'We're coming,' replied Antonio.

They emerged, hands loosely held together. Antonio squeezed hers reassuringly. It was not long before they were enveloped by journalists and a blitz of cameras. Antonio left her side but she took it all in good stride. She felt buoyant and happy. She answered all the questions with practised efficacy and not once did she make eye contact with anyone. She focused on that statue in the middle of the room. She posed dutifully for the publicity shots and smiled gaily like this was something she had been doing all her life.

It was only hours later, after the speeches and the clinking of glasses, that Chenai stole a moment to chat to Chamunorwa. He was lingering in the corner of the room with Lerato, Dumisani and Nomonde. They had hung on the periphery, away from the limelight.

'I almost didn't recognise you,' said Chamunorwa, throwing his arms around his sister.

She laughed. 'I don't recognise myself! I keep wondering if it's really me!'

'No one would believe you're the girl who was jumping fences last year,' teased Dumisani.

The three of them laughed. Nomonde and Lerato were the only ones who were not privy to the joke.

'All I can say is you clean up well, sis,' remarked Chamunorwa.

'That she does,' agreed Dumisani.

His eyes lingered on Chenai long after he spoke. He was mesmerised by her astounding beauty; she had undergone a

196

transformation of sorts. Nomonde edged closer to him and wrapped a protective arm around him.

'Well, we came to support you on your big night and we have,' continued Chamunorwa, 'but we must go. Work tomorrow and we left the baby with a neighbour.'

'I really appreciate it,' replied Chenai. She waved to the cameraman and asked him to take a picture of her with her brother.

In that moment no one would have believed they'd been born from the same womb. But the warmth and love that radiated between them was undeniable. It was Antonio who came to steer her away.

'Oh, I wanted you to meet my brother,' said Chenai disappointedly.

'Some other time,' replied Antonio. 'I'm sure there will be plenty of time for us to meet.'

There were more important people to meet. More photos to be taken.

By midnight all of the guests had left. The band was packing up. The waiters were picking up glasses and clearing plates. There had not been much to eat. Chenai had got a glimpse of the fare, which comprised dainty hors d'oeuvres. Stuffed mushrooms, tomato tartlets, mini crab cakes, shrimp tarts and other delectable eats had been circulated on glass platters. They were enough to appetise the palate but inadequate to fill the hollow hunger that consumed Chenai.

The three cocktail spritzers had gone a long way to quench her thirst but her hunger remained unabated. So when Antonio suggested they go and get something to eat, Chenai agreed. They drove around aimlessly looking for a restaurant. They found none. Most of the restaurants were closed and so Antonio invited her back

SUE NYATHI

to his place; a duplex apartment with a huge kitchen that seemed to take up all the space as it opened up into the lounge and dining area. All the walls were covered with life-sized photographs of some of Antonio's iconic work.

Chenai looked everywhere trying to capture it all in her head. Antonio poured her a glass of wine. The dark red wine was bitter and tasted like one of those concoctions a *n'anga* had prescribed for her. She wanted to spit it out but did not want to offend Antonio. Perched on a high stool in the kitchen she sipped her wine slowly watching with keen interest as Antonio busied himself preparing the food. He shoved a pizza into the oven and then began making a salad, tossing together tomatoes, rocket, peppers, cheese and other ingredients whose names she did not know.

'I'll have you fed in no time,' he declared.

Chenai had no affinity for salads or anything leafy but figured she should eat it anyway. There was a part of her that was desperate to win his approval. He had done so much for her.

'Thank you for everything, Antonio. Your kindness.'

'Don't thank me, *cara mia*. It's all *your* hard work.'

He came around to her side and held her hands in his. His hands were so warm and soft. Hands that had known no hard labour or strife. He brought her hands to his mouth and kissed them lovingly. As he did he held her gaze, staring at her with intention and longing. Chenai looked away, overwhelmed by shyness.

'Look at me.'

She obeyed him and held his gaze. There was so much intensity in his piercing green eyes. She was so lost in the look that he gave her that she gasped in surprise when she felt his mouth on her lips.

He kissed her full soft lips stained by the wine.

198

'I want to make love to you, *cara mia*,' declared Antonio. 'Will you let me?'

'Make love to me,' replied Chenai.

With one sweeping motion he unzipped her ballgown, which fell to the floor around her feet. She kicked it aside. The dim light of the apartment illuminated her sinewy silhouette. Like a hungry baby he suckled on her breasts whilst his impatient hands tugged at her panties, which she eventually pulled down and pushed aside with her foot. Then he was kissing her all over, biting even, making her squeal in delight. In-between the fiery kisses his clothes came off, one item at a time, until he too was naked. He took her on the floor. Her long silky black legs curled around his buttocks, drawing him into her most intimate embrace. She clawed her nails into his back with a need that overwhelmed her. Her cries of unbridled pleasure filled the room. The pleasure transported her beyond the reality of the moment until her entire body exploded in a volcanic orgasm. Afterwards they lay panting; their hot sticky bodies wedged together. The smell of pizza permeated the air. The hunger for food had now been replaced by a primal hunger for the flesh. They consumed each other with a searing passion that had been ignited between them.

# TWENTY-NINE

May was cloaked in an air of iciness. However, she was nothing compared to the coldness that embodied her sister, June. As early as six p.m. Johannesburg was veiled in darkness. Chamunorwa pulled his jacket tighter around him as he walked along Lenin Drive on his way home. The day had given way to night. No longer did the children play in the streets till seven as they did in summer. Preparing for the encroaching winter, the trees had already started shedding their yellowing leaves.

Chamunorwa now went to work alone as Lerato was on maternity leave, nursing their newborn child who they named Rudo. As Chamu walked into the shack he was greeted by the aroma of stewing chicken and Lerato's sparkling smile. She handed him a steaming mug of coffee and two slices of bread smeared with margarine and fruit jam. In-between mouthfuls he recounted the tales of the day.

'I also got promoted, sweetie! I'm now cashier!'
Lerato threw her arms excitedly around him.
'Congratulations!'

200

Chamunorwa was chuffed with himself. He handed Lerato a letter indicating his new position and salary of R6 500 a month.

'I've found us a decent back room to rent in Orange Grove. This is no place for a child to grow up.'

Rudo lay fast asleep in the crib on the floor. Oblivious to the world around her. They made a small fire in a metal bucket and the warm coals kept the draught out.

'Chamu, I don't know what to say. You take such good care of me.'

'And I will continue to take good care of you. We are a family, Lerato. You, me and the baby. I will keep working harder and things will get better. As soon as I have saved enough money, I will go to your parents and pay lobola.'

Lerato threw her tiny arms around him and showered him with kisses. Chamunorwa's face creased into a smile. He had not believed such happiness was possible. A joy he had found in the eyes of this girl he had met on the dusty streets of Alexandra.

After supper they reclined in bed. Chamunorwa was going through the manual of what his new role and responsibility would entail. Lerato was breastfeeding Rudo, who soon fell back to sleep. Soon enough Chamunorwa followed suit, drawn into a deep slumber. However, in his dreams his father awaited him. Unlike in other dreams, he was not bloodied and bruised. He was whole and larger than life. Just like Chamu remembered him when he was a child. The days when they were happy. Before their mother had disappeared from their lives. He reached out his hand to Chamunorwa.

'Come with me, son,' he cajoled. 'Come with me.'

Huge tears rolled down his face as he said this.

'I forgive you for everything you have done, my son. Just come with me.'

'I'm not coming,' replied Chamunorwa. 'Go away!'

'You will come with me. I am not leaving you behind.'

As he said this he started to approach furtively. Moving closer to the bed.

'Go away!' screamed Chamunorwa.

He woke up with a start. Afraid he might have startled the baby. Rudo was fast asleep. Lerato's voice attempted to placate him.

'You're having those dreams again, aren't you?'

Chamunorwa nodded mutely. He had not dreamt about his father in weeks. Months even. She stroked his back and encouraged him to go back to sleep but he couldn't. Instead he turned on his side and stared at the asbestos sheet that formed the wall of their home. At some point in the night sleep drew him into its deep clutches. He had no idea how long he had been asleep for but he was soon roused by a noise outside. Gently he manoeuvred himself, pushing Lerato off his arm. She looked so peaceful, her messy black hair splayed across the pillow. He sat up in bed straining to hear what the commotion was. He finally woke Lerato up.

'Did you hear that?'

'Hear what?' replied Lerato, rubbing her eyes.

At first Chamunorwa thought they were caught in a violent hailstorm but quickly dismissed the thought when the sounds were accompanied by a chorus of deep baritone voices who sang in unison: *'Phansi ngamakwerekwere. Phambili ngenkululeko.'* Down with the foreigners. Forward with the liberation. The voices got louder. They got closer. Chamunorwa leapt out of bed. He reached for his boxer shorts on the floor.

'Where are you going?' asked a panicked Lerato.

'I need to see what's happening,' replied Chamunorwa.

'Chamu! Wait!'

As he turned to look at her, the door fell to the floor. Flattened by an onslaught of men wielding pangas, machetes, sticks and axes. All types of men. Tall, thin, wiry, ungainly and muscled. Men fuelled by testosterone and anger. They encircled Chamunorwa and bulldozed him into the corner of the room. The shouts of 'makwerekwere' became louder and more visceral. The yelling was accompanied by physical force. Hard blows of rage.

Chamu buckled under the attack and fell to the floor. They kicked him like he was a soccer ball. The baby had woken up in the commotion and was wailing in alarm. Lerato's pleas for mercy only served to incite their violence. As they beat him they admonished him for defiling one of their own. We will teach you a lesson, they promised. A lesson you will never forget. Lerato grabbed her baby and fled from the room. They were not interested in her. It was Chamunorwa they were after. They dragged his body out into the street leaving behind a trail of blood. Vociferous chanting floated above his body. Someone supplied a rubber tyre, which was doused in petrol. They necklaced Chamunorwa with it before setting it alight.

The raging fire, a collage of yellow, red and orange, engulfed Chamunorwa in a hot embrace. It singed his dreadlocks, which burned like paper. The ferocious flames danced off his body eliciting a crackling sound as his flesh began to roast. The acrid smell of burning tissue filled the air. It was pungent and nauseating. The fire was fanned by their fury; fuelled by their resentment of foreigners who crawled across the borders and stole their jobs, stole their houses, stole their women. The foreigners were rude and abrasive. They disrespected them in their own country. They did not even want to learn their languages. They deserved to die. Every one of them. They deserved to be consumed by the fires of hell.

The fiery revolution continued even after the charred remains of Chamunorwa's body were collected by the police an hour later. The fire had obliterated his face. A charred version of his former self remained. His hands were held up in resignation as he capitulated to the flames. He would not be the only one to be caught in the sweeping blaze of anger. The fire spread to the north of Johannesburg to areas like Diepsloot, Thembisa and Kya Sands. Somali and Pakistani businesses were looted before being razed to the ground. Conspicuous foreigners resident in the area were beaten to a pulp and robbed of their belongings. Unsuspecting women were raped. Many were forced to flee to camps of safety, which started to sprout up in response to the scorching campaign of discontent against foreigners.

The tsunami of disgruntlement migrated east. Waves of destruction displaced foreigners in Primrose, Germiston, Olifantsfontein, KwaThema, Thokoza, Emlotheni and Emandleni. The flood of anger swept through Jeppestown and Hillbrow. Ethiopians, Malawians, Mozambicans, Nigerians, Somalians and Zimbabweans were drowned in the frenzy of madness. The deep south was not spared either. Violence broke out in Soweto. Black on-black violence; brother against brother. It was a rising tide of enmity ready to sink any foreigner that stood in its path.

# THIRTY

It was midday when Portia waltzed into the office in
six-inch Gucci heels. She wore a micro-mini skirt and a cof-
fee-coloured blouse. Kopano noticed the shoes before she
noticed the rest of Portia's outfit, which looked like something that
had been put together from the latest issue of *Cosmopolitan*. Had
she not been irritated, Kopano might have complimented Portia
but instead she pretended to be dialling a number.

'I almost thought you weren't coming into work today,' began
Kopano.

'I told the boss I was going to be late,' replied Portia flippantly,
sinking into her chair.

She opened a takeaway box and started munching on a fried
chicken drumstick.

'You know the boss is pretty clear about us not eating in
reception.'

Portia wiped her mouth and feigned shock.

'Oops. I had forgotten. Man the switchboard whilst I'm gone.'

She flipped back her long mane of Brazilian hair and headed
off to the boardroom leaving Kopano enveloped in a cloud of Hugo

Boss. Kopano shook her head in disdain. She stood up and marched into Advocate Hirsch's office. The door was wide open but still Kopano knocked. He looked up from the file he was reading, dropping his glasses onto the bridge of his nose so that he could look over them.

'Yes?'

'Sir, I have an issue with Phakama and her erratic working hours. I have to come in at seven in the morning while she only gets here at midday.'

Advocate Hirsch looked away, mildly irritated.

'Well, she was here till midnight typing client depositions for Advocate Hulisani. I left them here. I think the agreement is if she works late she comes in late.'

Kopano was not amused by the response but it muted any further objection she might have had.

'Was there anything else? If there is, please raise it with Advocate Hulisani.'

He focused his attention back to the file on his desk and without being told, Kopano knew she had been dismissed. As she walked back to her desk she was cursing. Everyone knew the only reason Phakama was working late was because she was sleeping with Advocate Hulisani.

'You know, if I were you, I would end this thing with Advocate Hulisani,' warned Kopano after Portia had returned from her early lunch.

'End what thing?' replied Portia fluttering her eyelids.

'Look, we all know you're sleeping with him.'

Portia rolled her eyes heavenwards.

'Even if I was sleeping with the man it is none of your business. Secondly, if you do want to make it your business, there is absolutely nothing wrong with sleeping with Advocate Hulisani.'

'I have been here longer than you have. All the women who threw themselves at Advocate Hooligan are gone. It doesn't last with him! Even his marriages don't last. He has been married twice. Both of his marriages ended in messy divorces. He is not a nice man.'

The door opened and Advocate Hulisani came sweeping through in his court attire; two frightened-looking legal assistants trailing behind him. Like a hurricane they swept through reception.

'Bring me coffee!' he shouted to Portia.

She obeyed him without question and rushed to the kitchen. Kopano merely shook her head. They had a cleaning lady for that but Advocate Hulisani insisted his coffee be brought to him by Phakama. He said no one else made his coffee like she did.

The moment Portia entered his office, Hulisani dismissed the legal assistants with a wave of his hand. He sat back in his chair, putting his feet on the table. He folded his hands behind his head.

'You know I could watch you all day, Phakama.'

She merely smiled and looked down, her eyes not meeting his. That alone drove Advocate Hulisani crazy; the combination of coyness and sexiness. She put the coffee in front of him and he beckoned her to sit down. As she settled into the chair opposite him he gestured for her to come closer.

'You are too far away.'

So Portia perched on the desk in front of him, folding one leg over the other. Hulisani held the coffee with one hand and started stroking Portia's thigh with the other. She giggled, pushing his hand away.

'Advocate, someone might come in!' she chided gently.

'Everybody knows to knock when they come into my office.'

He stared at her heart-shaped face and those big brown eyes mollified him somehow.

'We had a shit session in court. Judge threw my witness out. We are adjourned till tomorrow.'

Having spent a lot of time in Hulisani's company she had come to understand a lot of the legal jargon. When she asked he took pains to explain it to her.

'I'm sorry you had a bad morning in court.'

Portia stood up to massage his shoulders. She did it because he told her he liked it. And each time she did it, it elicited quiet moans of appreciation from him.

'It's going to be all right,' she reassured him. 'Tomorrow you will walk into that courtroom and blow his mind. You are the best advocate in Joburg.'

'Fuck Phakama! You're turning me on!'

She quickly responded by sitting on the advocate's lap, straddling him with her thighs. With one swift move her tiny skirt was bunched around her waist. She wore no panties and the advocate groaned heavily as his fingers touched the warm flesh of her buttocks.

'You are going to drive me crazy,' he gasped.

Portia silenced him with a kiss while her other hand freed the burgeoning erection from his starched trousers. She impaled herself onto him and with practised ease began to move up and down on him. He came hard and fast, expelling all the tension that he had bottled up inside.

'You are going to finish me,' he reiterated as Portia cleaned him up with some wet wipes that he kept in a drawer in his desk.

She just smiled back at him; that demureness returning.

'Get yourself something to eat.'

'Thanks, boss.'

She was almost out the door when Advocate Hulisani called out to her.

'Phakama!' he yelled, almost sounding desperate. 'I will come by again this evening.'

He came by almost every other evening. Her son had even started calling him 'malume'. Portia would go out of her way to cook his favourite meals. He particularly loved *mashonzha*, what she grew up calling *amacimbi*. To most, the mopane worms were not a culinary delight and would have scratched rather than tickled taste buds. But for Hulisani it was like eating caviar. Every Saturday Portia would go to the Yeoville market to stock up on them.

'See you later.'

She blew him a kiss before she sashayed out of his office, her buttocks bouncing together in synchrony.

When she returned to the reception desk she found Kopano, who was highly annoyed. The whiff of sex in the air infused her with irritation.

'Can I take my lunch *now*?'

'With pleasure,' replied Portia. 'Please get *us* something. Get Advocate Hulisani something filling. Nothing fried. He needs to watch his cholesterol. Keep the change.'

She handed Kopano a R200 note. The money appeased Kopano and her mood lifted considerably.

Portia sat down behind her desk and actually turned on her computer. She was going through her mailbox when Advocate Hirsch informed her he was going out and would only be back the next day. It was his wife's birthday and he had a whole afternoon planned. This she had heard from Kopano who had done the bookings at some fancy spa. They were going to spend the night there as well. Portia had taken the name down. It was in Fourways. She had never been there but had heard the name often enough. For her birthday she was going to ask Hulisani to take her there too. He did everything she asked of him. Sometimes she did not even have to ask. He paid her rent. Paid her son's school fees. Gave her money for groceries. Money for clothes. He even promised to buy her a car, as soon as she learnt how to drive. And all he wanted from her was that she give herself to him, fully and without restraint.

The phone rang, breaking into her reverie. It was Advocate Hlomani. He was calling to say he was still stuck in court and all his afternoon appointments should be rescheduled. As soon as she put the phone down there was a buzz at the door.

'Who is it?' she asked.

'Superintendent Lwaile and Morule,' came the reply in a deep baritone voice.

Portia let them in. The male officer was tall and lanky and his female compatriot was short and stocky, her uniform hugging her generous curves.

'How can I help you?' she greeted them with a sunny smile.

'We are looking for a Miss Phakama Hlophe,' stated the officer.

'That's me,' replied Portia boldly.

'Well, you are under arrest,' replied Inspector Lwaile. 'For identity theft.'

Portia's face dropped and her chin almost hit the floor. The female policewoman started to read out her rights.

# PART FOUR

**The Homecoming**

'Behold, I am with you and will keep you wherever
you go, and will bring you back to this land. For
I will not leave you until I have done what I have
promised you.'

*Genesis 28: Verse 15*

# THIRTY-ONE

Whenever anyone asked where Christine was her mother would promptly reply, '*use*London'. It was said with great pride because having a child living and working abroad was something to be proud of. It did not matter that Christine actually lived 58 kilometres outside London in the county town of Aylesbury. That in the five years she had lived in the UK she could count the number of times she had ventured into the capital. All these things were inconsequential. What mattered was that Christine was doing an admirable job of supporting her. Beyond that she had no comprehension of how Christine spent her days. Had no idea that on most days Christine did not want to get out of bed.

That particular Saturday morning was no different. Christine pulled the covers over her head after her alarm buzzed. She swore because she had forgotten to turn it off. It was her day off and for once she did not have an extra shift lined up. Christine worked as a full-time nurse at the Stoke Mandeville Hospital. A few years before she would have used her days off to work extra shifts at the Royal Buckinghamshire Hospital. That was because she needed to make the extra money to support her children back home.

When she had first arrived in the UK, sending money home had been a delight because they converted it on the black market into billions and trillions of dollars. However, along came dollarisation and it was now a pound for a pound, wiping out all those fabulous arbitrage opportunities. Not that it mattered anymore because Dumisani was now able to support the children. He had made it clear that they did not need *her* money.

She should have been relieved to have the extra time to herself; to have the time to relax but in all honesty she had no idea what to do with herself. She debated about whether to take a sleeping tablet to numb her body and senses. She did it at times, even when she did not need to. She was about to head to the medicine cabinet when her phone rang. Busi's name flashed across the screen. Christine contemplated ignoring it. Then she felt a momentary stab of guilt. It was Busisiwe, her cousin, who had facilitated her move here. Busisiwe who had taken care of her. She answered the call.

'Hello, lurve!' Busi chirped like a hummingbird.

She was always in an effervescent mood like a bottle of champagne. It annoyed Christine no end.

'Hey cuzzie,' she replied, trying to feign some enthusiasm.

'I was thinking about you; why don't you come and visit? The kids miss you! Doug is lighting the barbecue. It's such a beautiful day out.'

Christine started to scratch her head hoping an excuse would fall out like the flecks of dandruff that landed on her shoulders. She needed to get her hair done.

'I would love to Busi but–'

Busi cut her off. 'Well, call us when you get to the station.'

She hung up before Christine could even protest. Christine

exhaled into the mouthpiece. She decided to shower and get ready.

The 70-minute bus ride to Milton Keyes was dull and uneventful. If anything it lulled her to sleep. When she arrived at the station, Busi was already waiting for her in her sporty Range Rover. Busi and her husband lived ten minutes from the station. They lived in a massive four-bedroomed bungalow with an entrance hall, spacious, airy rooms and a massive garden where the children played on sunny days. Busi's husband was a cardiac surgeon and made tons of money and they had met in hospital while Busi was undergoing her nurse training. She never did finish her studies and instead graduated to become Doug's housewife. Four kids, three cats and two dogs later they lived in the heart of suburbia with a picket fence and picture-perfect life. Busi was always trying to hook her up with Doug's single colleagues.

'Karl is going to be there,' declared Busi. 'He's really keen on you.'

Karl was a podiatrist from Germany who had relocated to England two years before. He was also divorced with two teenage children. They had dated a couple of times.

Christine rolled her eyes. 'If I had known he was coming, I would never have come.'

'Come on, lurve! Be a sport! You have got the kind of body that white men like.'

What Busi really meant by that was that she was thin and shapeless. When Christine looked at herself in the mirror she saw a skeletal frame draped in ill-fitting skin. She looked the way she did because she did not eat. She found no joy in cooking for one. She had tried to survive on frozen dinners but they got boring, as did takeaways and fast foods. On those rare days that she attempted to string a meal together she would lose her appetite before she even served it.

215

'I would kill to have your body,' continued Busi. 'If I had a body like yours I could get laid all over London.'

Christine laughed at her cousin's brazenness. She wouldn't mind swapping bodies. Busi had big bountiful breasts and a curvaceous body. Of course Busi was always on some diet or caught in the latest exercise fad. Zumba was the latest craze and she was on some maple syrup diet. 'Rich-life problems' she called them as she laughed good-naturedly.

'You can take my body any time,' replied Christine.

'The problem is you need to get laid. When was the last time you had sex?'

Christine shuddered. It must have been a year ago. With the dreaded Karl. The sex had been terrible; like a lawnmower with blunt blades. The engine had roared as it had flattened the grass leaving it uncut.

'You see! You don't even remember!' cried out Busi. 'You need to move on, dear. Dumisani has moved on.'

'So you always remind me.'

Dumisani was now married to a woman called Nomonde, a nurse by profession. Christine could not help thinking he really had a penchant for women in uniform. They still had friends in common and Christine had felt betrayed by those who had attended his wedding. Not only did they sit and ululate at Dumisani's nuptials but they also had the nerve to call her and impart every detail of the elaborate ceremony.

She had tried to sound nonchalant when they said Nomonde was an exquisite beauty and that Dumisani had met her while he was recuperating in hospital after his accident in Johannesburg. Apparently she had nursed him back to health with her undying love. They had tied the knot at a luxurious lodge in Victoria Falls and the who's who of

Bulawayo had attended. A wedding so big it had obliterated the memory of their own wedding. It was like they had never been married.

Christine had searched for the pictures on the internet and found them. There was a whole website dedicated to their wedding: Dumi and Nomonde ~ A Celebration of our Love. His new wife had a mocha-coloured complexion and a buxom figure. She was even more beautiful than her friends had described her. Christine had slept for an entire week after seeing those pictures.

'I *have* tried to move on,' said Christine.

'You're not trying hard enough,' retorted Busi.

Christine was glad when they finally pulled up to Busi's home. Ainose, Kunle, Folasade and Abiola came rushing to the car and assailed her with hugs and kisses. They ranged in age from four to twelve. They all had Yoruba names whose meanings were tied to praising and honouring God. Their father followed suit, wearing a blue ankara with geometric squares. He often liked to dress in his native Nigerian clothing on the weekends. He was a tall dark man with an imposing stature and crown of white hair.

'Hello, my dear,' he spoke, opening his hands out to her. 'We don't see you often enough.'

Listening to Doug speak you would never know he was Nigerian. He spoke eloquently with a lyrical twang and had been educated at Cambridge and Oxford. His father had been a career diplomat and his mother the charming hostess. Now his parents were retired and lived in Lagos. Doug really bucked the prominent misconception that *all* Nigerians were drug dealers with big dicks. However, Busi had verified the dick size. She claimed it was one of the reasons she had married him.

'I'm busy at work,' explained Christine as she sank into his embrace.

They led her out onto the patio where their other friends were congregated. It was a mixed masala of associations from Europeans to Senagalese to Zimbabweans. The Diomes, the Shoniwas and the Thomases. She and Karl were the only unmarried ones. They were all professionals with well-to-do jobs and lived in well-to-do areas. None of them worked back-to-back shifts trying to balance the bills or lived in a tiny one-bedroomed ground-floor maisonette like she did.

The men manned the braai and spoke vociferously about politics between beer swigs. Then the conversation moved to the English Premier League. The women, on the other hand, spoke about the breaking Oscar Pistorius case and more inconsequential things like the *Real Housewives of Atlanta*. The only thing Christine enjoyed during these conversations was the steady flow of sparkling wine. Fearing she would get too drunk, Christine abandoned her glass and slunk away to play with the children, chasing them all over the garden. They all spoke perfect English. They reminded her so much of her own children. Sipho would be eight now and Silindile five. She only saw them in pictures and even though she called them every week they sounded so distant on the telephone.

Dumisani had assumed full custody of the children. The court had ruled in his favour since he had accused her of abandoning them. Her no-show at the hearing only solidified the judgment. Her failure to show up at the hearing had not been deliberate; without papers it would have been impossible for her to travel home. Only a few weeks ago she had been granted permanent stay in the United Kingdom. It was too late now. She felt like she had already lost everything. This was why she hated visiting Busi. It was a constant reminder of what she had lost.

She was glad when the day's festivities came to an end. Karl offered to drive her home. Christine was sufficiently inebriated not to be bored in his company. She laughed at all his jokes till her own laughter veered on the edge of hysteria. Against her better judgement she invited him up for a nightcap. Her liberal consumption of wine had made her frisky so she was quite engaging when Karl started rubbing his hand up and down her thigh. However, when Karl banged her head against the headboard with her legs suspended in the air she knew she should have passed up on the offer. The head-banging sex made her sober up very quickly. He offered to stay the night but she lied and said she had an early-morning start at the hospital. She saw him to the door and was glad to see it close behind him. She sank to the floor with the weight of her misery. She got angry then and went to call Dumisani.

'I want my kids,' she screamed into the telephone.

'Christine,' he replied in a more subdued voice. 'Calm down.'

'Why won't you let me see *my* children? They are mine!'

'Christine. You gave up the right to those children the minute you got onto that flight to London.'

Christine was used to Dumisani being abrasive and unkind on the telephone.

'How did you become this person?' she screamed. 'What happened to the Dumisani I married? He would never have been this cruel!'

'Christine, have you been drinking again?'

Christine started to sob uncontrollably, her tears wetting the mouthpiece of the telephone.

'Christine, I am going to put the phone down,' declared Dumisani.

He did and the line went dead. Christine sobbed harder as she confronted the futility of her own life.

# THIRTY-TWO

Dumisani stared at the phone for a long time. He kept thinking about what Christine had said. How did you become this person? The words resonated with him. It was then that the door to his study swung open and Nomonde's body emerged in full view. Her ungainly form almost filled the door frame. She was wearing a tiny négligée with her breasts spilling over the top. Her dimpled caramel legs were fully exposed. He wondered how long she had been standing there like a fly on the wall. Listening in on his conversation.

'Who was that?' she asked.

Her voice was thick with jealousy. Envy coated the words that fell from her acid tongue.

'Who was what?' he replied dismissively.

'On the telephone? Who were you talking to?'

'If you must know it was Christine.'

'Yeah right,' hissed Nomonde. 'It's one of your bitches isn't it?'

Dumisani slammed his fist hard on the oak desk as if in a deliberate attempt to leave an imprint of his anger. Even the picture frame of him and Nomonde on their wedding day shook nervously.

It fell to the oak-panelled floor with a resounding thud.

'Don't start. I am not in the mood!'

'You are never in the mood! When was the last time you touched me? When?'

'Nomonde, I am not in the mood for this.'

She exhaled deeply. She could not even remember the last time he called her baby or sweetheart. She was now Nomonde.

'*Ucing'uba ungcono?* You think you are better? *Uyachoma* Dumisani. *Mxm! Tsek!*'

Dumisani braced himself for the vitriol of Xhosa she spewed on him. Once upon a time he had been turned on by her anger. He would have actually grabbed her and screwed her on the floor. Now he wanted to grab her and throw her out of the window like his uncle had done to him. Though he doubted he had the strength to lift her. Her body embodied the Woolworths croissants and chocolate cupcakes that she gorged for breakfast every morning; the fish and slap chips she had for lunch and the pap and vleis she had for supper.

'I don't have time for this, Nomonde,' he replied searching his desk for his car keys.

The baby broke into a loud wail. The nursery was just a few doors away from his study. Xhanti was a colicky three-month-old baby. His conception had been a desperate attempt to salvage a marriage that was falling apart at the seams.

'I'm going out,' declared Dumisani.

'So I must take care of the baby?' shouted Nomonde, her hands resting squarely on her hips.

'*Angithi* you are the mother!' shouted Dumisani.

'And you are not the father?' she shouted back.

'I don't know, hey. That kid looks nothing like me. *Angina siphong'esinjalo mina.* I don't have a forehead like that.'

Nomonde slapped him hard across the face. Dumisani grabbed her by the neck and pushed her into the wall. He could see a vein pulsing.

'Go ahead and abuse me, Dumisani. I will call the police. You will be deported so fast your head will spin.'

Dumisani loosened his grip on her. He turned his back on her and walked out of the study. Nomonde's threats and Xhanti's cries followed him all the way downstairs. He even felt her slipper hit his back. He was glad the other children were safely cocooned in boarding school away from their harrowing fights, which had become more frequent and louder. He jumped into his Porsche Cayenne and sped down the winding driveway of their sprawling Kyalami home till it looked like a dollhouse in the distance.

He walked into Maestro, his favourite cigar lounge in Sandton. As he did, he saw beautiful coiffed heads perking up with interest. But he was not easily baited by the allure of easy sex; no matter how beautifully it was packaged. He was more discerning and tended to prefer sophisticated and intelligent women. He met many of those in his line of work.

'Hey *baws* man!' sang one of the waiters.

He was a regular there; he was familiar with the waiters who greeted him by his first name or referred to him affectionately as 'baws'. Most of them were Zimbabwean and he liked to commiserate with them because he knew that he could easily have been one of them. They all looked up at Dumisani with adoring eyes. To them he was success personified.

'What can I get you, *baws*?' asked a bubbly young waiter.

'The usual,' replied Dumisani.

It was always a privilege to serve him because he tipped

generously. But beyond the tips, Dumisani was helping two guys to study towards their degrees. He wished he could help more. To give more people a step up the rung in the ladder of life. He called it an investment in the future of others. His own life would not have been what it was had Solomon Kaufman not invested in him. Back then he earned a meagre salary of R6 000 at Investage Asset Management. He had a natural aptitude for trading. He had an innate knack for swaps, options and futures. It gave him a rush that could only be rivalled by sex.

He had made his mark as a derivatives trader and was pro-filed on many financial publications from the *Financial Mail* to the *Financial Times*. Dumisani Khumalo, one of South Africa's success stories. None of the publications ever alluded to his Zimbabwean origins. That was because somewhere along the way he had bought his South African identity. It had seemed like the right thing to do at the time. Now he regretted it. Especially when other Zimbabweans had achieved immeasurable success without having to hide behind an assumed identity. He had wanted to come clean but the price he would have to pay was just too much. He was now CEO of Investage, which had since changed its name to Vukani Securities, and he was one of the shareholders. Beyond his position at Investage he served on several boards of JSE-listed companies.

Work kept him sane; it also kept him away from his wife. The less time he spent in her company, the more peace of mind it gave him. Lately he found himself asking what he had ever seen in her. He'd even suggested divorce but Nomonde had threatened to expose him to the whole world for what he was. He sighed heavily and signalled to the waiter to bring him another drink. His marriage had now become his biggest source of unhappiness. During the fights there had been the sporadic bouts of angry sex. He suspected that Nomonde had been fooling around so he was not entirely sure Xhanti was his.

Many times the tracking company would report that her car had been spotted in the strangest of places, like Katlehong or Tembisa. Not that he could claim to be faithful. He was seeing someone, Keneilwe. She had a sweet disposition that reminded him of Christine in so many ways. It was at times like this that he missed the calmness of Christine. Missed the camaraderie they had enjoyed. As Silindile grew she looked more and more like her mother and the poignant resemblance was a constant reminder of what they had had. He wanted that back. The innocence. The authenticity. He often wondered if it was too late to get it back.

He was drawn from his introspection by loud arguing at the next table. The waiter was demanding that a young woman settle her bill. The woman was belligerent, insisting that she did not have the cash to pay. She tipped the contents of her handbag onto the table, totally oblivious to the fact that she was now the centre of attention. Dumisani decided to settle the bill for her. It was a mere R400. The lady then sashayed over to his table to thank him. She could barely walk straight she was so drunk. He recognised her from the billboards. He would have recognised her face in his sleep.

'Chenai?'

Clearly she did not recognise him. She smiled instead.

'Iwantedtothankyouforpayingmybill.'

'It's not a problem. Sit down, Chenai.'

She slumped into the chair with no elegance at all. Her mini-dress climbed up her thighs and she made no attempt to pull it down. He had a full and unrestrained view of her crotch. Dumisani looked away as he feared he might be tempted.

'Youwantsome?' she asked pointing to her crotch. 'Iamgood.'

Dumisani shook his head.

'I'm Dumisani; your brother was a good friend of mine. I don't think you remember me.'

Her eyes perked up. 'YouknewChamunorwa?'

'Yeah. I knew him very well. He was a good friend to me. He died such a horrible death. God rest his soul.'

'He comes to visit me at times. In fact all of the time. Him and my father,' she replied with a vacant look in her eyes.

Dumisani figured it was the alcohol speaking. She had certainly consumed a lot of it. And had expensive taste too. Glenfiddich Single Malt Whisky did not come cheap.

'How is the modelling going?' he asked.

'Itsbaaadnoworkforusblackmodels,' she replied.

She breathed noisily and her chest heaved in frustration.

'How's your boyfriend? The white guy? You were with him at the funeral.'

'My fiancé,' she replied, stretching out her hand to show him the platinum ring, 'WeareengagedWehavebeenengagedforyears.'

She continued to fidget with the ring. Dumisani just looked at her. He didn't trust a word she was saying.

'Wehavetoomanyproblems.'

Her voice faltered and Dumisani instinctively knew that tears would emerge.

'Are you okay to get home? I can give you cab money.'

Her eyes lit up and shone with expectation.

'Thankyou!Thankyou!'

Dumisani dug into his wallet and pulled out a wad of R100 notes. He had drawn it to pay for something or the other. He had forgotten what it was. He asked for her number. She gave it without hesitation, thanked him profusely, stood up and stumbled out of the lounge. The waiter who'd observed what had transpired came up to him to sympathise.

'A sad case that one. She's often in here drunk and picking up men.'

Dumisani opened his eyes in disbelief. 'Seriously?'

'One of those high-priced hookers, *baws*.'

Dumisani made it a point to call her the very next day. He had to help her. Chamunorwa would have wanted that. He remembered painfully how Chamunorwa had died a few years ago. His death had been front-page news for a long time. However, it was all forgotten now; yesterday's news. There were new struggles, new conflicts. He looked up and sitting at the bar, smiling suggestively at him, was an attractive young woman. He contemplated going to book a room at the Michelangelo and having his way with her but decided against it. He called for the bill instead and went home.

# THIRTY-THREE

Chenai got home with the rising sun. She fumbled in her bag searching for the keys. It was Antonio who finally let her in and she stumbled into the apartment, almost crashing into the coffee table. She tripped and fell, her legs splayed on the floor. Her thighs were encrusted with dried sperm. He stared at her, looking exasperated.

'You're using again?'

She grunted something inaudible. Antonio shook his head and returned to their bedroom to sleep. It was midday when he felt Chenai snuggle up close to him, her pert breasts pressing into his back. She smelled fresh, like a bouquet of pink roses sprayed with white chrysanthemums.

'Antonio?'

'Hmmm.'

'Are you awake?'

'Yes.'

'I'm sorry.'

He turned around to face her. Cupped her face with both his hands.

'It's been two days, Chenai. Two days. You are using again, aren't you?'

She could not look away. She cast her eyes downwards in shame. The tears fell. The tiny droplets encapsulated the sadness in her soul.

'I'm sad. I keep thinking about my brother.'

'It's been five years, Chenai.'

He held up his hand for greater emphasis. Everyone had a card they liked to play. He strongly believed she had milked the grieving card.

'Please forgive me, Tony.'

'I forgive you, *cara mia*. I always have. But you know we can't be together. I can't do this anymore.'

He pulled his hands away and sat up in bed. She followed his example.

'I landed that job in Europe. Being of Italian descent makes things easier for me so I got the permit. I am going to give it a try.'

'So that's it. You're just going to pack and go. You're leaving me?'

Antonio nodded. 'I can't do this anymore. I can't do *us* anymore. I've tried. You've been in and out of rehab, Chenai. I've been at your side but I can't anymore.'

She started to cry. It came from a deep place and it was raw and gut-wrenching. He knew if he reached out to hold and comfort her he would be overwhelmed by her emotions. So he chose to remain detached.

'I've paid the rent until the end of the year so you can stay here until the lease expires. You can keep everything but after that you're on your own.'

'Please Antonio, I promise I'll stop using. Please don't leave me.'

'Chenai, I'm leaving. I'm going to move into a hotel until I go. You need to take charge of your life.'

Antonio got up and headed into the bathroom escaping Chenai's dry, anguished sobs. They finally lulled her to sleep.

When Chenai woke up her eyes were swollen and red. Her heart was heavy and her soul desolate. She stretched out her hand to feel the space where Antonio lay. It was empty. She got out of bed and went to his cupboard. Only the empty hangers were left. He had gone. Really gone this time. Throughout the course of their relationship he had often threatened to leave. This time he had really done it. She started to cry again. The sobs echoed through the entire flat. When she was all cried out she decided to visit her mother. It had been many months since she had last seen Sibongile. When she arrived her mother was outside hanging the washing. She looked considerably thinner and even older. Her mother said the same of her.

'Are you not eating with that *white* man of yours?'

'Antonio left. He has found work in Italy.'

Chenai started fiddling with the ring again.

'And the wedding? When are you getting married?'

'We'll see. Maybe in Italy.'

Sibongile stopped hanging the washing to look at her daughter. Her eyes were gleaming in excitement. Chenai could not bring herself to tell her mother the truth about her failed relationship, her failed career and her failed life.

'I can't wait to tell the others. My daughter getting married in Italy! I will be the envy of the street!'

She clapped her hands together animatedly.

'I would also come to Italy, right? You would pay for my ticket?'

'Mama, calm down; it hasn't happened yet.'

Sibongile pulled her face and returned to hanging the clothes.

'Since Chamu died I have had nothing to be excited about. You know the Lord is punishing me for leaving you behind? He wasn't even here for long and he ...'

Sibongile's body heaved with her cries. She cried so hard she fell to her knees. Chenai hugged her mother from behind. Trying to console her. Fighting back her own tears. After the last tear had fallen, Sibongile hung up the last dress wordlessly. She then invited Chenai back into her tiny flatlet where she had some food in the freezer. Leftovers from the Hirsches' supper, Chenai guessed. There were roast potatoes and slivers of roast lamb. Chenai nibbled on a piece of meat before putting it back on her plate.

'You need to eat.'

'I'm not hungry,' replied Chenai.

'It's that modelling thing of yours.'

'I just don't have an appetite,' replied Chenai.

'You look tired. Do you even sleep at night?'

'How can I when Chamunorwa visits me? Every time he comes to me and he's burning, Mama. I touch his body and it's hot.'

'I don't know if he'll ever rest in peace. He died a terrible death,' replied Sibongile.

She had a distant look in her eyes. Then as an afterthought she added: 'You just need to pray, Chenai. I have started to pray,' she pointed at the Bible at the foot of her bed. 'They say God forgives our sins. It doesn't matter how big.'

Since Chamunorwa's death, her mother had started attending some Pentecostal church in Randburg led by a Nigerian man and his wife. Revival Ministries, it was called. They promised to awaken even the deadest of souls.

'The blood of Jesus will set you free. Cleanse you of all your sins!'

'I don't have any sins,' replied Chenai dismissively.

She decided to leave before her mother launched into a sermon and said her goodbyes hurriedly. She was sitting in the taxi when she received an sms on her phone. It was a banking notification that R10 000 had been deposited into her account. A deep smile spread across her face. Suddenly the thought of spending the afternoon drinking was not such a bad one. She started to call her friends. She was about to make her third call when an incoming call flashed on the screen. She did not recognise the number but answered promptly thinking it might be an agency calling her for work.

'Hello! Is that Chenai? Dumisani speaking.'

Dumisani. She rummaged through her brain trying to look for an image of him. Trying to place him.

'Dumisani Khumalo. Chamunorwa's friend.'

'Oh right. Yeah I remember you! Long time!'

He sounded annoyed on the other end.

'Anyway I sent through some money. I just wanted to confirm you had received it.'

'Thank you so much. I wanted to call you but I realised I didn't have your number.'

'Not a problem. Take care.'

Dumisani ended the call. Chenai promptly saved his number; she decided he was an asset to have in her life.

She met up with her friends at a trendy sidewalk restaurant in Melrose Arch. They air-kissed before settling down into their chairs. They all professed it had been ages since they had last seen each other. Estelle, Priyanka and Anele were all friends Chenai had met through the modelling industry.

'So doll, what's happening with you?' piped up Anele, lighting a cigarette. 'You are so thin; I'm jealous!'

Chenai laughed. 'Liquid diet!'

They all laughed in unison.

'I'll try that diet once I've given birth,' chortled Estelle.

The blue-eyed blonde was a former Miss South Africa finalist, now married and expecting her first child.

'How are you finding pregnancy?' asked Priyanka.

Priyanka was a model who had morphed into acting. With a cameo role on a local soapie, her face was easily recognisable.

'I'm finding it hard to get dressed,' replied Estelle. 'Maybe Anele should consider designing a line for pregnant women.'

Anele smirked and blew smoke into the air. 'There isn't a market for it!'

A waitress came to take their drinks order. Chenai immediately recognised Tryfina and looked down at her menu and made no attempt to say hello.

'Hello! My name is Tryfina. I'll be your waitress this afternoon.'

'I'll have vodka and cranberry to drink. Then the seared tuna salad with jalapeño dressing,' said Chenai, keeping her eyes fixed on the menu.

The ladies ordered other exotic salads. After Tryfina had gone, Anele cracked up.

'Only a Zimbo could be called Tryfina. What does that mean?'

Chenai shrugged. 'Don't look at me!'

The leafy orders came but no one ate. Instead they pushed the food around with their silver forks. They talked and laughed and the afternoon gave way to the early evening. Estelle kissed everyone goodbye and left. Priyanka followed suit as she had a date with a hot young man. Anele and Chenai moved off to drink at a bar in Sandton. But even Anele could not outdrink Chenai and pleaded she had a long day ahead and left.

Chenai was seated at the bar by herself when she was approached by a suited man. He greeted her in Shona, which implied he was fully aware of her origins.

'I have been following you for a while. Watching your movements.'

Chenai was about to get up but he slammed his hand on the counter.

'You might want to stay and listen to what I have to say.'

Chenai exhaled noisily, 'I'm listening.'

He pulled out a badge. It read: Criminal Investigation Department. Captain Gomo.

'A crime never dies.'

As he said this his hand stroked Chenai's lightly. She felt her blood curdle.

'Your father supposedly died under mysterious circumstances. Is that not true?'

Chenai nodded mutely.

'There was foul play there, madam. You know this very well.'

Chenai remained silent. The alcohol no longer numbed her senses. She craved something stronger.

'Look, I can make this crime disappear. We can strike it off the database. For a price.'

'How can I trust you?' croaked Chenai.

He laughed, 'You think I went through all this trouble to find you for nothing? Your modelling career won't be much use to you in prison. What's ten thousand dollars between friends?'

Chenai felt a shiver down her spine. Who did people take her for? Naomi Campbell?

'I don't have that kind of money.'

'Find it,' replied the captain replacing his smile with a nasty smirk. 'You won't survive a month in a maximum prison.'

He scribbled his number on the back of a business card that he handed to her.

'Call me when you have the money. I am giving you till Friday next week.'

He left. Chenai followed suit. The joy of drinking had dissipated with the enormity of the captain's threats. When she got home she had a throbbing headache that would not subside. She felt like a heavy metal band was rehearsing inside her skull. She lay on the bed feeling restless. She reached for her phone and scrolled through it. She desperately needed a hit and called several of her suppliers. It was a Nigerian dealer named Kayin that responded. He was reliable and always had good quality coke. She had met him at a hip party in Sandton a year ago.

'Hello, Kayin is that you? Can you score me some coke?'

'Do you have the cash?'

'Of course I have the cash. Would I call you if I didn't?' snapped Chenai angrily.

After she hung up she felt much happier. Her mood lifted as she thought of the line of coke she would soon sniff. It would take her to greater heights. Realms far and beyond. And as her mood lifted, she knew too where she would get the cash. Dumisani was the answer to all her problems. She was pacing the apartment frantically when Kayin arrived. She snatched the tiny pack out of his hands. He looked around the apartment; it was empty. She had sold the entire contents to feed her drug habit. He shook his head in disdain. Addicts were a pitiful sight. He looked away; it was not his fault that she had ended up like this. He was merely a middleman. If she didn't get the drugs from him she would get them elsewhere.

'I need to borrow some money,' she began. 'My mother is sick and she needs an urgent operation.'

Kayin's eyes widened in disbelief.

'You seriously want to borrow money from me? How the hell do you intend to pay it back?'

She removed her dressing gown to reveal her naked emaciated body. Her breasts had shrivelled up like dried peaches; the imprint of her ribcage reminded him of the rack of lamb he had eaten for dinner. Her hip bones jutted out awkwardly; her stomach had hollowed out and her kneecaps looked swollen and disproportionate to the rest of her bony legs. He felt as if he was staring at a corpse that had escaped from the mortuary. Kayin turned away. The emaciated look did nothing for him. He would need electric prongs to get turned on.

'Look, if you want to make extra cash I can help you.'

Chenai took the cue to fasten her nightgown. She turned away, embarrassed that she had even offered herself to him.

'Why don't you sell your kidney? There's good money in it.'

She eyed him circumspectly, 'Are you serious?'

'Very. It's a quick, harmless procedure. You will be in and out in no time.'

Kayin explained to her that there was a waiting list of over a thousand people who needed a kidney transplant in South Africa. In a few sentences he was able to convince Chenai that after a quick operation she could easily make half a million rand. When Chenai went to bed that night she was already counting the notes in her head.

# THIRTY-FOUR

Every Sunday she forayed into the deep south. Turning her back on the lush northern suburbs, Nomonde veered off onto the Soweto Highway in her Mercedes Benz. She turned onto Klipspruit Valley Road in the direction of Orlando where she had grown up. Orlando was the first and oldest township of Soweto, born in the thirties to house the growing black population. Her grandfather had been an *umaWasha*, working in Braamfontein washing laundry for European miners. He lived in a modest two-roomed matchbox house on the corner of Mooki and Magoye Street. After he died the house had passed onto her father. A mineworker himself he had made a few modifications to the house and added two more rooms.

Nomonde was born in 1980 at Chris Hani Baragwanath Hospital. It was four years after the infamous 1976 Soweto Uprising and the Hector Pietersen Museum had been built to commemorate the event. Even though it was close to where she grew up, Nomonde had never been there until a year ago when Dumisani's parents came for a holiday. They had all made an afternoon of it.

Like the multitudes of tourists who were bussed in on a

daily basis they had thronged like bees to Vilakazi Street, which had gained pre-eminence for being home to two of the world's Nobel Laureates: Archbishop Desmond Tutu and the late Nelson Mandela. The main attraction was house number 8115 where the late Nelson Mandela had lived with his first wife, Evelyn Mase, and later Winnie Mandela. The house had been transformed into a living museum and the public could walk through the rooms trying to get a feel for how the Mandelas had lived.

Nomonde had found the whole experience bordering on cheesy but Dumisani and the kids had enjoyed it immensely. However, instead of trekking to Sakhumzi's or Nambitha's for lunch like most tourists, they had gone to her mother's home for her seven-colour Sunday lunch. Now Nomonde attended Sunday lunch alone or with the kids when they wanted to come with. Unlike her, they had no sentimental attachment to Soweto. She had grown up playing on dusty Mooki Street; long before it was paved; long before the Bus Rapid Transit System cut through it. Their house was a stone's throw away from Orlando Stadium, which had received an overhaul in the wake of 2010 World Cup fever.

As a child, Nomonde had always yearned to live in the more affluent neighbourhood of Diepkloof Ext. The residential fabric was a mixture of single- and double-storey homes that were walled and gated. Often it felt like a dream that she had outdone her Diepkloof aspirations and now lived in the heart of the affluent north. Some of the girls she grew up with were still languishing in Soweto. They had kids and their kids had kids. She saw them every weekend when she came back to Soweto and shuddered to herself, as she could have been them. As she pulled up to the house, her mother was already waiting with an annoyed look on her face.

'We're going to be late, Nomonde.'

Her mother was dressed to the nines as always. Now that she had retired from cleaning people's homes in the plush northern suburbs, Yondela spent her days looking like a beauty queen. Sis Yondi, as she was known in the neighbourhood, was wearing a pristine pink Chanel suit courtesy of Nomonde. Her mother was a happy recipient of all of Nomonde's outfits, which could no longer fit past her expanding waistline or generous hips.

'Mama, I'm sure if I slimmed down I could fit into that outfit again.'

'Slim down first and we'll see,' replied her mother flippantly. 'You don't take care of yourself.'

'I'm trying to lose the weight, Mama.'

Sis Yondi settled into the Benz, crossing one leg over another. Her manicured hands sat in her lap. Every Sunday they went to church together. For Nomonde it was out of habit as opposed to any spiritual edification. For her mother it used to be for spiritual edification but now it was more for egotistical reasons.

'Is Snowy coming with us?'

'Snowy is asleep. She came home at the break of dawn.'

'Mama, how can you let her stay out till dawn?'

Her mother held her hands up in resignation. 'I've lost control of that child of *yours*.'

Snowy, as they called her, was Nomonde's first-born child. One she had birthed at the tender age of fifteen. A fact she did not often disclose; not even Dumisani knew how they were related. She was more honest about Khaya, who had come a few years later when Nomonde was in nursing college.

The name Snowy came about when, at the age of three, the little girl made her first attempt at baking and ended up covered in Snowflake Cake Flour.

'I will speak to her when we get back from church.'

'It's your fault. You give her too much money.'

Nomonde shrugged. She did it to soothe her guilty conscience. For not being there for her daughter. She turned the key and the engine purred to life. They drove off. Nomonde pulled to the side of the road to buy *amagwinya* from a lady seated outside a spaza shop.

'Do you want one, Mama?'

Sis Yondi shook her head vehemently. *'iCholesterol yam' iyenyuka. Angithi ngivele nginesugar ne high high.'*

Nomonde ignored her mother as she wolfed down a greasy koeksister with syrup dripping down the sides.

'Then you wonder why you don't lose weight.'

Nomonde ignored her mother and looked ahead.

They attended mass at the Regina Mundi Catholic Church in Rockville. Nomonde drifted in and out of sleep during the two-hour service. She would either be jarred awake by her mother jabbing her in the side or by the enthusiastic singing accompanied by the rhythmic pulsating sound of African drums. When mass ended they spent an hour afterwards chatting to her mother's friends, all of whom offered nothing but glowing admiration for Nomonde. She smiled good-naturedly; even when they pointed out that they no longer saw Dumisani anymore.

'You must bring him to church next week,' insisted her mother as they drove home.

'You have no idea how stubborn Dumisani can be.'

'Nomonde, I don't understand what you did to that man. He used to eat out of the palm of your hand.'

'Mama, have you ever stopped to think that maybe *he* changed?'

Sis Yondela shook her head once more. 'That man takes care of us. Treat him well.'

Nomonde rolled her eyes. No one ever talked about him treating *her* well. She was tired. Exhausted with the ill treatment and abuse.

'Enough is enough, Mama.'

'What are you going to do? Leave him? We are Catholic. We don't divorce!'

Nomonde drew her mouth in a tight line. She had it all figured out. She had a plan that would put an end to all her misery.

'Can we stop at Woolworths? I need to get some salads.'

'Sure, Mama.'

They made a detour at Maponya Mall, one of Soweto's newest and possibly largest shopping malls. Not that there had been a dearth of shopping malls as there had been Jabulani Mall before that and Dobsonville. Now all investors had their eyes on the expanding black middle class and had realised the untapped potential Soweto had to offer and so mall after mall sprouted up in quick succession.

'It's not Sandton,' murmured Sis Yondela as they made their way back to the car. 'Would you want to come back and live here?'

'Off course not, Mother. Whatever happens I'm keeping the Kyalami home.'

'Nomonde … some of these divorces. Mary's daughter is back in Pimville. She didn't even get a cent from that man. She came out with her car and a trunk full of clothes. She can't even service that car!'

'Mama, don't worry. It won't come to that.'

'It better not. I couldn't live with the embarrassment. How would I face the ladies at church?'

Dumisani had bought her mother's allegiance after he renovated and extended her home on Mooki Street. He had paved the driveway and built a pretty wall with an electric gate.

When they got home, Snowy was warming the Sunday lunch. The table had been set with her mother's special crockery from the display cabinet and her shiny cutlery that only appeared on Sundays. Sunday lunch was a revered tradition in the Zondi household. Nomonde's older sister and her three children joined them. Nandipha had never worked a day in her life and subsisted on the social grant that each of her kids received as well as whatever maintenance she had been able to siphon from their fathers.

Their oldest brother, Monty, also lived at home. Monty occupied the back room. At forty he had just come out of serving a ten-year jail sentence for strangling a man in a beer brawl. Sis Yondela had raised his two children abandoned by their mothers just after he had been sentenced. Then there was Xolisa, Sis Yondela's niece who had recently graduated from university and had moved up from Mthatha seeking a job in Johannesburg.

'Don't you need someone to help with the kids?' asked her mother. 'Xolisa could help out until she finds something more permanent.'

'Xolisa is a graduate, Mama!' replied Nomonde. 'I will ask if Dumisani has something for her in his office. And besides, we don't need extra help at home.'

They already had a full staff complement. Maxwell had been a former chef at a luxury hotel in Victoria Falls and Keepmore, their gardener was a former farmworker from Murewa. Then there was Everjoyce whose sole mandate was to do the housework. Dumisani took good care of them all. He was even paying to put Everjoyce's son through school.

'I'm sure Dumi can create a post. He owns the place,' said Monty. 'But funny how he couldn't create a post for me.'

'With your jail credentials who is going to hire you?' replied Nomonde snootily.

Monty smirked and sucked on his oxtail bone.

'She can even start as a receptionist,' suggested Sis Yondela.

Nomonde exhaled deeply. 'Xolisa, email me your CV and I'll see what I can do.'

'Nomonde, don't forget I need to pay the deposit for my residence fees,' piped up Snowy.

'I don't know why you can't live here and commute every day.'

'It will interfere with my studies. I can't. I want to stay in res.'

'So you can party all night? Mama told me you only came home this morning!'

'Please don't stress me. I've passed my matric. I'm going to study law. What's wrong with a party once in a while?'

Snowy picked up her plate of food and stormed off to the kitchen.

'She should have just gone to UJ.'

'Why UJ when you can afford Wits?' replied Sis Yondela pointedly. 'This is why you need to be nice to Dumisani. Snowy has four years of university.'

Nomonde pushed her plate aside. 'I have to go.'

The burden of responsibilities often took away the joy of being with her family. They could not even have a simple conversation without the mention of money.

'Can you see me at the back before you go?' said Monty getting up.

'I guess you also want a hundred rand? People here think I'm ABSA!' hissed Nomonde.

'But you *are* married to the bank,' replied Sis Yondela saucily.

Nomonde shot her a glare before following her brother outside.

Monty was smoking a joint. Without prompting he lit one for Nomonde.

'I got you a name. One of my guys in prison said this guy is reliable.'

Monty handed her a card. On the back was a name and a number. Jackson Mdluli. 0714535523.

'Where do I find this guy?'

'He's based in Hillbrow. I spoke to him. He wants fifty thousand rand. Half upfront and the rest after they've topped him.'

Nomonde took the card from him and shoved it in her handbag. As she walked to the car she wondered if it had been prudent to let Monty in on what she was planning.

# THIRTY-FIVE

The pretty, painted and pleasant-smelling madams of Sandton and surrounds converged at the Hirsches' home for their monthly book club meeting. It was Adrienne's turn to host their small group of ten. Two had apologised to say they would not make it. Two were a no-show. Adrienne had seen the WhatsApp messages in the group but had been too annoyed to read them. They were all married but none of them belonged to the First Wives Club. They were either second or third wives. When they were not discussing books they swapped colourful stories about baby mama drama and unruly stepchildren while nibbling daintily on pretty hors d'oeuvres and drinking pink bubbly champagne. Normally they read a book recommended by Oprah but a few months ago, at Mrs Molefe's insistence, they started reading authors from the *Sunday Times* shortlist.

They met on the third Saturday of each month with no exceptions. That afternoon they were having a boisterous discussion on *White Wahala* by Ekow Duker.

'Posh, what it was about the prison scene that particularly resonated with you?' probed Mrs Hirsch.

She was well read and Portia aimed to emulate her. She now sounded like most of the women in her book club when she spoke. At times she slipped up with words or lost the right intonation but she would brush it off with a smile.

'The prison scene. I could relate to Cash. It is the one time I felt he was weak and vulnerable,' replied Portia.

Portia was referring to a scene in the book where the main protagonist called Cash, a loanshark/gangster, ends up in prison. Having once been incarcerated herself she could relate to this. Her stay in prison had been short-lived; Advocate Hulisani had come for her the following day and bailed her out. She was mandated to appear in court a month later but the case had been dropped after the docket disappeared. So did the crime.

The incident of Phakama Hlophe was never mentioned again and she went back to being Portia. Then later she became Portia Mulaudzi. She and the advocate were married in a small civil ceremony. The advocate bought her a big shiny ring with a cluster of sparkling diamonds. Afterwards he adopted her son and Nkosi also changed his last name to Mulaudzi. She never ever again set foot in Hulisani, Hirsch, Hlomani and Associates. Never even to visit. She just assumed her new role as Advocate Hulisani's wife and ran his home.

They moved into a massive house in Houghton and Advocate Hirsch's wife, Adrienne, helped her with the décor and gave her several paintings that hung on the high walls. In no time Adrienne introduced her to her circle of friends and soon Portia was initiated into their way of life. They only knew her as Mrs Mulaudzi and nothing of her sordid past. A past she was not about to reveal to them. She saw this as a new chapter in her life with a new set of friends. Even when they called her name it sounded posh and light like a soufflé. She had also adopted their interests; she did cardio three times a week, met her friends for yoga and pilates twice a week.

In-between ferrying and picking children up from school. And in-between sports days, ballet recitals, PTA meetings and other fundraising initiatives, they read books, went for manicures and pedicures, lunched and shopped. Once in a while they would all meet for dinner at some charity event with their husbands in tow. Husbands who had come into their own with very colourful CVs and fat bank balances.

'But he deserved it,' piped up Mrs Molefe vociferously. 'If you do the crime pay the time! So many *black* people in this country commit crimes and go unpunished!'

'Sometimes poverty and desperation force you to do things you wouldn't necessarily do otherwise. Most of us are not able to appreciate this because we don't come from a place of need; we have all that we want,' responded Portia.

There was a quiet moment of introspection as the ladies chewed on Portia's words. 'Such great insight, Posh,' remarked Mrs Hirsch.

'It's something many privileged whites would not appreciate,' commented Mrs Khumalo.

Nomonde went on to explain that she grew up poor in Soweto. 'Ten of us slept on the kitchen floor. I *know* the struggle!'

'But don't you think the new blacks are equally oppressive? You have merely replicated the system!' pointed out Mrs van Tonder.

Estée van Tonder was a pampered housewife too. Her husband Danie played golf with Adrienne's husband. That was how they had become friends and later she too was incorporated into the book club.

'What do you mean by *new* blacks?' hissed Mrs Molefe, who took offence to the term.

Seipati and her husband had been the recipients of lucrative black economic empowerment tenders. Nomonde's husband handled their investment portfolio.

'She means new wealth,' replied Mrs Ledwaba.

Thobile Ledwaba considered herself old wealth because she had grown up in money. Her father made his wealth in taxis and shebeens and then later diversified into property development. With the new dispensation of 1994 her family had migrated from Diepkloof to Waverley. Thobile had married into an equally wealthy family and looked down on all people she considered nouveau riche, complaining they lacked class.

'The Nicholsons were old wealth,' spoke up Mrs Mussa for the first time, drawing them back to the book. Reena Mussa knew how easy it was for the discussion to veer off track and deteriorate into something ugly. Reena had struck up a friendship with the ladies because they all sat on the PTA committee.

'Agatha did typify old wealth,' agreed Estée. 'She reminded me a lot of my own mother. '

Nomonde did not care who Agatha was or the Nicholsons for that matter. As always, she bought the book but never got a chance to read it. She came to the meetings for the social aspect more than the constructive debate. She called out to Sibongile to bring out more Veuve Clicquot. Portia decided to make a hasty exit at this point.

'Ladies, I have to go!' she announced.

Mrs Molefe glanced at her watch then looked back at Portia.

'It's not even six yet. What's the rush?'

'I have to make dinner for the advocate.'

Nomonde rolled her eyes and refilled her glass of champagne.

'Portia, that's why we have hired help,' pointed out Mrs Ledwaba. 'You need freedom from the kitchen!'

The ladies erupted into laughter. Most of them could profess to not having cooked a meal in years.

'The advocate refuses to eat anyone's cooking besides mine.'

'That's what he tells you to keep you chained to the stove. Don't cook and see if he will die of starvation,' responded Mrs Molefe acidly.

Portia laughed it off, promptly said her goodbyes and left. As she pulled up to the gate outside her home she noticed the guards arriving for their evening shift. Normally she didn't pay attention to the guards manning the property but this one she noticed because it was her son's father. Her former husband. The badge on his uniform read: Vusani Sibanda. Her heart started to beat faster as she contemplated him possibly recognising her. Then again not many people from her old life would be able to recognise her now.

She waved from behind the window of her sporty GLE 400. It occurred to her that Vusani would never in his wildest dreams imagine her in this kind of setting. She drove up to the house but remained unsettled. What if her son decided to ride his quad bike down to the gate? What if Vusani recognised Nkosi? It was one thing not to recognise her but he would undoubtedly recognise his own son.

'Nkosi,' she called out as she walked into the house, the echoes bouncing off the walls.

'He is outside by the swimming pool,' replied a uniformed maid who appeared with a baby in her arms.

Portia took the baby from her and threw her in the air a couple of times. Lufuno giggled in delight and broke into a wild wail when her mother handed her back to the maid. Portia quickly swept outside to ascertain that Nkosi was indeed in the pool. He was happily playing with his older brothers Vhongani and Makhado. Advocate Hulisani was lying on the sun-lounger with the newspaper covering his face. After she had married him she had also inherited his two boys from his previous marriages. They were a solid family now. The last thing she wanted was for Vusani to ruin everything for her. She reached for her cellphone and dialled through to the security company.

'I have a request,' she said, 'one of your guards. Vusani Sibanda. He is very rude. Please make sure he is removed from our premises. No, I don't want to lay a formal complaint. Just make sure I never have to see his face again or we will terminate the contract. Thank you. Bye.'

After she hung up she exhaled deeply and then busied herself with making dinner. It was hours later when the advocate walked into the kitchen, lured by the aromas.

'I had no idea you were back,' he said, sliding his hands around her waist and hugging her from behind.

'*Aaa, ndi masiari.* Good afternoon. I was here a while ago. You were sleeping. I didn't want to disturb you.'

He kissed her on the side of her neck while Portia continued stirring the gravy.

'How was book club? Did you discuss anything or were you ladies just gossiping?'

'Yes we did. We do more than just gossip!'

He kissed her and declared he was going to shower before dinner. Every Saturday they had dinner out on the patio. Portia laid out the food in ceramic pots on the heated server and prayed over the food. She thanked God for the food before them, for their children and most of all her loving husband. Advocate Hulisani always squeezed her hand when it came to that part of the prayer. Then they all said 'amen' in unison. After the prayer, she got up with a bowl of water to let him wash his hands. Then she dished food onto his plate. Pork trotters. Fried cabbage. Stewed Beans. Steaming hot pap. When their father had been served the boys knew it was their cue to help themselves. Portia always ate last.

The dinner conversation was dominated by the boys regaling their father with stories. It was the only time they sat down to dinner with him. During the week the advocate got home way after their bedtime. After he had polished off the last bone the advocate declared he was going out for drinks with his colleagues. He told Portia not to wait up for him but she did anyway. After putting the baby to bed she curled into a ball on the couch, watching television. She fell asleep only to be woken by a kiss.

'*Aaa, ndi madekwana.* Good evening,' she responded half asleep. Her voice was soft and sensuous. She sounded like she was deliberately stroking his ardour.

'Let's go to bed, my darling.'

Hand in hand they made their way upstairs. They made hot passionate love. Just the way Hulisani liked it. They fell asleep. Portia fell into an even deeper reverie of contentment. This was her life now. And it was a fulfilling one too. She could think of no better way to live it.

# THIRTY-SIX

Dumisani sat at the end of the oak-panelled table. Nine men in crisp linen shirts and tailored suits sat at the table with him. Their faces were taut; their lips drawn in tight smiles. Only two women sat at the table with them; one of whom was hurriedly tapping onto a tiny tablet. The other merely stared at him, eagle-eyed. He wondered if this was how Jesus felt at the Last Supper.

'The board has reached a resolution. We are calling for your *immediate* resignation as CEO.'

It was the woman who spoke with sound authority. The words fell from her cherry red lips. On another day he might have deemed them sexy but today he found them callous as they mouthed his fate.

'… the board also wants to take this time to thank you for your contribution over the years. We wish you the best in your new endeavour.'

Dumisani jumped to his feet.

'Please don't be hasty! I can get us out of this mess!'

His eyes circled the room, desperately pleading with those

who were able to meet his gaze.

Most cast their eyes away. Many he had considered friends. They had given him firm handshakes and warm hugs when he had been elevated to the post of CEO five years ago.

'I have made billions for this company,' implored Dumisani. 'Billions!'

'And you have lost us billions too. This is shareholder money. People's livelihoods are vested here. This isn't Monopoly,' spoke the woman, reminding him of what had necessitated his dismissal.

'We can cover this position. I swear! I will personally cover it!'

None of the board members were moved by his contention. The chairperson, Kirsten Fairguard, continued with the meeting, while her assistant next to her continued to type hurriedly into her tablet.

'I will take over as temporary CEO until we find a suitable candidate.'

Dumisani held up his hands in resignation. His whole body slumped. Ms Fairguard motioned to the guards to escort him out. Dumisani refused to be held by them. He shrugged off their hands. Why were they treating him like a criminal?

On the tenth floor of his office suite, with a panoramic view of the Sandton CBD, his teary-eyed PA helped him pack his personal belongings into boxes. Sonia de Venter had run his diary effortlessly for the past five years.

'You don't deserve this,' she said.

She lifted framed accolades off the wall. Removed the pictures of his family from his desk. Finance journals and financial publications that sat on the bookshelf found their way into boxes. A trophy he had won at the Nedbank Golf Challenge followed. Soon there would be no trace of him left in the building. He could feel the tears bubbling beneath his calm exterior. It would serve him no good to give into them at that moment. The door swung open and Nomonde's whale-shaped form filled the doorway.

'I was in the area and thought I would drop by.'

Many years ago she used to drop by with his lunch. Or accompany him to lunch. Now all she had was a piece of paper in her hand.

'Give us a few minutes,' he told Sonia, who shuffled silently out of the room.

'What's going on? Are you moving office?' asked Nomonde as she paced the room.

'I have resigned,' he replied.

His pride would not let him admit to her that he had been forced to resign and been thrown out of the organisation like a stray dog.

'Why? What happened?'

'One of the traders has been betting on futures on the Hang Seng Index. He's been making loss after loss and in trying to cover his position he's incurred more losses. By the time we picked it up it was too late.'

When Nomonde stared at him with a blank look on her face he knew the enormity of the statement was lost on her.

'So what does this mean? Are we going to lose everything?'

Dumisani shook his head, 'We'll still have our houses and cars. I will get a package and everything. But I won't have this ...'

His voice cracked and he felt the tears resurface, threatening to overwhelm him again.

'It's okay,' comforted Nomonde, drawing him into her arms.

As he rested his head on her shoulder he felt the reassurance he craved. He was vulnerable; something he had not felt since the day he met Nomonde in hospital many years before.

'We will get through this.'

Their embrace was cut short when Sonia entered the room. The urgency in her eyes communicated to him that he had to leave. Nomonde helped him and was the one who walked with him out of the building. He had not even paused to say goodbye to the traders in the dealing room or the back-office staff. As they descended in the elevator, a sinking feeling of failure enveloped him.

The minute they got home Dumisani declared he wanted to lie down for a bit. Nomonde gave him his space as she slunk away to the garden to make a call. She ignored the furtive stares of the gardener. Hours later she returned to the study with some lunch for Dumisani. He was on the phone when she walked in. He looked excited and his mood had lifted somewhat. When he hung up he had a huge smile pasted on his face.

'I was just talking to Advocate Hulisani.'

In the past the advocate had assisted them with many legal battles on the corporate front. They had also forged a private relationship in the process.

'And?'

'He says I could actually sue them. Screw Kirsten and the team! I made that company into what it is today. He said he could even get me reinstated.'

Nomonde looked back at him, unconvinced. 'What would that mean? Shuffling back and forth to court for years?'

'Not necessarily. He says chances are they will want to avoid messy litigation. So they will probably be willing to settle out of court.'

Nomonde clapped her hands excitedly. 'That's good news then! Does this mean you would go back to your old job?'

Dumisani shook his head. 'I realised I don't want my old job, Nomonde. Maybe it's time I started something new. Something of my own. Advocate said there is room for transformation in the financial services sector. He really got me thinking and it's about time I did.'

He beckoned Nomonde to bring his food, which he ate with relish. In-between mouthfuls he told Nomonde that Advocate Hulisani said he could walk away with millions more than what he thought he would receive.

# THIRTY-SEVEN

The heaving mass of fat emerged from beneath the Quantum. His face was smeared with grease from tinkering with the engine of the car.

'I fixed it,' declared Givemore, with a smug smile on his face.

He was now the proprietor of Jack's Auto Spares and Repairs. He had joined the team a few years earlier as an apprentice, then later bought out Malume Jackson, and also managed the fuel station that had been closed for years. But they continued to work together on other ventures and Givemore still sometimes respectfully referred to him as 'Boss'.

'After two hundred kilometres this car will pack up, but that's not my problem,' said Givemore.

'You are evil!' grinned Malume.

'I learnt from the best!'

They both cracked up. Their laughter was cut short when a short, light-skinned woman walked in with a cellphone in her hand.

'Malume, it's for you,' she announced.

'I said I don't want to take any calls. I'm busy. I told you I was busy!'

Malume Jackson was in his seat, one heavy leg crossed over another. His belly spilled onto his lap. From where he sat he had a vantage point of the showroom.

'This woman has called ten times. She insists on talking to you!'

'I don't care,' replied Jackson dismissively.

He figured it was one of his girlfriends looking for *papgeld*. Malume Jackson had lost track of the number of children he had fathered outside of his marriage. There were some that he did not believe were his; he believed many of the women were just trying to swindle him of his hard-earned money.

'Bring us coffee,' he ordered, 'with those nice cream dough-nuts from that bakery.'

The young girl nodded and walked away.

The car business was a front for more lucrative pursuits. Givemore had earned the money to buy the garage in a cash-in-transit heist. He had even taken a bullet during the episode. The scar was small compared to the scar that Lindani gave him when she'd knifed him in the throat. He fingered it absent-mindedly as he remembered that incident so many years ago. That whole issue with Lindani had created a rift between him and Melusi. They had parted ways shortly after that. It was about then that he called Malume Jackson looking for a job. He still saw Melusi every now and then but their lives had followed very different paths. Melusi still continued with his cross-border business while Givemore had moved onto more lucrative ventures.

'That's the guy we need to take out,' declared Malume Jackson casually, like he was talking about an outing to the local bar.

Givemore sat down across from him. There was a picture on the table and the name 'Dumisani' was scribbled across it.

'*Ke batla ho mo bolaea.* I want to kill him. However, you will have to do it for me. I can't have the blood of my sister's child on my hands.'

Givemore eyed him quizzically.

'So why kill, Malume? Just break his knees *nje*. Teach him a lesson.'

'But no. *O ne a robala le mosadi wa ka*! He slept with my wife. He disrespected me. In my own house.'

As he spoke his eyes began to widen, the pupils flashing anger.

'I brought him here. To Johannesburg. He is here because of me. He is what he is because of me.'

His voice was thick with hate.

'Not once did he wake up and say, here, Malume, thanks for everything you did for me. But no. *O ne a batla ho ja le mosuli ua ka.*'

Malume Jackson picked up the picture and stared at it for a long time. Then he started to finger it.

'Yi shit!' declared Givemore.

He could not understand how anyone would want to abuse the generosity that Malume bestowed upon people.

'We must fix him,' continued Givemore.

'That we will.'

The young girl returned with a tray in her hand. Jackson quickly covered the picture with the thick palm of his hand. She handed him his cup of coffee; he told her to take a sip.

'One must always test for poison.'

Givemore concurred with him and began to finger the pendant that hung around his neck. After Malume had given the coffee a nod of approval they drank and wolfed down the doughnuts.

It was about that time that Nomonde arrived. Malume Jackson could smell her even before she presented herself. Her signature

Bvlgari scent filled his nostrils, almost obliterating the oily smells from the workshop. Her breasts bounced as she walked. He was sincerely torn between staring at her heart-shaped face or that inviting cleavage. She was wearing tight jeans that looked like they were painted onto her legs and outlined her curvaceous form. As she walked in her stilettos her body swayed so much that he was afraid she would topple over.

'It would be nice if you answered your phones!' she snapped.

There were no pleasantries. Nomonde's voice was icy. Even the warm weather had done nothing to thaw her chilly demeanour.

'We are having coffee. Want to join us?' asked Malume Jackson.

'I didn't come here for coffee!' she replied curtly.

Malume Jackson grinned sheepishly. 'So what did you come for?'

'I want to call off the hit on my husband. *O seke oa mo bolaea.*'

He stared at her blankly then erupted into laughter like she had cracked a bad joke. Nomonde was not moved.

'Why?'

'*Akukho nto.* It doesn't matter. *Ayidingi wena leyo.*'

'I don't refund. No cash back here,' replied Malume Jackson acidly.

He even pointed to a poster on the wall that declared words to the same effect.

'I don't care about the money,' replied Nomonde.

As she said this she waved her hands in the air and walked away. Her gold bangles clanked together as if in agreement.

Nomonde had pawned off a gold ring and a Tanzanite necklace to get the cash as Malume had insisted on a 50 per cent deposit. Although it had pained her to lose that money, she knew R25 000 was not the price tag on Dumisani's life; he was more valuable

SUE NYATHI

alive than dead.

Long after she had left, her scent lingered. Givemore was utterly mesmerised by her.

'*Mochana oa hao o ja monate! Moer!*'

Malume Jackson threw his head back and laughed. 'He has good taste like me!' and patted his chest proudly.

'When he first came here I told him to forget about *izishwepe* from home. At least he took my advice.'

'*Hayi* ah …' said Givemore shaking his head.

'Well, once you top him you can get a piece of that!'

Givemore eyed him quizzically. 'His wife said we must not– '

Malume Jackson cut him off brusquely. 'This is not about his wife anymore. It's about me and him. I want to settle this score.'

Malume Jackson shoved the last of his doughnut down his throat. He chewed on it as he contemplated how he would destroy Dumisani once and for all.

# THIRTY-EIGHT

Three Cuban cigars later, half a bottle of Johnny Walker Platinum between them and Advocate Hulisani decided to call it a night. They had met earlier for some drinks to celebrate the successful outcome of his challenge to his unfair dismissal. As Advocate Hulisani had predicted, Kirsten Fairguard and her team had been keen to settle out of court. It was clear they did not want the expense and publicity of a drawn-out legal battle and Advocate Hulisani had assured them it would have been long and messy.

'I can't thank you enough!' gushed Dumisani.

Advocate Hulisani laughed. 'Oh you thanked me all right. My bank balance is grinning!'

'But honestly must you leave? It's not even 11 ...' implored Dumisani.

'I know my wife is waiting up for me. It would be unfair for me to keep her waiting any longer.'

'Come on, Huli! You used to go home at six a.m. when you were married to your other wives.'

'It's different now.' He paused, seemed reflective. 'I don't have to try hard with Portia. Loving her is like second nature. Do you understand that?'

Dumisani nodded slowly, as if the words were just sinking into his head.

'She doesn't have to call me to come home. I *want* to go home.'

Dumisani expelled a deep breath. 'I stopped feeling that way a long time ago. '

Advocate Hulisani motioned for the waiter to bring them their bill.

'Life is too short. Leave if you are not happy. You know I have your back. Always.'

After the advocate had left, Dumisani decided to follow suit. He would have liked to carry on drinking into the night but drinking alone only brought misery, not mirth. He pulled out his cellphone and dialled Christine. She answered on the second ring. She sounded frantic.

'Is everything all right with the kids?'

'Everything is fine with the kids,' he assured her. 'I was just checking on you. Is everything fine with you?'

There was a long pause on the other end. Christine did not respond to his conciliatory approach; she was used to him being abrasive and abrupt.

'Well, everything is not fine with me, Christine. I miss you. I miss us. I miss talking to you.'

There was still no response from the other end.

'I have been thinking a lot. You are right. I have become this person that I don't know. It's not fair. You should see the kids. I'm going to send them over to spend Christmas with you. I might even come too.'

Christine started sobbing into the phone.

'Sshh … it's going to be all right. I promise.'

After he hung up he still felt pensive. Maybe he was pining over a past that was not even worth holding onto. He started to think maybe he needed to give his marriage another chance. He had been crazy over Nomonde once, surely he could reignite that crazy feeling once again? But the advocate's advice kept ringing in his head. Advocate Hulisani was always right. Dumisani finished off his whisky and his phone buzzed. It was a WhatsApp message from Keneilwe. There was an image attachment of her wearing a flimsy red négligée.

'I am putting on a show. You might miss out on the action!'

His groin stirred to life. He punched in a quick reply.

'I'm coming.'

He grabbed his car keys and made a hurried exit. As he drove he played his voicemail messages. Three from Nomonde. Two from the kids. One from his mother. He felt the guilt creep up his throat like bile. He made a stop at a forecourt store that was open all night and bought some chocolate and drooping daffodils. He drove past the Morningside Shopping Centre. The lights were on and he could see cars in the parking lot. As he sped down Rivonia Road he noticed a sporty red VW Golf tailing him. He ignored it. Instead he turned up the music and continued driving. Minutes later he was on the highway pushing his car at a fabulous speed. He turned off on Allandale and drove past the new Waterfall development.

He was thinking it might actually be a good idea to buy some property there. He had always wanted to view the development but just never seemed to have time. Well, now that he was officially unemployed he decided he wanted to spend more time doing the things that he liked. Like spending more time with his children. As he drove past the Kyalami racetrack he thought about taking the boys there when schools closed in two weeks' time. It was Sipho's favourite place to hang out during the holidays; he wanted to become a Formula 1 driver. It had also rubbed off on Khaya, who was Nomonde's son from a previous relationship. Khaya was two years older than Sipho but they got along famously with a shared passion for fast cars. Silindile's ambitions were more grounded. She wanted to be a ballerina. At five she already knew she wanted to be the lead dancer in Swan Lake. Three-year-old Mondli, on the other hand, envisioned himself as a painter. He scribbled on everything he could get his grubby hands on. He had no idea what Xhanti's dreams were. At such a young age his mind was a blank canvas.

He wondered which of his children were going to follow in his footsteps of tremendous wealth. He could not be faulted for having set the right foundation for them. He looked through the rear-view mirror and the VW Golf was still tailing him. He decided to slow down. When the car overtook him he shoved his fears aside but then the car came to a sudden halt. Dumisani slammed on the brakes, bringing his own car to a screeching stop. He cursed. Instinctively he wanted to jump out of the car but they beat him to it. Before he could even blink two masked guys were coming at him, armed with guns. Without even thinking, he pressed the panic button. The door swung open, he was yanked out of the driver's seat and landed on the ground with a loud thump. His knees hit the tarmac and he fell flat on his face. He banged his head against a rocky outcrop hidden in the grass along the side of the road and the skin on his forehead split open. He grimaced. Then a gunshot rang out.

'Please just take the car!' he screamed. 'Don't hurt me!'

He felt utterly helpless. Powerless. Weak. His legs started to convulse of their own accord. His arms and body followed suit. An incoherent prayer fell from his trembling lips.

'*Mbulale!*' screamed a voice.

Dumisani recognised that voice. He would've recognised it anywhere.

'Malume Jackson!' he screamed. 'Please, Malume! *Ngimi!* uDumisani!'

The gun went off again. Three shots in quick succession. Like those noisy fireworks during Diwali celebrations. The sound almost eclipsed the screams as the bullets tore through Dumisani's flesh. The blood sprayed the grass, painting it a brilliant red.

His lifeless body lay on the side of the road. He would probably occupy a few sentences in one of the daily papers. Then tomorrow he would be yesterday's news. He would be buried and forgotten and a year later no one would even remember him. Or care about him. He would be another tragedy. Another crime statistic to be reported in the South African Police annual report.

# THIRTY-NINE

**M**elusi stood in the basement garage directing his men who were loading goods onto his fleet of trucks. All his trucks were emblazoned with an emblem of an eagle in flight with Asambeni Enterprises written boldly in black. He had developed eyes at the back of his head to ensure nothing went missing. He could not afford to have things go missing. After collecting all the merchandise his guys would pack it into the fleet of taxis he now ran. He merely supervised.

He now had a million-rand operation transporting everything from alcohol, to chemicals, electronics and foodstuffs. He rubbed his sprouting belly lovingly. Five years later and he was 15 kilograms heavier. Not only was Melusi involved in the logistics business but he also dabbled in property. His portfolio had grown to include a number of flats in the Hillbrow area. He had two in Esselen. Three along Cavendish. One at the corner of Kotze and Claim. Four on King George Street overlooking the noisy Noord Taxi Rank. They might not have been aesthetically pleasing but the rental yields were pleasing to his bank balance. He had bought himself a big bungalow in Kempton Park. 'Careful with that TV!' he shouted.

It was a 48-inch Samsung Smart TV with an LED screen. Costing almost R10 000 he could not afford to have it broken or scratched. He could not keep up with the television technology. First there had been LCD screens, now it was LED. A lot of his clients were buying them.

'You almost forgot these,' said a woman handing him a plastic bag full of green passports.

He would take them across the border to get stamped so that it would appear that the holders had exited the country within the stipulated three-month time frame granted under the stringent entry regulations. Yet most of the passport holders were gainfully employed in South Africa, even without the requisite permits. It was a lucrative business for him. He charged R1 000 to get each passport stamped. It cost R2 000 for those who had overstayed. In such instances you needed a stamp that could be backdated and this service invariably cost a lot more.

He had forged strong relationships with some border officials who took their cut and he pocketed what was left. It was easy money and less stress than carrying live cargo back and forth. Even when he did carry live cargo he would give them one of the passports and they would assume the identity of that person for a day. Even if there was no resemblance. The business of human trafficking had become sophisticated. Very rarely did you hear of people drowning in the Limpopo these days. Even his cargo business was seamless. He now had a trusted friend at SARS who had issued him with a Goods Export Permit and as a result his cargo was never inspected.

Melusi carried a lot of things in his vehicles. Sometimes he even had noxious gases and ammunition. He did not care what he carried; his only concern was that he got paid for it. He even carried dead bodies. For a cool R15 000 he transported a body along with the mourners. The singing would keep him company during the six-hour journey but the crying annoyed the hell out of him.

'Thanks, my darling,' he said, grateful for her efficiency.

'So when will you take me to Zimbabwe to meet your parents?'

'I will. Soon,' he replied.

Lungile eyed him circumspectly. He had been saying that for the past three years. Her parents suspected he might have a wife across the border. She insisted he didn't but she was no longer sure.

'How soon is soon?'

Melusi became annoyed. He hated having to explain himself. Especially to Lungile. He had met her a few years before and she was one of his many girlfriends who had conveniently fallen pregnant. They lived together because he did not want his daughter growing up in squalor. Lungile kept pressing him for marriage but he kept telling her he wasn't ready.

Lungile pursed her lips in annoyance. Her feelings had been dismissed with little regard. Melusi reached into his shirt pocket and handed her his debit card. Lungile's face lit up.

'Buy something for the kid. Make sure you get yourself something too.'

She started to dust his shirt and then kissed him playfully on the cheek.

Of every week he spent three days in Zimbabwe and four in South Africa. He was building a massive house back home. He showed her pictures of the progress on his Samsung tablet. She had even helped him pick out the furniture and fittings. The Zimbabwe he had showed her was nothing like the Zimbabwe she saw on the news. In the news all she heard was that Zimbabwe was run by an old dictator and that the economy had ground to a halt. But the money that Melusi was making in Zimbabwe told a different story.

Lungile waved and walked away. Melusi stood there in quiet contemplation. He wrung his hands together nervously as he began to contemplate his future.

'Come on, guys, let's work this. Time's running out. The cars need to get on the road.'

Later, as he drove to the border, Melusi thought that he should stop exerting himself with this gruelling drive. But he was the one who had forged the relationships with the immigration officials and they would not risk talking to anyone else. It was a high-risk operation but with the high risk came high returns. It was just after seven at night when he arrived at the border. It was never good to do any of their shenanigans in the glare of broad daylight. The night provided a cloak of discretion over their illicit activities. He drove through the gate and waved at the guard on duty. He knew nearly all of them on a first-name basis.

He circled the parking area for a while before he could find a spot to park. Musina border post was always swarming with people. It did not matter what time of day it was or what season. He was certain that some people lived at the border. With his portfolio of passports tucked safely under his arm he made his way to immigration. There was a queue snaking all the way into the building but he avoided it. The guard kept calling the people to order. They were restless. Some were moaning that they had been standing in the queue since three in the afternoon. Melusi was relieved not to be part of *that* struggle. He made his way to the front of the queue. The overzealous guard almost stopped him, trying to pull rank at the door.

'*O tseba seo ke leng sona?* Do you know who I am?'

A scuffle at the door ensued. The crowd rallied behind

the guard accusing him of jumping the queue. It was only after an immigration official appeared that the hubbub died down and Melusi was given entry. The guard was put in his place and returned to harassing the people in the queue. Ordering them to stand in a straight line. A young woman with a baby strapped to her back came forward.

'Please, my child is restless. Can't you let us through?'

The guard did not flinch.

'Mama, thet iz nun of my bizness.'

He dismissed her with the threatening wave of his baton. The woman shrank away in defeat to join the queue. A pregnant woman with swollen feet had decided to sit on the bare ground. She was convinced her waters would break before they got a pass to proceed to the other side.

Melusi reached the immigration counter. A beautifully made-up official with high cheek bones and hair swept back in a bun greeted him. They exchanged a few pleasantries. The first passport made it across the counter. Then she asked Melusi to step into the side office. Confidently, Melusi marched to the side office. He plonked himself on the seat and even put his legs on the table. The portfolio of passports sat on the desk. He understood that they were busy. Weekends were always busy. This is why he wanted to retire now. He had been doing this job for too long; it was physically exerting. He was often bothered by an ache in his back that would only subside after he had nursed it with strong painkillers.

A few minutes later the division head appeared with a stamp. Money changed hands under the table. There were no bank transfers in this business. It was cash upfront. He quickly started to stamp the passports, cursing as he did so. He was halfway through when the door swung open and four men in black overalls armed with rifles burst into the room. Melusi jumped to his feet in surprise. Before he knew it he was up against the wall. One man restrained him while the other one handcuffed him. He was too distracted to notice the immigration official scuffling beneath the table and being dragged out on his hands and knees.

*'You are under arrest for contravening the Immigration Act 13 of 2002 as amended in ...'*

# FORTY

Sibongile reached for her daughter's cold hand. The length of her arm was bruised with piercings like a diabetes patient. An intrusive intravenous tube ran down her arm. The nurse had already informed her that the prognosis did not look good.

'What is it?' she kept asking.

No one seemed willing to provide her with a substantive answer. She had once found a doctor hovering over her who merely said Chenai had an infection of sorts. Caused by what? No one could tell her. One nurse implied HIV complications and had gone on to deliver a diatribe about how many young women were affected by the disease. Drugs, said another nurse. Sibongile did not understand. She tried in vain to communicate with Chenai who lay prostrate on her bed.

Sibongile had kept vigil by her side for many days and many nights; however, it appeared her daughter remained unmoved by her presence or concern. Undeterred, Sibongile continued to pray persistently for God to save the life of her daughter. How was it possible that she would outlive both her children? She did not want to bury yet another child.

Chenai was fully aware of her mother's presence at her bedside but was unable to communicate the pain she felt. The pain that Kayin had omitted to tell her she would feel after the operation to remove her kidney. Two weeks later the pain still clung to her like the IV tubes that were stapled to her limbs. She was bleeding profusely and the doctor had said an infection had set in. As each day passed, Chenai felt like the world was slipping through her fingers. However, her brother stood at the edge of the bed beckoning her to come to him. To leave it all behind. He stood there with a sunny smile reassuring her that it was going to be all right. He was just the way she remembered him. Not with his charred burnt body but whole, robed in white, his dreadlocks framing his face.

'Please don't die. Jesus please spare her life,' Sibongile murmured.

And she got down on her knees and begged and pleaded with the Almighty to be merciful. As she was kneeling beside the bed she heard a piercing scream. It startled her. The scream had not come from Chenai's lips, however, and prompted Sibongile to follow the sound to its source. She hurried out of the room down the corridor. There she found a young girl cowering in the corner of a ward like a frightened dog.

'It's okay, my child. Mummy is here. I am here!'

'I want Gogo!' she screamed. 'Where is Gogo? These monsters are coming for me! Help me! I want Gogo!'

There was already a crowd at the door. Sibongile manoeuvred herself to a vantage point to observe the scene unfolding before her. The nurses had to sedate the girl.

Sibongile hung back and watched in awe as the young woman closed the distance between her and the child. They embraced. It was a heartfelt moment.

'What's going on here?' asked Sibongile.

One of the nurses exhaled deeply. Confidentiality did not allow them to reveal the details of their cases but she whispered sotto voce, 'This child was found in a hotel room with cigarette burns all over her body. She was raped several times.'

Apparently the only thing she knew was her name and her granny and these monsters that had done terrible things to her. Sibongile shook her head slowly and the tears fell from her eyes. Even as the nurse spoke, she could see the pain she felt as she articulated the ordeal the child must have suffered. For a few minutes her mind was deflected from the pain of her own suffering to that of this child.

They were still commiserating when another nurse came rushing down the corridor with her hands flailing in the air.

'It's the patient in Bed 19. Her heartbeat is fading. Call the doctor.'

Chenai was in Bed 19. Sibongile followed the mad rush to her room. She watched, dumbstruck, as they tried to revive her daughter. And just like that, Chenai's soul departed the room leaving behind a cold, lifeless body. Defeated, the doctor slunk away. The nurse pulled a sheet over the dead body and ushered everyone out of the room. Sibongile sat in the corridor sobbing profusely. Though immersed in the tragedy of the moment she felt a hand on her shoulder.

'It's okay, mama, it will be fine.'

Sibongile looked up and her eyes met those of the mother who had been embracing her child earlier.

'I just lost my daughter,' cried Sibongile. 'I am far away from home. I have no one here. No one!' she wailed.

The woman edged closer to her. 'Where are you from, mama?'

'Zimbabwe. I came here in the early nineties. But it's been hard. So hard. I thought my kids would have a better life here but they are both dead. Dead!'

Sibongile wiped her face, trying to present a brave front.

'I almost lost my child,' said the woman. 'For many years I thought she was dead.'

'What happened to her?'

The woman edged closer to her. She looked around and then began to whisper.

'I came to Johannesburg in 2001 to join my husband. I left my child with my mother. We were trying to sort ourselves out. It was a struggle but finally we were settled. My daughter did not have a passport and the only way I could get her here was to smuggle her across the border. I knew of someone. He had often carried my groceries so I asked him to bring my child. The day before they arrived, our flat got raided. They took every foreigner with no papers. My husband and I both spent almost two weeks at Lindela Repatriation Centre.'

She paused as if she was reliving the ordeal. She exhaled deeply before continuing with her narrative.

'When we came out and went to look for my daughter we were told she had died. That she had drowned in the river. It killed my mother. She died shortly afterwards. I think she died of heartbreak. I also thought my daughter was dead until a week ago when I was watching the news. I knew it was her. I just knew …'

'Oh thank God your daughter was found!'

Sibongile reached and embraced her. 'They say God gives with one hand and takes with another. But I don't understand. Why does He make us suffer? Why are we here? Why?'

The woman shrugged. 'I stopped trying to understand it. I have just learnt to accept it.' She stood up. 'Let me go and be with my child. She needs me.'

In another hospital, in a private suite, in another part of Johannesburg, Dumisani was propped up in bed reading a newspaper.

*A young girl believed to be eleven years old who only identifies herself as Gugulethu was found abandoned in a hotel room in the Johannesburg CBD by one of the cleaners. The child was left for dead but due to the actions of the cleaner her life was saved. It is believed this young girl is a victim of child prostitution, a growing trend in Johannesburg. Syndicates involved in human trafficking are selling the children for anything between R2 500 to R10 000 ...*

He did not finish reading the article but he threw it aside.

'Is there any good news in this world?' he asked, feeling exasperated.

'Well yes, the doctor said you are getting better and he will discharge you soon.'

'When? I want to go home.'

'We also want you to come home,' said Nomonde earnestly. 'I am so sorry this happened, Dumisani.'

Her eyes misted with tears. She cried on a whim nowadays. Dumisani squeezed her hand lovingly.

'It's okay, darling. I am fine now.'

'This is my entire fault,' she replied.

'How could this even be your fault? It happens. We should thank God I am alive.'

'If we didn't fight so much you would have been home.'

She squeezed his hand tightly. Nomonde wanted to confess to him that she had played a role in orchestrating his demise. But she knew that a confession of that nature would not unite them but destroy them forever. It had been three weeks since the gruesome botched carjacking incident. He had been shot several times in the chest. The doctors kept saying it was a miracle he had survived, as one of the bullets had narrowly missed his spinal cord. The newspapers had reported that one of the suspects, Givemore Ncube, had been apprehended and was in custody awaiting trial for attempted murder. The other one, Jackson Mdluli, had been shot and killed on the scene as he tried to get away.

When Nomonde first heard of his death, untold relief had washed over her. The last thing she needed was for anyone to tie her to this. As Dumisani lay on the bed she realised she really did not want him dead. All she had meant to do was punish him for his disloyalty. He had suffered enough these past couple of weeks. Nomonde had prayed earnestly, together with Sis Yondela and the other ladies from church. They had begged and pleaded with God to restore his life and help her to become a better wife.

Nomonde had often prayed before but it had been without conviction. Just words she had recited in a parrot-like fashion. Now her words were covered with passion and zeal. She had reached a plea bargain with God and she was going to spend the rest of her life atoning for her sins. She was sorry for what she had done. She was ashamed of herself. To think she had been so desperate to have extinguished her husband's life for a few pieces of gold.

'Do you remember how we met and fell in love in a hospital?' asked Dumisani, cutting into her thoughts.

Nomonde nodded. She was taken back to her days as a nurse. The days when she walked the corridors until her ankles swelled with pain. She had been filled with so much passion and dedication to her work back then. She was a much nicer person then.

'You know I fell in love with you again, Nomonde. Every day I have woken up and you have been here it reminded me of the love and devotion you once had for me.'

Nomonde touched his forehead. She wondered if it was him speaking or the medication.

'I miss that, Nomonde. I really do.'

Nomonde kissed him lovingly on the forehead.

'It's going to be different this time around. I promise you.'

Dumisani smiled at her. He was filled with conviction; it *was* going to be different this time around. He was determined to make things work between them. He believed he had only survived because life had given them a second chance and he was determined not to waste it. And so they held hands and looked into each other's eyes which spoke of untold promise for the future.

Sibongile was left to bury a painful past. She had texted everyone in Chenai's phone, alerting them of her passing. Some expressed their condolences. Dumisani was one of those who had called her back. He had said he would not be able to make it to the funeral but had deposited R15 000 into her account to assist with the funeral arrangements.

They laid Chenai to rest next to the remains of her brother in a cemetery in Chiawelo. Like her son's funeral, only a handful of people attended. Amongst them were Mr and Mrs Hirsch who had bought the coffin and paid for the funeral. They were there in the same way they had been when they had buried Chamunorwa a few years earlier. Connie, Milly, Patricia and Rue were also there standing in solidarity with their friend. They were all kitted out in black for the mournful event. Connie had on a huge black hat, which shielded her and half of Milly from the blazing sun. She had explained it was the hat her daughter had worn to the Durban July the year before. Her new hair extensions cascaded down her back. She could have easily passed as one of the madams they served from Monday to Friday. Afterwards her friends came to the Hirsches' home and congregated in Sibongile's staff quarters. Rue had brought with her three bottles of wine, which she proudly professed she had misappropriated from her boss's wine cellar. The wine was poured into tall drinking glasses as none of them owned wine glasses. They drank the rich berry-flavoured liquid until the tears of pain were replaced by tears of laughter.

The irony hit her then. That she had come all this way in search of a pot of gold at the end of the rainbow. She had not found it. Not even an ounce of it. Instead she had found something more valuable. Her relationships. That was the real treasure. Here she was surrounded by a rainbow of women who loved her. In that moment it did not matter whether Sibongile came from Zimbabwe or Zim-bub-we. They stood by her with unwavering love. This was the gold. For behind that glittering façade of Johannesburg were fleeting smiles and faux love. To find that deep lasting connection was certainly worth more than any gold bullion ever formed in the belly of Johannesburg.

# ACKNOWLEDGEMENTS

This year, 2018, marks the tenth anniversary of my living in Johannesburg, the place I now consider my home. Although I did not jump fences or swim across a river to get here, my struggle and the struggle for many immigrants, whether political or economic, is real. This is the inspiration behind *The GoldDiggers*. I want to acknowledge all the lives that have been lost as a result of xenophobic violence; those whose stories were never told.

I would also like to acknowledge the many individuals and resources who contributed to my knowledge of the city. Some of the research did not make it into the final novel, but it certainly enhanced my own understanding of the city, its origins and how it evolved over the years.

To Paula Marais, who got sight of this manuscript in its early stages; it was your direction and criticism that finally got it into a form that was worth selling! To Phumlani 'Ndo' Mzongwana, who read the first draft of this manuscript and affirmed that it was indeed a work of gold!

I also want to thank the publishing team at Pan Macmillan.

To Andrea Nattrass, who read the manuscript and decided it was worth publishing. Thank you for buying into my dream. To Jane Bowman, who worked diligently while editing the novel. I loved her attention to detail no matter how minor. To the publicity and sales teams at Pan Macmillan, who worked tirelessly to make sure this novel ended up in your hands.

To my parents, Max and Judith, you gave me the foundation. Thank you for your continued belief in me and my writing. To my brothers, Nduna and Kwanele, and their wives, Sanelisiwe and Nobuhle. You remain a formidable support base as I try to balance a career, write novels and raise a child. To my sister, Minenhle, the last born but not the least, thank you for always being there.

To my niece, Rebokile, I know you are a closet writer and I hope my writing will encourage you to come out! To my nephews, Kabelo, Andile and Vuyisile; may you continue to be my biggest cheerleaders. And to my son, Sabelo, I can never acknowledge you enough. I hope I continue to do things to make you proud of me.

To my friends, the golden oldies. You were there when it started and you are still here cheering me on. To my friends, the newbies. The ones I have met through book clubs, our bonds have evolved beyond words. To the virtual friends, the Tweethearts, some who have connected with me beyond cyberspace. Thank you.

And finally, to the readers. None of this would have been possible without you. We started with *The Polygamist* and now we are here. I live to write for you.